LANA POPOVIĆ

Poison

# Priestess

AMULET BOOKS • NEW YORK

Cataloging-in-Publication Data has been applied for and may be obtained from the Library of Congress.

ISBN 978-1-4197-4592-8

Text © 2021 Abrams
Jacket illustration © 2021 Jen Wang
Book design by Hana Anouk Nakamura

Printed and bound in U.S.A.
10 9 8 7 6 5 4 3 2 1

Amulet Books are available at special discounts when purchased in quantity for premiums and promotions as well as fundraising or educational use. Special editions can also be created to specification. For details, contact specialsales@abramsbooks.com or the address below.

Amulet Books® is a registered trademark of Harry N. Abrams, Inc.

**ABRAMS** The Art of Books
195 Broadway, New York, NY 10007
abramsbooks.com

*To Anne, for helping me bring some very bad and bloody ladies (sort of) back to life*

## PROLOGUE

Sometimes when I fear I may expel my very soul into the cauldron's fumes, I like to imagine that the fabrique is truly hell itself and I one of its lesser demons. A wraith, a capering imp, a nightshade wreathed in wisps of smoke. Some diabolical creature made entirely without mercy.

Anything but the prisoner I am in truth.

My ghoulish fancy requires only the barest stretch of imagination. Despite its soaring ceiling, the converted ballroom of the hôtel particulier that houses Maître Prud-homme's candle factory feels as cloistered and scorching as any furnace. Cast-iron cauldrons of tallow and beeswax bubble all along the great room's length, two dozen of them suspended by chains above roaring braziers. Each is tended by a barefoot girl clad only in a flimsy, sweat-soaked chemise, the linen slipping sideways to reveal jutting collarbones like blades, whetted by the ruthless wheel of hunger. In the room's relentless heat, any more clothing would only be a punishment.

Though perhaps, I remind myself as I wipe searing spatter off my cheek, it could be worse. Perhaps we are all fortunate the maître has not yet decided we would work more ably in the nude.

I would not put it past him to strip us of the few scraps of dignity we have left.

As they bend over the kettles, shoulder blades flexing like little wings with the effort of churning each blistering mass, the stirring girls remind me of nothing so much as fallen angels. Discarded and cast into perdition, forced to tend to the instruments of their own torment in penance. *Save that my fellow captives are innocents*, I think bitterly as I stir. Guilty only of being girls, unwanted and poor enough to wind up in this enfer.

The ballroom's curdled decadence only bolsters the illusion of hell. Above our heads swing ruined chandeliers, studded with blackened crystal shards like rotting teeth, dangling from rafters smeared with the tallow's fatty smoke. While beeswax melts much more cleanly, releasing a warm, delicious smell, not even the royal candlemaker can afford to ply his craft in costly wax alone. Instead, only the maître's favored girls are assigned to the five beeswax cauldrons, while the rest of us choke in the tallow's charnel reek. The rendered sheep fat is bad enough, but the pig lard that yields the cheapest candles could roil even an iron stomach. Only the wildest girls, the banshees who court daily thrashings by the overseers, are consigned to that particular misery.

For all my quiet wickedness, the curses I whisper into the tallow, I make sure never to be a banshee girl.

But the new dipper who attends to my cauldron does not take such heed.

Instead, she mutters mutinously to herself as she works, uncaring of who might hear. "May the pox speckle his manhood until it rots like grapes left too long on the vine," she hisses, dipping the lines of cotton wicks looped over her broach into the tallow. "May his own maman grow to loathe the sight of his vile face."

Though she is plainly furious, the turmoil does not disrupt the deftness of her movements. She expertly dips, then lifts the broach, letting the tallow harden just enough before lowering it again. Never allowing it to linger in the molten heat too long.

At least this one will not bring a beating down on our heads by overdipping the candles or melting them with haste.

"May everything he touches fade and crumble," she continues, "turning to the palest ash and sourest dust."

The ferocity of the words, the eerie malevolence of their rhythm, plucks some deeply buried string inside me and sets it aquiver. Though she does not rhyme, it still sounds like some wicked song, a perverse sort of prayer not intended for the ears of notre Dieu but something altogether else. Though I doubt the devil attends to mortal pleadings any more than God himself, who is certainly all but deaf to our predicaments, the savage sound of her curses appeals to me nonetheless.

But for all that I like it, I am certain the foreman would not feel the same.

"Would you *hush* already," I snap at her under my breath, flicking her a barbed arrow of a look. "Unless you yearn to feel a bullwhip on your back. Beelzebub may not be near, but those cabbage ears of his are keener than you'd think. If he thought you might be speaking of Maître Prudhomme, I wouldn't wish to be in your shoes."

She pauses in her labor, knuckling away a trailing drop of sweat. When she meets my eyes, hers are as dark as banked coals and unaccountably amused.

"Did you say 'Beelzebub,' p'tite?" Her chapped lips quirk, tugging to one side, and her eyes ignite with interest. "That is what you call the foreman, I take it?"

I hesitate, cursing myself for this slip of the tongue. There was no need to allow this stranger such an undue glimpse into my mind. Not when the morbid fancies it devises are the only things I can still afford to call my own.

"It's all right, p'tite," she coaxes. "You can tell me of your thoughts. I will not turn them against you, I swear it."

I hesitate another moment, but there is something beguiling about her interest. She looks about nineteen, a little older than most of the young women indentured here; at thirteen, I am among the youngest, though little Berthe is only ten. In the sallow gleam of firelight reflected by the tallow, the girl's face is stern and wary. Her mouth sits slightly askew, dragged sideways by the sliver of a scar where someone must have split her lip. But though she is

4

as flushed as any one of us, with damp hair plastered to her head, there is something oddly regal about her bearing.

As if she is some secret queen merely disguised as a wretch.

"Yes," I admit, casting a look over my shoulder to make sure no one else is listening. The foreman, Etienne, is still nowhere to be seen, though he usually drifts stealthily about the floor like some malign wind. "Beelzebub, because he is le Diable's general and his right hand."

"So we are in hell, then," she surmises with a solemn nod. "And Prudhomme our presiding Lucifer, I suppose. Stands to reason, sure enough; certainly reeks like the very pit in here. Tell me, p'tite, how long have you been here?"

"Three years," I reply, gritting my teeth as the tallow resists my stir. "Since the bonnes soeurs at the orphanage indentured me to the maître. There is a contract, they said, a sum I must repay for my freedom. But if there is truly such a paper, I have never seen it."

"Such an irony, to be sentenced to this miserable enfer by a clutch of nuns," she mutters, her mouth twisting viciously against the seam of her scar. "I'll tell you, should I ever find myself cast into true perdition, you had best believe I will have earned my own way there, rather than allowing myself to be tricked by a man again."

"What happened to you?" I cannot keep myself from asking. "How did you come to be here?"

"I gave my heart to a gutless canaille with a cherub's face," she grinds out, spitting into the tallow. "He dragged me to the gaming halls in Montmartre nearly every night, gambled on my sight. But even a gift of prophecy like

5

mine may sometimes grow clouded with such overuse. And then when I could not always see which cards would come, the bastard sold me to repay his debts! Can you imagine such a bedamned, shortsighted fool, to sell a divineress into servitude?"

*A divineress.* I sneak another look at her, wondering if it could be true. If those shrewd eyes, the sense of steel and outrage about her, are truly the marks of a sorceress rather than a mere survivor.

"And to be indentured to one such as Prudhomme . . ." She shakes her head bitterly. "You are right to liken him to the devil, p'tite. I have heard vile rumors of him for years, never thinking myself unlucky enough to wind up in his domain. They say he likes to inflict punishment for his own twisted pleasure." Her eyes narrow with revulsion. "Sometimes, even, to kill."

I swallow hard, an icy flurry coursing down my spine despite the stifling heat. I have only seen the maître a handful of times, a smallish man strutting about the floor in his thread-of-gold waistcoat and red-soled shoes. Bewigged and powdered like a fop, yet gimlet-eyed in his inspection of the candles. The rest of the time the overseers act as his hands, whisking away the comeliest older girls from the floor and ferrying them to his rooms. Most times the girls return, wan and mute but dressed in finer chemises, allotted larger portions of our morning gruel at dejeuner.

Sometimes they do not.

"Maybe it's only stories," I attempt, more to reassure myself than because I believe it. Several of the girls around me have heard her, too; I can see them turning over their shoulders to flick fearful glances at her, murmuring uneasily among themselves. "Empty breath and bluster. People will say anything to stir up scandal."

"Not to a divineress, they won't," she counters. "Most would not risk crossing the likes of Agnesot Brodeur with lies."

The girl at the cauldron next to mine scoffs through her plump lips, rolling her eyes disdainfully. Seventeen-year-old Eugenie is as lovely as the icons of Marie-Madeleine that hung on the orphanage walls, her face a dainty oval, eyes enormous and velvety brown.

"A divineress among us! How very lucky we are, to have such a sorceress amidst our ranks," she croons mockingly. "And what are your powers, Agnesot, besides poor taste in men? Perhaps you can inflict the overseers with such dreadful cauchemars that they wet themselves in the night, and wake too afraid to whip us? Or no, that is too modest. Perhaps you can *fly*."

Agnesot laughs lightly, almost to herself. "That depends," she replies, twitching one shoulder in a careless shrug, "on what I am called to do. What do you wish for, Eugenie? What do you want most, in all the world?"

There is something about the way she says Eugenie's name, like a menacing caress, that unnerves the other girl. I can see Eugenie tremble, as if nails have been raked down her spine. She blinks rapidly, struggling to compose herself.

"A . . . a husband, I suppose," she finally manages, faltering a little. "A wealthy one like the maître, so I need never be anyone's drudge again."

"Easy enough," Agnesot replies, inclining her head. "It will be done."

Eugenie stares at her with flat incredulity, then sweeps her gaze theatrically around the room. "And yet here I still stand, with beef suet in my hair and burns all along my arms. My miracle of a husband nowhere in sight."

She shakes her head contemptuously, turning back to her cauldron. "Don't waste your time listening to her idle talk, Catherine. She is nothing but a charlatan. If she could do real magic, why on earth would she be stuck here toiling with the rest of us?"

"Because magic takes time and sacrifice, chère, much like anything worth doing," Agnesot responds with another shrug, transferring her blithe gaze back to her dipping broach. "And whether you believe or not makes no difference to me."

I watch her for a long moment as she dips her broach again, mesmerized by the conviction that radiates off her like heat. As if she is powered by an inner furnace of her own belief. "Can you truly grant Eugenie's wish?" I ask, unable to keep a shade of marvel from my voice.

She favors me with a smile, small and secretive. "I think you already know I can, p'tite. And I can grant yours, too, if you tell me what you want."

I think on it for a moment, frowning, but I cannot quite imagine what I might wish for, beyond the impossible dream of being away from here.

"To be truly free," I say finally, because it is true. Freedom is what I crave. To be unfettered, owned by no one but myself.

"True freedom," Agnesot repeats thoughtfully, drawing out the word. "That is harder than a husband—but not impossible, given enough time and the right tools. But, are you sure that this is what you want? No wish is granted without a price, and true freedom comes only at the dearest cost. Much more than most would choose to pay."

"All the same," I say, lifting my chin in an attempt to mimic her enviable steel. "If this is all there is to life, to be forever shackled and in service to some cruel master or another, why even bother to live it?"

In truth, I am nowhere near as bold as I strive to sound, my innards roiling with doubt; what sort of cost might seem high to a brash divineress like her, whose tongue flows so easily with curses? As if she can sense this hidden weakness, Agnesot searches my face for a long, fraught moment, her eyes sliding between mine. The firelight from the brazier licks up her face, flinging her cheekbones and eye sockets into stark relief. For a moment her youth seems to desert her, as if some withered crone peers down at me instead. At once ageless and ancient, delving past my eyes and into my heart.

Then she seems to come to some internal decision, her lips pressing white and thin as she gives me a brisk nod.

"Freedom it shall be, then, for petite Catherine."

"Cat. I prefer just Cat."

"Cat," she echoes, reaching out to tip my chin with a light fingertip. "Un petit chat. You have the feel of a canny little soul, Cat. Tell me, have you found that you sometimes . . . see things? Perhaps know what might happen even before it does?"

My mouth drops open. How she might know this is beyond me, but she isn't wrong. Sometimes, when I stare into the creamy runnels of the tallow, it is as if my sight softens and parts, like a curtain sliding open to reveal a glimpse of what lies ahead. A few months ago, I saw a fortnight before it happened that Patrice would lose an arm when her cauldron slipped its chain and overturned. And when shy Mathilde's belly began to burgeon, swelling with child, it was a surprise to everyone but me.

"Yes," I whisper, through a throat suddenly full of sand. "But I thought . . . I thought perhaps I only imagined it."

"Now you know better than to doubt yourself again," she says, a touch reprovingly. "Given the chance to come into your own, mon petit chat, you will grow strong. Stronger, even, than I could dream of being. And I mean to make sure you have the opportunity you deserve. Once I've slipped loose from here and regained my strength, you can be certain the first Messe Noire I cast will be to set you free."

Before I can ask her what a Messe Noire might be, Beelzebub appears behind Agnesot, snatching her by the hair like a cat seizing a kitten's scruff. Her head snaps back so hard her eyes fill with tears, but she doesn't make a sound.

"Is this what you're here for, you trull?" he snarls into her ear, his crude face contorted with wrath. There is something base about his features, his massive, ungainly limbs. Bernadette calls him a golem—a lumbering clay monstrosity of Jewish legend, animated by its master's will and malice. "To fill hardworking girls' ears with such fanciful rot, instead of seeing to your work?"

Agnesot swallows hard, her lips compressing into a defiant line. When she does not respond, he shakes her by the head so fearsomely that I cringe, afraid for her neck and spine.

"Fine," he grinds out, turning on his heel and whipping her around with him. "Have it your way, you impudent dolly-mop. If you won't deign to speak, then I mean to make you weep instead. The rest of you, back to your tasks," he commands over his shoulder as he drags her to the dim corner beside the candle-drying rack—the alcove reserved for our discipline. "And do not let me see your efforts slacken even a jot, unless you aim to be next."

I bend over my cauldron, stirring furiously as another dipper steps up to take Agnesot's place. With each crack of the whip and muted howl, I grit my teeth harder, force myself not to flinch. *Her pain is not your pain*, I remind myself. *This is no place for sympathy.*

Still, hours later, when the foreman and his minions come to herd us to the dormitory, I creep over to the corner where Agnesot sprawls in her bloodied shift. As she slings an arm over my shoulders and slumps gratefully against me, she whispers in my ear.

"See how it is done, p'tite? Given the chance, always resist."

"But he beat you to a pulp," I whisper back vehemently. "How could that *possibly* have been worth it?"

She shakes her head as she staggers along beside me.

"Pain is unpleasant, but it ends," she rasps, almost panting with the effort of speech. "And it is a . . . a good reminder that evil exists. Always remember this, and let no one tell you that salvation might be found through your woman's goodness. Protect a measure of your evil, p'tite. Keep it safe in cupped hands, and nurture it."

She stumbles on a crack in the floor, blanching as the movement jerks her ravaged back. And for just a moment, her bitterness seeps through.

"Else men like these will break you on their will."

The next morning, we wake at the matins bells to find that Agnesot has vanished from the dormitory. Though our pallets are crammed so close we nearly sleep atop one another, somehow none of us heard anything in the night. Not even a stray creak or whimper to betray her departure.

"But where could she have gone?" I wonder, dragging a comb through my unruly hair. "The doors are still barred."

"They must have taken her," Eugenie insists as she dresses hurriedly next to me. "You saw how she was yesterday, styling herself after the martyrs. Refusing to submit. She should have known the maître wouldn't stand for it."

"Or maybe," little Berthe offers timidly, "she walked through the walls. You heard her say she was a divineress. They can do such things, you know."

"Oh, please," Eugenie retorts, starting toward the doors. "As if a sorceress would have allowed herself to fall under a whip."

They are still debating as they join the swarm of girls by the doors, eager for our morning repast of barley gruel. I linger by Agnesot's pallet instead, running my hands over its threadbare quilt, as if her bedding might yield some silent answer. I find nothing beneath the thin square of her pillow, nor captured in the tangle of her sheets. But caught between the prickly straw-tick of the mattress and the wooden frame, my fingertips meet the corners of something hard and cool.

My heart drumming, I ease out a black bound book, casting a quick glance over my shoulder to ensure I am not being watched. Whatever Agnesot left behind, I find myself loath to share it with the others. The leather cover flips open to reveal yellowed pages dense with text and odd illustrations—sketches of creeping plants with labeled parts, and charts of strange and angular symbols. I cannot read the words, having never been taught letters, but as I cradle the pages to my chest so tightly they seem to hum against my skin, I am struck with the certainty that someday I will.

Because wherever Agnesot has gone, I know beyond the cobweb of a doubt that she escaped on her own power.

And whatever this book is, I suspect the divineress left it behind for me.

# ACT ONE: ASCENT

**CHAPTER ONE**

# The Sigil and the Door

PARIS, FRANCE
**June 5, 1667**

*Should the waters guard their secrets close, make certain you have not overlooked the strongest of the scrying herbs.*

"But I *added* the agrimony already, devil take you," I grouse into the grimoire's pages, resisting a powerful urge to slam the spellbook shut. "Why won't it simply work properly for once?"

As if sensing my high dudgeon soaring to even greater heights, Alecto slithers up my arm, tucking her wedge-shaped head against my collarbone. Her tongue flickers against my skin in a ticklish caress, urging me to settle down. I take a calming breath, running my hand gratefully along her cool, muscular length. In my view, anyone who believes snakes to be cold or unfeeling has never taken the proper time to get to know one. And of my three king snakes, Alecto is the most affectionate, supremely attuned to the shifting squalls of my whims and moods.

If she were a person, one might call her solicitous.

"I know, mon trésor," I murmur to her, tracing the outline of her dainty head with a fingertip. "Failing to conjure a vision is hardly the end of the world. But it is galling to be foiled when one is so very close, n'est-ce pas? Perhaps we try again, just one more time?"

Alecto tightens briefly on my arm before relaxing again, the serpentine equivalent of a long-suffering sigh. But it seems she is willing to indulge me for at least a little longer. When I rest my hand on the table's edge, she pools down my arm like a sentient spill of ink, arranging herself in a coil around the obsidian scrying bowl. I refill the bowl with the mixture called for in the book: ewe's milk, water strained through cheesecloth to rid it of impurities, a blend of herbs, and a dash of my own tears. After my years in the fabrique, precious little moves me to weep, and I had to pinch myself rather viciously to eke these out.

Against the unremitting black of the bowl, the murky liquid roils like a storm front crawling over an eventide sky. It lurches into tantalizing shapes, which scatter into ripples as my breath skates across the water's surface.

*Once the waters are waiting, bring the sight to bear upon them— but gently and with forbearance*, the book directs, somewhat prissily. *Do not be insatiable in your hunger to know, nor overeager in your demands. The veil does not bend readily to the will of a boorish divineress.*

Be patient, in other words. Reasonable enough, yet the enjoinment still rankles me. Patience has never been among my virtues.

Taking another breath, I do my best to heed its command. I let my eyes go hazy, my vision thinning at the edges like unraveling gauze, letting the swirling of the water lead the way. As if sensing the slow gather of my focus, Alecto begins to seethe around the bowl, her body forming a circle around a circle. This addition is of my own devising; there is no mention in the grimoire of snakes. Yet the few times I've managed to fish a full-fledged vision from the water, it has always been with my girls' help.

But today, not even Alecto can tip me over the edge. The milky water remains obstinately inert, speckled with herbs and on its way to curdling.

With a sigh, I stand and gather Alecto up, carrying her back to the immense glass vivarium she shares with Megaera and Tisiphone. Antoine built it for me as a birthday gift, and installed it close to the fireplace so my snakes might bask in its heat. As I lower Alecto into its mossy depths, the sight of its clever compartments tempers my disappointment and reminds me of my new life's many blessings. I am now a jeweler's wife with a stately home near the Pont Marie, wed to a husband who loves me in his way. Enough, anyway, to permit me my snakes and cabinet of occult treasures, when another man might have had me clapped in brodequins or even burned at the stake.

But we understand each other well, Antoine Monvoisin and I. Well enough to know that certain forbidden desires must be given their head.

This life is so much more than I could have imagined during my years of drudgery, that I cannot help but believe in the magic of Agnesot's grimoire. Out of all the girls desperate to escape their indenture, Antoine chose me to wed. Which means that wherever she is now, Agnesot managed at least part of what she swore to do; she sprang me free from the fabrique, set me loose to pursue my own power. The power that she predicted would one day surpass even hers.

And if the spells in her grimoire yet fail to corral the wild tempests of my visions, to bring them fully under my control, then I must only work the harder. Perhaps, once I have come into my own as Agnesot predicted, the true freedom she promised me will also follow suit.

A freedom far beyond the small one I have now, ever hinging on my husband's continued beneficence.

A light knock sounds at my door, followed by a courteous pause. Enough time for me to clear the scrying bowl away, tuck the grimoire behind the more innocuous books that line my shelves, and sit back down by the fireplace with embroidery spread across my lap. I trust Antoine, but not enough to have him entirely privy to my doings.

A moment later, the door creaks open to admit my husband.

"Bonsoir, Catherine," he says mildly, crossing over to blandly buss my cheek. Though we've been man and wife for almost three years now, he has never laid a hand on me in passion. When he came to Prudhomme's fabrique to avail himself of an amenable young wife, it was not the allure of the marital bed he wished to purchase, but the outward trappings of marriage. A respectable veneer. "Am I interrupting?"

"Oh, not at all." I set aside the embroidery, which has not progressed beyond the odd thread in well over a year. I cannot abide such insipid pursuits, not when I can always feel the grimoire's tidal pull. "Are you finished at the atelier, then? Shall I see to dinner with Suzette?"

"Ah, no, actually." He pulls a regretful face, stroking his silver-shot beard. "I'm meeting with my colleague Sebastien for dinner again tonight. I . . . I expect it will go late. I'm sorry, I should have thought to tell you earlier."

My practiced eye runs over his hair, neatly clubbed and pomaded away from his silvering temples, his dove-gray satin justaucorps and crisply tied cravat. Though we leave each other quite unmoved, Antoine can be handsome when he tries. And not only has he put effort into his appearance, but this makes three times that he has seen Sebastien this week. Their romance must be flourishing indeed.

Though I reap the benefit of his false life, it still gives me a pang that they must steal this time together, that my husband cannot simply have the love he truly wants. Especially when the king's own brother, the duc d'Orléans, rides into battle bejeweled and rouged, and it is widely known that the Chevalier du Lorraine shares his bed.

But while the noblesse dally as they please, such latitude does not apply to common folk, especially not when it comes to any love beyond the pale.

"Do not trouble yourself over it, cher," I tell him, waving a hand. "Perhaps I will meet a friend tonight as well." My heart lifts joyfully at the prospect of seeing Marie, a light fluttering like a lacewing swarm tickling in my belly. I have been so consumed with studying the grimoire that over a week has somehow flown by since I last spent time with her. "See you in the morning?"

Antoine's face slackens with relief at the lack of judgment in my voice, as though I would ever see fit to condemn his predilections when they are not so unlike my own.

"Bien sûr, we'll have breakfast together," he says. "But you will be careful tonight, yes? Colbert has hiked the taxes yet again; it seems the Sun King's Dutch war has gnawed the royal treasury so thin that the peasantry must yield ever more of their meager earnings to replenish it. I wouldn't have you assailed by some malcontent staggering about after drowning his woes."

I smile at Antoine, moved by his concern, even though I have no fear of the city's restive streets, no matter how many times Louis XIV's royal comptroller sees fit to turn the screw yet tighter. Anyone fool enough to cross me and Marie would soon live to regret it. I always carry a knife belt on our outings, while Marie wears vicious little stilettos strapped about her person at all times, along with hollow rings filled with corrosives ready to be flung into an offending face.

"I'll be fine," I reassure him. "I always am, non? Though before you leave, could you see to your haberdasher's bill, cher? It arrived over a fortnight ago."

"Bien sûr," he replies quickly, drawing a palm over his pomaded hair. "I had meant to attend to that already, but . . . the shop has been such pandemonium that it must have slipped my mind. Thank you for the reminder, Catherine. Though you really need not fret over our finances."

"Oh, it is no trouble. And I do not want us to find ourselves in accidental arrears again," I add a touch pointedly, referring to an incident a year ago in which Antoine "misremembered" to pay his irate tailor for over a month. "Now go enjoy your night, mon cher."

Excusing himself, he withdraws from my study. As soon as he is gone I rise, casting the embroidery away with an exasperated huff. My mind already tumbling ahead to when the last rind of sun peels away from Paris, revealing the dark and inviting pith of night.

Before I pen an invitation to Marie, I move to the window to twitch aside the heavy brocatelle curtains. Beyond the ranks of mansard rooftops still glistening slick from a brief afternoon shower, the sky is a velvety plum. At the sight of it, a sense of vast potential strains inside my rib cage, unfurling against my lungs. I have little use for the Paris of the day, marinated in horse piss and hazed with chimney smoke, clamorous with carriage wheels, church bells, and the racket of a hundred thousand shrilling voices.

But night . . . night is another matter altogether. A beguiling province of promises and whispers, secrets traded like coins behind shielding hands.

Night is when the dark sun of my city truly rises.

By the time I arrive at the Pont Neuf bridge to meet Marie, Paris has plunged fully into darkness. The river ripples like an oiled snake hide, winding through the stone arches of the bridge that spans across the water to the Île de la Cité—the city's oldest district and its beating heart, an island suspended in the silty lifeblood of the Seine.

Marie waits for me by the bridge's base, torch in hand; after nightfall, Parisians make their own light if they must have it. She always undertakes to arrive before me, as if even a few minutes without her might land me in some grave peril. Though she's my elder by only a year and a half, she was my fiercest protector at the orphanage as well as my best friend, before I was indentured to the fabrique and she took to the streets. While I've severed all other ties to the wretched girl I used to be, I pined for Marie during the years we spent apart, and sought her out almost as soon as Antoine sprung me free.

Though I have never said it to her aloud, I cannot remember a time before I loved Marie.

"Ma belle," she cries out now, surging forward to embrace me with her free hand, her thin brown cheek brushing mine. Everything about Marie is sleek, including her narrow face, slim frame, and shining spill of hair dark as chestnut shells. My skin tingles where our cheeks press together, and I breathe in the familiar, subtle scent of her, orange blossom and sandalwood, a faint and spicy sweetness that makes my heart swell like a waxing moon.

She draws back to pout playfully at me, with lips that are ripe and full and creased down the center just like midsummer cherries. "I thought perhaps you'd cast me aside in favor of that bedamned grimoire. It has been *ages* since you last came out to play."

"Hardly ages, chérie. And as if I could ever forsake you for much longer than a week," I soothe, looping my arm through hers. "It's only that I have been so busy."

"Yes, busy attending to that book-shaped devil's snare," she replies, her mien darkening. "As if you have any notion what evils you might unleash with all your idle tinkering."

This is not the first time Marie has cast aspersions upon the grimoire's worth, suggested that a strange divineress's spellbook might contain dangers best left untouched. But for all that she can cut a purse as deftly as pretend to read a palm, Marie is only a talented grifter. She could not possibly feel or understand the pure power that beats from within the grimoire's pages like a living heart—much less judge its nature.

"The grimoire is a tool, and a tool cannot be evil," I reply by rote, as I have the countless other times we've had this conversation. "Besides, you of all people should know that a little evil can come in useful."

"My evil is only of the most innocuous sort, ma belle. The kind meant to keep me in cheap wine and baguettes." She presses her lips together disapprovingly, then gives over. "But since you insist on prodding at it, at least tell me it has been going well?"

"I wish," I reply as we merge onto the trottoir. A troupe of fire-eating acrobats capers past us like a demonic horde, swallowing curved blades alive with flames. As we pass by the half-moon alcoves set atop each stone pile, the wheedling voices of quacksalvers and merchants assail us, peddling their wares from covered stalls. My stomach stirs at the smell of crisp-baked wafers and nuts roasted in sugar and cinnamon, sweet above the river's brackish tang.

"But the scrying spells are damnably difficult to master," I continue as we dodge a cackling guttersnipe pelting away with someone's purse. "Sometimes I can nearly feel how they should work. But they almost always evade me in the end, wriggling between my fingers. It is beyond maddening. I was meant to do such magic, Marie, I can *feel* it— and yet I simply cannot summon it up at will."

I am articulating it poorly, which is nothing new. I have never been able to properly explain it to Marie, the potent yearning that I feel for dominion over my magic. The sense that drawing it under my control will also bring forth the freedom I so crave, as if the two are somehow inextricably linked.

Marie cants her head to the side like a sparrow, tiny replicas of the torch flame dancing in her eyes as she considers me. Then she gives a little nod, as if she has come to some decision.

"Then perhaps there is another way," she says, picking up her stride as she tugs me along, until I nearly struggle to keep up despite my longer legs. "A better way than battering yourself against that book—and certainly safer."

"What do you mean? And why the sudden rush?" It is not as if our outings ever follow some set schedule. "Has

Stephane earmarked a particularly choice wine bag for us? An entire barrel, perhaps?"

Marie merely shakes her hooded head, cryptic as a sphinx. She maintains her silence as we walk, only piquing my curiosity further. By the time we set foot on the Île de la cité, I am so ablaze with anticipation I feel as though I could light our way myself.

The Île cleaves itself uneasily between the city's richest and its poorest, with Notre Dame's grand spire presiding over its eastern point, the king's Palais Royal and its lush gardens sprawling across the west. But Marie and I make straight for the island's shabby center, the cité itself, an ancient maze of run-down tenements and taverns, seedy hospitals and churches. And in it the notorious Val d'Amour, beating like a secret heart within a heart, with the Rue de Glatigny as its central artery. The wealthy only venture here when they have a pressing need, or some burning wish. The death of a rival, a glimpse into the morass of the future. Or perhaps only some stolen hours with one of the Val's many filles de joie, with their threadbare corsets and garishly rouged lips.

Though I do not live in the cité as Marie does, I've dallied in her demimonde enough to know that any twisted dream the mind devises can be purchased here.

As we whisk by shuttered storefronts, keeping our skirts hitched high above the mud-slick cobbles, I glance curiously at Marie.

"But we've passed La Pomme Noire already," I protest, naming our favorite tavern. "Surely you were not thinking of La Sirene et la Pierre, not after the rotgut swill we had there last time? My innards are likely to never be the same."

"Trust me, Cat," she replies, flashing me a sharp slice of a smile, firelight shining off her teeth. "I am not taking you anywhere you have been before."

Some minutes later, she draws to a halt in front of a hulking wooden door clasped with battered hinges. Standing on her toes, she brings the torch to bear just above the door, casting light on a sigil inscribed in the stone.

"What is that?" I ask her, an anxious swell surging up my throat. "That symbol?"

"One of the runes of les arts occultes," she replies, rapping on the door. "This one denotes chiromancy."

"But there are chiromancers every night at the Pomme," I remind her. "You read palms there yourself; I've seen you do it a time or two. Why come here instead?"

"The Pomme is merely good for the occasional diversion, ma belle," she scoffs. "Only unskilled dilettantes ply their trade in earnest there. The ones too simple to gain admittance here."

"But—"

The eyelet set into the door rattles open, and a gruff "Alors, dis-moi" filters through. Marie whispers something through it, too quietly for me to hear.

A moment later the door creaks inward, whining on its hinges.

Then Marie steps inside and draws me in behind her, and I'm left with no more time for questions.

## CHAPTER TWO

# The Haven and the Lady

The first thing I notice is the ceiling.

It is barrel-vaulted and flung high enough above us that the arching ribs vanish into gloom, as if the building has neither roof nor end. We must be inside one of the abandoned and deconsecrated churches that litter the Île, I decide, though this one is rather grander than most of them.

The second is the smoke. The air is so steeped in frankincense and myrrh that it gathers above our heads like trailing clouds, as if we've stepped outside rather than in. The first lungful leaves me a little dizzy, reinforcing the illusion of having crossed a threshold only to land in another world. It almost makes me want to trawl the dark above us for stars, or the winking glimmer of a miniature moon.

The third is the quiet.

"Why is everyone whispering?" I ask Marie, bringing my lips close to her ear and pitching my own voice low. None of the patrons seated at the room's many candlelit tables pay us any mind, so intent are they on their quiet conversations carried out over upturned palms. But a thrumming sense of tension pervades the space, and I find myself loath to disturb it. "And there is no music."

"What is spoken here is to not be shared beyond these walls," she whispers back, reaching up to gently tug my hood farther over my head. "As to music, well. No one seeking mere amusement can afford to seek it here."

Wreathing her cool fingers through mine, she leads me over to the colossal bar top that takes up the room's left wall, like a standing stone toppled on its side. As she orders from the gruff barkeep, I lean forward to sweep my palms over the bar's scarred surface, pocked with age and scratched with obscure sigils. Eight-pointed stars, spirals trapped in circles, hands with too many fingers and palms turned up, inscribed with overlapping lines. With a spurt of shock, I realize that some of them are familiar—I have seen these symbols in Agnesot's grimoire. Some of them I know to be astrologers' runes, but others I have never been able to identify.

*And yet they are here*, I think with a rising thrill. Perhaps this was once the divineress's haunt.

"What is this place?" I breathe to Marie as I dip my head to examine the markings more closely, until I can smell the stone's rusty mineral odor. "And why have you kept it from me all this time?"

"It's a haven of divination," she replies. "One of many

in the cité, and my favorite. As to why I have never taken you . . ."

The barkeep interrupts her by sliding two sloshing goblets across the stone, tipping Marie a brusque nod as she drops a clutch of sous into his waiting hand. The wine the goblet holds is rich and red, better than I expected. It burns furiously down my gullet, like a falling star escaping the firmament.

"The lawless dealings that transpire here are not for the faint of heart," Marie continues, her eyes glinting secretively above her goblet's rim. "I wished to keep you clear of it for another few years yet, at least. But were I to wait any longer, I fear that blasted book might swallow you whole. At least here, I can be certain you do not sell your soul to le Diable all unwitting."

Her impulse to keep me safe never fails to warm me, unnecessary though it is in this case.

"While I appreciate the thought, ma chère, I'm quite certain Lucifer has far more pressing things with which to occupy his time than lurking in wait for me," I scoff, rolling my eyes. While I do not doubt that notre Dieu and le Diable wage their eternal war against each other somewhere far beyond our ken, I do not truly believe now, any more than I did back at the fabrique, that either of them deigns to meddle directly in the affairs of men. "And what do you suppose I shall learn here, that all my failed attempts with the grimoire haven't taught me?"

Marie makes a thoughtful moue, lifting a single finger. "Not *learning*, but the right sort of *practice*. Those born with the true gift, like you, ma belle, are few and far between.

And though the chiromancers here are exceptional grifters to the last, most of them have about as much real magic as I do—which is to say, not a jot of it. But I put up a lively enough pretense when there is coin involved, do I not? And if even I can convincingly pretend to read the future in a palm, think what *you* might be able to do."

I frown at her, cocking my head. "But I have never even tried to read a palm!"

"Not yet, you haven't. But a certain woe-struck lady who wishes to remain unnamed comes here tonight, seeking a stolen glimpse of what lies ahead."

She leans in closer to me, her dark eyes sparkling with mischief. "And I've a mind to have you read for her in my stead."

A quarter of an hour later, Marie and I sit at one of the tables with the nameless lady across from us.

"Pardonnez-moi, but I came for *your* talents, Mademoiselle Bosse," the lady protests, her cultured voice barely above a breath. She is wealthy but not highborn, Marie believes, most likely some well-heeled tradesman's wife. "You come highly recommended, whereas your companion . . . Catherine Monvoisin, you say? Well, I've never heard so much as a whisper of her name."

"Catherine is my apprentice," Marie lies smoothly, the corner of her plush mouth quirking when I dart her a peevish look. "And an exceptionally promising one. Her star is on the rise, madame. Soon her name will be on everybody's lips—and *you* will have been the first to sample her gift."

The lady's eyes shift to mine, clouded with uncertainty. "But . . ."

"What harm can it do to try, my lady?" Marie cajoles. "Allow me to ease your mind. Should you be dissatisfied with the reading, I shall take over for Catherine—free of charge, bien sûr."

The lady weighs the offer a trifle longer before deciding that she has little to lose. When she extends her hand to me, I bend my head over her proffered palm, thinking furiously. My sight has always been unpredictable, tempestuous as a summer storm; if I can barely claw it up with the grimoire's exacting guidance, why should it heed me now?

But, I tell myself, I have watched Marie do this same thing so many times. Drinking in the intent lines of her face as she subtly scanned her targets, reading intentions from the cast of their expressions, discerning hidden desires from their eyes.

If she can lie her way through a divination, then surely so can I.

"A . . . a fearsome cloud hovers over your path, madame," I improvise haltingly. "I can see its outline casting a shadow on your palm . . ."

And then I sputter out, unable for the life of me to think of what might come next.

As the lady gives me a dubious look, I take a few deep breaths to calm myself, under the guise of letting magic build. I allow my eyes to drift up to the lady's face, taking stock of her. The sort of troubles that drive people to a soothsayer tend to hail from a common source—health, or wealth, or matters of the heart. This woman is too young and clearly hale to be besieged by some deathly ailment. Nor, from her fine skin and the rich fabric of her cowl, does she seem to lack in means.

Which very likely leaves us with love.

"Alors, you wish to know what will become of you and him," I venture, searching her face for confirmation that some "him" exists at all. When the skin at the corners of her eyes crinkles minutely, I take heart and plow ahead. "And given what has come to pass between you, whether his attentions will hold true."

"And will they?" she whispers, eyelids fluttering to contain sudden tears. "Now that, now . . ."

Though I am only spinning a grift, something about the raw fervor of her need calls to me. I sink my teeth into the inside of my lip, sweeping my thumb over the lines that lattice the lady's palm. For a moment they remain no more than creases of the skin, meaningless and inert—then they begin to waver like shifting runes, to writhe and realign.

A buzzing starts to build low in my nape, the sense of swarming pressure that often accompanies the sight.

"You took a lover, madame. Betrothed to another, but under your thrall," I intone, the words suddenly tumbling past my lips seemingly of their own accord. "Breath to breath, mouth to mouth, entwined beneath the darkened boughs. And when he said he loved you, that he only needed time—that he would withdraw his given ring and pledge it to you instead—you did not think to doubt him."

Her story unfolds in flickering spurts and starts, inscribed in her palm but suddenly coming alive in my mind's eye. I see her slipping out of a fete with her giddy lover in tow behind her, all flushed cheeks and swallowed laughter. I watch as they shed their clothes, sinking together into passion in the tangled space within a hedgerow. I hear their heated promises as though I am there myself, a silent ghost bearing witness to their ardor.

Then the lines swirl and coil again, melting into nothing before taking on another shape. When the roiling darkness finally clears behind my eyes, I can see the lady curled like a forlorn comma into a cushioned alcove, hand hovering above her belly.

"But instead of his ring, you bear his seed," I murmur, looking up to meet her stricken eyes. "And now you stand at a crossroads, abandoned and alone. Save for the unborn child he left behind."

This time her tears do spill over, glimmering on the darkened hollows under her eyes.

"I do not know what to do," she whispers, pressing trembling fingers to her lips. "Should I tell him, in hopes that it will spur him into wedding me instead? Or will the knowledge only make him cast me away for good?"

I shake my head vaguely, swaying it from side to side. When I strive to see past her sitting at the window, the vision slithers away from me, clotting into a denser darkness. Yet I can feel something lurking just beyond, more secrets hidden in her palm.

But how do I coax them forth into the light?

A snippet from Agnesot's grimoire surfaces, a maddening explanation of a rune that only ever vexed me before.

*If you should find yourself well and truly stalled, remember that circles make for openings.*

I had no notion of what this might mean before, but now I think of the spiral sigils inscribed into both the bar top and the grimoire. With my ring finger, I begin to draw slow, concentric circles into the lady's palm. As though I am stirring away the obscuring darkness, wheedling the vision forth. Her lines shudder and dance under my touch before falling firmly into place, the truth of them like the breaking of a new dawn.

Dazzling and irrefutable, a certainty beyond reproach.

"If you tell him, he will ruin you," I say bluntly. "He will paint you a harlot, a strumpet who flung herself at him with no care for decency. A siren calling to a sailor until he dashed himself against the rocks. He will leave you disgraced, madame, and thoroughly alone."

*He will, he will, he will.*

She flinches every time I speak, each of my pronouncements striking her like a ruthless blow.

"But that is not fair," she says, her shoulders slumping pitifully. My heart swells with sympathy for her, even as I wonder what sort of unduly sweet life she's lived thus far, that has led her to expect fairness as her rightful lot. "What shall I do now?"

I shake my head, my body slackening with fatigue as the last whorls of the vision melt away. "I do not know, my lady. I've told you all that I can see."

"S'il vous plaît," the lady presses, gulping back tears. "Please, you *must* tell me what to do."

Though I have all but forgotten that she is here, it is Marie who rescues me. She reaches for the lady's other hand, folding it between her own.

"There is no need to weep, madame," she says quietly. "If you do not want this child, there are ways to go about things. Remedies I can suggest, procedures to help you should the tinctures fail. And if you do want it, well . . ."

She fixes the lady with a gimlet gaze, but not without sympathy. "I would suggest finding yourself an amenable husband with a great deal of haste."

## CHAPTER THREE

# The Moneylender and the Lord

I barely remember staggering home that night, drunk on elation and the haven's robust wine.

"You did gorgeously, ma belle," Marie whispered into my ear as she left me on my doorstep, the warm fan of her breath sending a spiraling tingle down my neck. "Just as I knew you would."

"But why was it so much easier to scry for her?" I marveled, the words sluggish on my tongue. "When I can barely dredge up a vision for myself?"

Marie tipped me a sly wink over her shoulder as she turned away. "Perhaps you might take this lesson to heart, chérie. And trust that sometimes I *do* know best."

The next morning, I break my fast with Antoine at a decadently late hour. We eat in companionable silence, both of us basking in the afterglow of a night well spent. I am idling over the gossip pages and spooning fromage and fruit compote into my mouth when Suzette cowers into the dining room in her diffident way.

"Pardonnez-moi, monsieur," she breathes, wringing her hands in her starched apron. "There are some men downstairs to see you. I told them you could not come to the door just now, but they would not be turned away."

"But who would be calling on us at noon?" I wonder, glancing over at Antoine, expecting to find a reflection of my own bemusement. Instead, I see that my husband has gone an alarming shade of suet gray.

When my gaze lands on him, he fumbles clumsily for a smile, dabbing at the corners of his mouth.

"Nothing of any import, I'm sure," he says weakly, pushing back from the table and waving me down when I begin to stand as well. "No, please, Catherine. Do not trouble yourself. I will go and sort it out."

But the cheese has already soured in my mouth, a premonitory dread surging up my throat like bile. Whatever this interruption is, I suddenly know that it bodes far from well.

Gathering my dressing gown closer around my shoulders, I whisk out of the dining room and down the carpeted stairs, until I reach the landing overlooking our foyer. Below, Antoine confers with a burly man, menacing despite his grubby wig and tiny pince-nez. Beside them two muscle-bound roughs wrestle our claw-footed credenza out the door, followed by a third lout with one of our Gobelin tapestries slung like a corpse across his brawny shoulders.

"Antoine?" I call down, my voice more strained than I intended. But I cannot help the shrillness of my tone, not when my throat has turned into a vise. "What is happening? Where are they taking our Gobelins?"

When Antoine and the stranger glance up at me, I do not know if I am more terrified by the sheer blaze of panic that streaks across my husband's face or the flat disdain in the strange man's beady eyes.

"I told you there was no need to interrupt your petit déjeuner, Catherine," Antoine chides feebly, jogging up the stairs to meet me on the landing. "I have everything quite under control."

"Of course there is a need, Antoine," I hiss under my breath, flicking a pointed glance below. "When there are *men* taking our *things*, I should say there is decidedly a need. I am sure my fromage will keep while you explain all this to me."

He wets his lips with his tongue, his eyes skittering nervously to the side before resettling on mine. "It is truly nothing. Only that earnings at the shop have dipped a bit of late, and I have had to be . . . somewhat more enterprising in keeping astride our debts."

"Our debts?" I repeat, simmering with rage. "*Ours*, Antoine? Surely I misheard you."

What my well-intentioned wastrel of a husband means to say is that he spends his jeweler's income like water, streams of coin sieving through his fingers. Even his lively trade cannot keep pace with his refined tastes. Antoine is a helpless connoisseur of every sort of beauty, drawn to luxury like a moth to any open flame. Rich clothing, the objets d'art tucked into every corner of our home, exorbitant love tokens for his petit copains; he can resist none of it. I suspect that even I was such an acquisition, with my bramble of foxy curls and cinnamon spattering of freckles, my hazel eyes that edge toward amber. Though I am not beautiful in any fashionable way and certainly do not stir his particular passion, I know Antoine finds me outwardly arresting.

I have never begrudged my husband this weakness for finery, not when he cares for me so well, indulges my own appetite for matters of the dark.

But though there have been other debts, repossession men have never come traipsing into our house before. It has never come to this.

"Catherine, do not be like this," he pleads. "Please, ma chère, spare me a little understanding."

"And how should I be instead, when you have beholden us to a moneylender?" I demand, striving to even out my faltering voice. "When we cannot pay what is owed?"

"It is only a few pieces to tide us over," he soothes, squeezing my hands. "You know our profits are always scarcer over the summer, when so many of the noblesse abandon the city for their country estates. But I have several commissions lined up in the coming months, for the Vicomtesse de Polignac and the Duc de Bouillon, to start. Once they are complete and I am paid in full, I can reclaim whatever we have lost. This is only a temporary thing, Catherine. I promise you. We will be fine."

So he says. And yet a hot reek boils up my nose, the memory of acrid tallow pierced with beeswax sweetness. I can almost feel the blister of a bullwhip falling across my back, cruel hands tightening on my shoulders, a vicious grip buried in my hair.

I do not need my scrying bowl to see a bad moon rising, its bloated outline cresting the horizon to leer above my head.

And even clasped between my husband's hands, mine begin to shake.

"Antoine, listen to me." I gird my tone with steel and search his eyes, trying to impress the truth into my kind yet feckless husband, whose downfall would surely spell my own. "I cannot be poor again. I would rather die, do you understand, than return to the squalor from which I came. Do you hear me, Antoine? I would rather *die*."

Because, where would I go if he loses everything of ours? What choice would there be for me, besides the poorhouse or the streets?

If he cannot find us a way out of this, I will lose even this small plot of freedom that I've staked out for myself.

"Oh, Catherine." Antoine draws me close, and though we are almost of a height, I allow him to tuck my head into his neck. "I promise it will never come to that. I am only sorry to have distressed you with this at all, and so needlessly!"

When I shudder against him with a restrained sob, he holds me gently away from him, attempting a reassuring smile.

"Why don't you go out again tonight, divert yourself with your friend? I will review our ledgers, make certain that all is just as well as I know it shall be in the end. Trust me, chérie. We may not be . . . exactly as other unions are. But you *are* my cherished wife. And I would not let any harm come to you on my account."

*And what am I to do*, I think despairingly as I look into his eyes, *if you step over the precipice and lead us both into ruin because you cannot help yourself?*

Because I know, as surely as I know that I owe my life to Agnesot, that it is I who will pay for my husband's folly, as has every wastrel's wife that came before me.

Then I remember the weight of the little coin bag Marie slipped into my purse the night before—payment for my session with the nameless lady, which Marie insisted that I keep for having done all the work. With that thought, the frantic gallop of my heart subsides a little in my chest.

Perhaps there is another way I might yet begin protecting myself.

The next night, I fashion myself into a proper fortune-teller.

Asking Marie to let me read for another of her new clients is even simpler than I had hoped. She is amused by how a single taste has whetted my appetite for selling prophecy, and though I fear that I may be encroaching on her territory, she assures me that she has amassed a reliable enough clientele that ceding one more newcomer to me will hardly affect her livelihood.

But if I am to make my own livelihood of this, I know it will take much more than just the sight. If life has taught me anything, it is that folk with means yearn to feel as though they have taken some clever advantage. Spent their coin uncommonly well in comparison to their less-savvy peers.

So I must learn to sell myself, to wear mysticism like an alluring second skin. To present the face of a true divineress.

When Marie's gentleman client meets me at the haven, I know just what illusion I have conjured up for him. I've draped a black lace veil over my curls, allowing only the stubbornest of ringlets to spring free by my temples. Thick kohl lines my eyes, and a much darker shade of carmine than is stylish stains my lips. I keep my face both taut and expressionless, teeming with possibility as I reach confidently for his hand. As though I am some oracle he has sought out on a mountaintop, poised on the breathless brink of revelation. Lovely and untouchable as she is secretive.

"And who might you be, mademoiselle?" His lips purse petulantly even as he allows me to take his hand. I asked Marie to make herself scarce while I read for him, though I know she watches from the shadows, ready to swoop in should I require her help. And there is also burly Alexandre to call upon, the rough who ensures that the haven's hush remains unbroken by customers displeased by their purchased prophecies. "I thought it was to be Mademoiselle Bosse who—"

"Mademoiselle Bosse is, alas, indisposed tonight," I interrupt, keeping my voice soft but unassailable, leaving no room for contradiction. "But I am her trusted colleague, Madame Catherine Monvoisin. Should you be unhappy with my services, Mademoiselle Bosse will read for you for free once she has recovered. But I assure you, messire, I am every bit her equal. You will not require a second reading once you have heard mine."

He blinks at my assertive tone, taken aback—exactly as I want. I mean to unsettle this man, set him back on his heels and tantalize him all at once.

I mean to make him remember me.

"I suppose that will do, for now," he allows, his smooth hand relaxing in my grip. An arrogant languor overtakes his patrician face even as his eyes spark with anticipation. Though he has offered her only an alias, Marie believes him so highborn that he may even have grown up in Versailles's gilded halls. Cosseted enough, at any rate, to render him mostly intrigued rather than alarmed by unexpected novelties.

*And why should he not be intrigued*, I think a trifle bitterly, *when life has offered him nothing but pleasantness and opportunities?*

Yet some real need boils in him, seething just beneath his pampered surface like a sulfurous spring. I can feel it tugging at me even before I properly begin. I have barely bent my head over his palm, following the furrows of his lines, when my nape starts to knell, tolling like a rung bell with the rising of the sight.

"Ever since you were old enough to know it, your father has favored your half brother," I begin, speaking the vision aloud for him even as it unfolds behind my eyes. "The silver-tongued son of your father's second wife. Though you are his better in every aspect, from riding to falconry to the keeping of the estate's books, it seems nothing can unseat him in your father's fond regard. And with every passing year he burrows deeper under your skin, lodged like a stubborn thorn festering in your side."

I can hear the breath snag in his throat, bright shock flaring in his eyes. He clearly expected his fortune told in broader strokes, was unprepared for such a specific truth.

"It is . . . Yes!" the lord exclaims. "That is Bernard, pardieu, that is him precisely! Go on, girl, what else do you see?"

Though it galls me to hear this uppity nobleman call me "girl," I set it to the side.

"You thought you had time to prove yourself his better," I continue, tracing my fingers over his palm in ornate designs. "But now your father lingers on his deathbed, and your brother does not leave his side, whispering sweetened venom in the old man's ear. Angling to steal the estate out from under you—along with your sire's title, if he can manage it."

The lord breathes raggedly, a savage fury twisting his handsome face.

"So he *is* plotting to usurp my inheritance, the weaseling blackguard," he growls through clenched teeth. "Well, he and his grasping chit of a mother cannot have what is mine by right, he will not take—"

"But he *will*, messire," I interrupt softly, spearing his eyes with mine. Because I can see the possibility of this loss looming in his future, like a long shadow cast upon a spreading fog. "Even now he is telling your father that you have failed him as a son, that you harbor no true filial love. Convincing him to redraw his will and testament, so that your brother may properly honor his legacy once he is gone."

The young heir's lips compress into a vicious line. He swears under his breath and slams a bunched fist to the table's surface, rattling the candle and his iron tankard.

I manage to retain my impassive facade only because I saw this outburst coming, but the patrons at other tables startle at the sound. They cast us curious glances from the corners of their eyes, which only pleases me the more. Let them wonder what it is I am telling him that stokes his passions so.

Let them wonder what I might be telling *them*, were they in his place.

"Then I must put a stop to his scheming," he mutters, a flurry of dark thoughts chasing one another across his face. "If he feels so very free to plot against me, why should I not do the same?"

"Perhaps you should, at that, messire," I agree placidly, flicking one shoulder in a shrug. "It does sound as though he has brought a reckoning upon himself."

His eyes latch ferociously on mine, though he takes care to corral his impassioned tone, shooting a wary glance over his shoulder.

"He certainly has, the ingratiating weevil. I . . . have heard of substances that might help at times like this. Poudre de succession, for one." He lowers his voice even further, lifting a fine brow. "And if I should ask you to procure some for me?"

A bitter chill whirls through my veins at how readily the request falls from his lips. I know what inheritance powder is, of course. Though she would never sell such a thing, I have heard Marie mention it, and Agnesot's grimoire contains many recipes for occult poisons meant to rid one of ham-fisted husbands and pestilential relatives. But it shocks me to hear it nonetheless, when I had been expecting something less insidious. Perhaps a duel at dawn to settle the brothers' differences, or counter-stratagems to regain his father's esteem. Nothing, in any event, so malicious and sly as arsenic.

The young heir's eyes narrow calculatingly at my hesitation. "I could make it worth your while, Madame Monvoisin," he offers in a whisper. "If you do not trade in such alchemy yourself, I would pay you for only a name. A reputable and discreet source for what I seek."

I waver for a moment, sorely tempted by the prospect of additional coin; surely the alchemist Marie uses for her tinctures and abortifacients would have something deadlier at hand. But I find I cannot bring myself to go that far. His wretched brother's death, should it come to pass, will not weigh on my soul.

"I'm afraid I do not deal in poisons," I demur, shaking my head. "Too illicit a business for my tastes, you understand."

The amiable facade disappears in an instant, like a candle guttered by a fearsome wind.

"*You* would refuse *me*?" he demands in a low, incredulous hiss laced with rage. "You, only a two-bit soothsayer without even a reputation to her name? Do you not realize how I could destroy you, with no more than a word in the right ear?"

I meet his eyes with a steely equanimity I do not feel, my stomach flopping like a landed fish. But if my spine is too fragile to bear me up against this overindulged brute of a peer, then I will surely never succeed in making myself a name.

"And do *you* not realize you are speaking to a divineress, who sees truths such as few others could possibly fathom?" I ask, lifting a cool eyebrow. "What else might I be capable of, do you not wonder? Other things . . . less pleasant, perhaps, than a stolen glimpse of your future?"

His eyes narrow, but I can see the fear that also flits within them, like fish glinting deep beneath the surface of a pond. "Are you truly threatening me? Surely you cannot be so brazen, especially when I have yet to pay you."

"No, messire. I am merely asking you to consider whether antagonizing me might not be in our best mutual interest."

Though I have mentioned nothing so overt as hexes, as his eyes rove a trifle fearfully over my carefully constructed sorceress's facade, I can almost see the notion of dangerous magics take hold of his mind. Which means it is time to take another, less aggressive tack.

"And perhaps you will require another consultation in the future," I add, gentling my tone a shade. "Would it not be better, for the both of us, if I were still inclined to grant you one at such a time?"

"Very well, then," he grinds out, wariness winning out over pique. As he balefully drops a clinking money bag onto the table before he pushes back and rises, a warm bloom of triumph opens in my chest.

"It was my pleasure, messire," I say, allowing a sphinxlike smile to curve my lips at his continued glower as he turns away. "And should you have a friend in similar need . . . please do not hesitate to tell them that they might find me here."

CHAPTER FOUR

# The Skeleton and the Magician

After the reading, I am far too galvanized to go straight home, my skin still abuzz with lingering excitement. Instead, Marie and I strike off for La Pomme Noire, her arm looped through mine as we traipse down the cité's night-shrouded narrow streets.

But when we reach the Pomme, we find our tumble-down tavern nearly deserted, the sagging tables bereft of their usual complement of merrymakers and scalawags. Exchanging puzzled looks, Marie and I sidle up to the bar, where the solitary serving wench fills our tankards in a sullen huff.

"Where is everyone, Jeanne?" I ask her, taking a bracing slug of abysmally cheap wine. "I've never seen it so quiet in here."

"They are all out back," Jeanne grouses, irritably wiping down a goblet. "Some new magician is putting a show on in our courtyard, have you not heard? It's only been the talk of the cité for weeks. Stephane left me to man the till, the heartless canaille. So now everyone will have seen Lesage's magic but me."

"Lesage . . . I *have* heard of him," Marie says slowly, her eyes agleam with interest. "A young magician newly returned to Paris after some years spent abroad. They call him an unparalleled prodigy of minor magic, though I shall believe that only when I see it."

"Then what are we waiting for?" I demand, tossing back my tankard before I seize her by the arm and drag her toward the tavern's back door. "Let us go see him for ourselves!"

We tumble together out into the courtyard, where it seems half the cité has gathered to watch the show. The crowd presses in against us from all sides, a shifting crush of ale-rank breath and unwashed flesh. Even standing on our tiptoes, we can barely see the wooden stage that has been hastily erected against the crumbling stone wall in the back.

"Well, this obviously won't do," Marie mutters, then raises her voice. "You there; move, if you please."

Disgruntled rumblings and mumbled oaths die almost as quickly as they're uttered, as soon as those being elbowed meet her basilisk glare. Marie's aptitude with her stilettos is well known across the cité; none of these spectators are quite so attached to their spots, it seems, as to risk being speared between the ribs for them.

It is not until we reach the crowd's lip that I hear the music.

I have seen minor magic shows before, of course, though most have left me cold. Even the most elaborate rely on benign deceits, sleight of hand, and cheap trickery of the eye. Most magicians keep up a steady stream of patter to assist in their misdirection, and wear billowing robes to conceal their multitude of props.

Compared to them, the magician Lesage might as well be a shadow cast onto the strange, pale smoke that roils across the stage.

He does not speak at all, relying instead on his accompaniment. A trio of black-robed violinists plays for him just beside the stage, their faces hidden by hooked plague doctor masks, their hands encased in black gloves. All three keep uncannily still even as they coax a macabre, meandering song from their strings. Their heads do not so much as twitch, and even the gusts of summer wind seem to barely stir the heavy pooling of their robes.

And yet they are not nearly so captivating as the magician himself.

He wears black, slim-fitting garb that matches his unfashionably short hair, which is inky as a raven's wing and cropped into feathery spikes. Even the ruffles that cascade above his trim waistcoat are basalt black. Though matching ruffles at the wrists are customary, he wears his shirtsleeves plain and rucked up to the elbows, leaving him with seemingly nowhere to hide the sly tools of his trade.

Yet he conjures an endless spool of scarlet ribbon out of thin air nonetheless.

And he makes the most arresting faces as he loops the blood-red ribbon around his wrists, a quicksilver deluge of them. Sly bemusement melts into rakishness, which gives way to sheer confounded glee, as though he himself cannot comprehend his own astonishing legerdemain.

"How is he doing that?" I ask Marie, thoroughly baffled. "I don't understand."

She shakes her head, her lips parted with wonder. She is so lovely that for a moment I cannot even look back to the stage, held captive by the unguarded softness of her profile, the enraptured luster of her eyes, even the way her paintbrush lashes swoop down to her cheeks with every blink. My best friend is always pretty, but rarely quite so overtly tender. The sight of it stirs something dangerous to life; a tenderness of my own that I prefer to keep firmly bricked away and hidden.

But for once, I let myself give in, reaching down between us to thread our fingers together.

She squeezes back, casting me a slantwise smile without shifting her eyes from the stage. "I've no idea, chérie," she replies in a whisper. "You know I have nimble fingers myself, but I cannot say I have ever seen anything quite like this."

As though he has heard us, the magician's gaze rakes our way. His dark eyes snare mine for a single heart-stopping moment, glimmering as if with unspoken promise.

*This is only the beginning*, they seem to say. *And you cannot begin to imagine what comes next.*

I lift my free hand to my plum-stained bottom lip, coyly tracing its outline as I wait with bated breath. Then he tips me a roguish wink and flings the mass of ribbons up— where they burst into a shower of petals so dark they must be either deepest crimson or truest black.

As they rain over him and fill his waiting hands, he tosses them up again, even higher above his head. There they transmute through some unknown alchemy into an unkindness of ravens, cawing shrilly as they wing their way above the cries of the crowd below. I wheel around to track their progress as they flap above the courtyard's wall and disappear into the dark beyond, where Notre Dame's colossal silhouette blots out the stars.

"Pardieu, that was marvelous," Marie crows beside me, breathless with shocked laughter. "Would you look at them, ma belle, they are real, they are still *flying*—"

*Surely that was the finale*, I think wildly, turning back to the stage with my heart still throbbing in my throat. For what could possibly follow such a coup?

Except there is still more; the magician no longer stands alone. A spectral skeleton has appeared beside him, all rictus grin and spindly, fleshless limbs, as though conjured up from beyond the grave. Against the clouds of smoke that billow across the stage, it flickers in and out of substance like a ghostly apparition, as though made of mist instead of bone.

A claw of fear scrapes in my gut even as Marie's hand clamps down hard on mine. A blanketing hush falls over the crowd, so encompassing I hear the rasp of breath catching in her throat.

"Mother of mercy, what is this?" I whisper to her through my own dry lips. "Surely it is not real, but how is it done?"

"Mirrors, perhaps?" she hazards. "Somehow positioned

to reflect an accomplice in costume? Hand to heart, I could not say."

A rippling whisper of "necromancy" snakes its way through the throng like a needle pulling thread, only to tie itself off as the magician and his bony companion launch into a dreadful dance. They shuffle along in jerky lockstep, a morbid pantomime of the sarabande so popular at court. It reminds me of paintings I've seen of the danse macabre, in which a skeletal Death whirls victims from all walks of life into a frightful jig. Evoking the final reaping that awaits all of us in the end.

And yet this is different and somehow almost worse, more chilling and enthralling all at once. Because it is the skeleton that dances at the magician's behest, as though this mortal man can not only call up the dead but demean them at his command. Like some cruel king or puppet-master, a despot of the damned.

From the wolfish grin that plays on his face, I gather that this is exactly the impression the magician Lesage wishes to convey.

When the whirling music reaches a crescendo, the skeleton removes its skull with a flourish, holding it aloft as the magician takes a triumphant bow—then the man turns on his heel and vanishes, engulfed by a shower of violet sparks.

Once he has gone, the skeleton winks out of existence as well. The music dies completely just as the last of the smoke fades, licked away by the rough cat's tongue of the breeze. When everything has cleared, I see the musicians have also disappeared, and the ensuing silence leaves the stage deserted and somehow bereft, as if we have all suffered an unexpected loss.

As if the eerie miracle we have all just witnessed was never truly there at all.

Afterward, Marie and I sit at the Pomme for hours, drowning more tankards of wine and speculating feverishly on how Lesage's magic was made. By the time we stumble out into the smallest hours, we may be no closer to unraveling the magician's secrets, but we are well and truly drunk. We trip together through the cité's echoingly empty streets, the summer night folding in luxuriantly all around us, soft as a mink stole rubbed against the skin. The crescent of the moon above glints like a cunning cat's eye in the dark. My heartbeat roars in my ears in a thunderous rush, the savor of cheap wine still lingering on my tongue. Marie's sandalwood and citron scent wreaths up all around me, stealing into my lungs.

It all merges into a singular sensation, throbbing and insistent as some voracious hunger.

A rising passion born of the night.

I am not sure which of us begins it. But suddenly we are pressed together in one of the Pont Neuf's half-moon alcoves, my back hitched up against the stones and Marie's plush lips sliding over mine. I can hear the slap of the water far below us, hear the forlorn calls of some lost bird wheeling in the dark. Perhaps even one of Lesage's impossible ravens. My hands tangle in Marie's silken hair as she kisses me like a succubus, tasting of red wine and almonds and just a trace of salt.

We have kissed each other many times before, in greeting and in parting, sometimes out of sheer affection bordering on something beyond a friendly fondness. But I have always been the one to draw back, too afraid to linger over it; afraid of what it would lead to, of the sweeping change that it might bring upon us both. Afraid of losing her to the upheaval and misery that would surely follow, should any romance between us ever fracture down the middle.

And afraid that pledging my love to Marie, binding my heart to hers even in such sweet and voluntary servitude, might somehow render me even less free than I am.

Even now, with my head awhirl with lust, the same tangle of fears rears up within me like a restive wyrm trapped inside my chest. Sensing my uncertainty, Marie pulls back to smile at me, her eyes a liquid glitter against the dark. She reaches up to cup my cheek and brush a gentle thumb across my cheekbone.

"What's the matter, ma belle?" she murmurs, soft as a breath, leaning forward to tip her forehead against mine.

"I am afraid," I say simply. "Of us. I *need* you, chère, as you are now. As my best friend. What if we ruin it, with . . . this? Whatever this is, whatever it might yet become?"

"I will be your best friend until my dying day, ma belle," she responds, trailing her fingertips down my throat. My skin heats under her touch like tinder catching flame. "No matter what else comes to pass. But if it feels too much, to consider anything more between us . . . then for now, let us savor this for what it is. No more than a dalliance between friends."

"Then we are of a mind," I reply, a sweet, vast relief washing over me as I slide my hands down her corseted waist. "So why waste any more breath with words?"

She laughs softly against my mouth, twining her arms around my neck and nipping at my bottom lip.

And it is a long time until we find the need to speak again.

## CHAPTER FIVE

# The Philter and the Marquise

Before I became one of its regulars, I thought I knew the cité reasonably well. Enough to be welcome in its choicest establishments, and to avoid the cutthroats and rookers that slink about its back-road nooks.

But I knew nothing of its hidden heart, the secret province of magicians and sorcerers.

The cité's network of occult havens marked by sigils, in which diviners peddle past and future alike.

Some are more tumbledown than the chiromancy haven, far seedier and less ostentatiously arcane. Marie takes me to all of them nonetheless, introducing me to adepts who practice physiognomy and tarot, or bespy the future via the movement of celestial bodies. Their mystical trappings are of little use to me, when it is the sheer force of a client's need that most reliably summons up the sight. The chiromancy haven remains my favored haunt, and in a handful of weeks I amass a tidy little clientele; apparently the irate nobleman chose not to speak ill of me after all.

Not all my clients are wealthy, nor do they need to be. Modest tradesmen and even peasants prove more than capable of mustering coin, when it comes to pressing matters like a child's illness or the roving of a spouse's eye. And with each night the contents of my strongbox swell, my stash of pistoles and louis d'or heaping steadily up.

Should the repossession men return, Antoine and I may still come out of it all right.

"You know, you are not at all as I expected," Francoise-Athenais de Rochechouart informs me languidly, soon after she has seated herself for our assignation.

Unlike my more bashful clients, who balk at so much as looking me in the eye, the Marquise de Montespan seems unafraid to take my measure. Just as unfazed as she was to provide me with her name and rank, if it meant I would make time for an earlier session.

It seems very little in life gives the marquise any great pause.

"No?" I respond, lifting my eyebrows with cool curiosity. "And if I may, madame, what did you expect?"

She furrows her forehead, knitting fine blond brows. The marquise is exquisite, as clear-featured as a cameo and blessed with larkspur eyes, a rosebud mouth, and a soft swoop of honeyed curls. Under her brushed velvet cloak her décolletage is cut fashionably low, exposing rounded shoulders and a milky expanse of bosom. Everything about her appears delicately wrought, like the spun-sugar confections I've heard they prize so highly at the Sun King's court.

But I recognize hers for a bayonet sort of beauty, shining with a dangerous edge. As inviting as it is likely to gut a careless lover.

"I confess I am not even sure," she says in a conspiratorial tone, resting her chin on interlaced hands. "Someone . . . more wizened, I suppose. Perhaps more sagacious in appearance."

"Is my lady implying that I do not seem clever?" I counter. "Perhaps I should consider taking offense."

She bursts into a silvery peal of laughter, uncaring of the looks it draws in the haven's hush.

"Come now, that is hardly necessary," she drawls with a dismissive wave of the hand. "I suppose I only thought you would be much older, and less fetching. More crone than maypole maiden. What are you, barely eighteen?"

"Nineteen, my lady."

"Such a lovely age, as I recall," she says, a touch wistfully, as if she is a great deal more than five or six years older than me. "Do savor the youthful blush of your beauty, my dear. It will vanish in a wink."

Though she says this in a flattering tone, there is a certain asperity to the words, a coolness to her scrutiny she cannot quite conceal. I make a note to myself; should I see the marquise again, it would be preferable to render myself more the dowdy divineress and less the alluring sibyl.

"May I ask what has brought you here tonight?" I ask, brushing past any further discussion of my appearance.

"Why don't *you* tell *me* what might have brought me to this charmless place?" she responds, giving a dainty shudder as she glances around the haven's incense-roiled expanse. "Surely an oracle can scry as much for herself. Believe me, I never would have ventured here at all had I not heard elusive little whispers of a talented divineress. Someone of a wholly different breed than the grifter scum that have the run of this place."

"Then perhaps we had best begin," I say, reaching for her hand. She obliges, still exuding that air of indolent hauteur. Yet I can feel her need writhing just below the surface almost as soon as I touch her, wriggling like an earthworm surfacing after a heavy rain.

There is something the marquise very badly wants to know.

"Someone stands in your path," I begin, tracing my fingertips over her palm in the intricate pattern of a clarifying rune from Agnesot's grimoire. Tonight it dredges up the hazy outline of a man, burning at the edges with a burnished glow, like the silhouette of the moon when it slides across the sun's radiant face.

"A powerful man," I continue, schooling my surprise. I have never before been visited by a vision quite so bright. "With a mantle of vast influence gathered about his shoulders. He seeks you out not only for your beauty, but for your esprit, your incomparable wit and lively tongue. You have been growing closer for some time now, but it seems something even more tender has recently come to pass between you."

I glance up at her, raising a teasing eyebrow. "It seems, madame, you have fallen in love."

She casts me a wide-eyed, girlish look, suppressing a grin. *Of course I am right*, I think, barely refraining from rolling my eyes. For this much, I scarcely needed the sight. She radiates new love, shining like a freshly minted coin.

"Oh, c'est vrai," she exhales, fastening her lower lip with her pearly little teeth. "I cannot deny it. Though I have often thought myself impervious to Cupid's bow, it appears my heart has finally bestirred itself."

Her gaze grazes over the wedding jewel on her left hand, her joy dimming a shade with guilt. *But*, I think wryly, *only a shade*. The man is not her husband, then, which comes as no great surprise. As I have heard it told, court is a den of vice and infidelity, in which romance flourishes most unabashedly between those not wed to each other.

"What more can you see of him?" she demands. "Does he love me, too?"

I frown, sifting the obscuring mists for a clearer picture.

"It seems he does, though with some trepidation," I allow. "But should he choose to forge ahead nevertheless, the love between you will grow into the stuff of legend. It will elevate you far above your station, set you high above your envious peers."

Every word is true, though not quite so clear as I make it sound. Visions of the future often unfold like a gauzy dream rather than any concrete depiction. In this one, I see the marquise standing on some high-flung battlement gilded by fiery sunrise, a towering headpiece akin to a crown set upon her head. A grand habit sewn from cloth-of-gold billows around her like a royal pennant.

And she looks triumphant, overjoyed, glutted with new-found power.

A newborn queen in all but name.

When a gasp tears free of her lips, I realize I have said the last aloud.

"A queen in all but name," she repeats, awestruck, having shed the last of her nonchalant veneer. "Yes. That is it, that is what I want! And now you must help me seize it, make certain that it comes to pass."

I cock my head in question, unsure what she means. "But I have seen all that I can. What further help would you have of me?"

She leans across the table, flinty determination hardening her delicate face. "You said that Lou— That he has some trepidation," she replies. "About loving me. Alors, we must sweep any such hesitation to the side, ensure that he becomes just as besotted as he wishes. Surely there are draughts for such things, non? Philtres d'amour and the like?"

*Ah.* I sit back against my chair, crossing my arms over my chest. So the marquise is angling for a love potion, an aphrodisiac. Thus far I have summarily refused all such requests. Though love philters are a far cry from poison, I have steered studiously clear of tangling myself in my clients' affairs by offering anything that might demand a guarantee of certain success.

"I'm afraid I am no quacksalver, madame," I reply, shaking my head. "I do not claim to influence the future, only to bespy it."

"And why ever not?" she demands, her nostrils flaring with consternation. "You are obviously a sorceress of considerable power, else you could never have known what you just told me. Surely if *anyone* could craft the future, it would be a skillful divineress such as yourself."

"Meddling with love is a risky business, madame," I warn. "Perhaps it would be best if you allowed these matters of the heart to unfold of their own natural accord."

"Hang what's best," she snaps, her eyes glittering with fervor. "We are meant to be, he and I, I know it in my bones. And I *deserve* his love, Madame Monvoisin—for all I am, and all that I can offer him."

She places both palms flat on the table, lips pursing with conviction. "I will not falter now, not when I am so very close. Not when I have more than earned his love."

It is this that sways me, the high esteem in which she holds herself. It appeals to me, somehow, that she should be so convinced of her own worth. And if a love philter is evil at all, it is certainly only the small sort of evil Agnesot instructed me to nurture, nowhere near the league of deathly poison. I think of one of the love concoctions detailed in the grimoire: a disturbing little mélange of dove's blood, ground peacock bones, and crushed iris petals. I have never had the cause or inclination to test it, so I cannot be certain of its potency. But even if it promotes ardor only weakly, its very presence may bolster the marquise's efforts to win the luminous man's heart.

And given the fever pitch of her desire, I've no doubt I can charge her an exorbitant sum for its preparation.

"There is something," I concede. "I will have it ready for you two days hence."

"Oh, marvelous," she purrs as she settles back in her seat, aglow with satisfaction. "And tell me, have you any suggestion on how I should dose him with it? He is . . . often surrounded by a fawning entourage. A great many attentive eyes that rarely stray from him. The delivery must be a subtle thing."

I think of the magician Lesage, his nimble hands and engaging face, and of Marie's hollow rings. Surely I could procure one such for the marquise.

"I'll send a clever little trinket along with the philter, and instructions on how to use it," I say. "All you must do is ensure that his attention is occupied elsewhere when you doctor his drink. If you practice enough to do it deftly, he won't notice a thing."

"Oh, I think I can manage as much," she muses, trailing idle fingertips over her collarbone, her eyes sparkling like polished gems with anticipation. "Thank you, Madame Monvoisin. And I assure you, you will have no cause to regret this. To the contrary—I believe you have made the future a great deal brighter for us both."

When I come home from Les Halles the following day with fresh flowers for the marquise's potion, the repossession men have returned en masse.

They troop past me as if I scarcely exist, lugging our paintings and fine furniture out the door like a conquering army's spoils, heaving them into dray carts that await on the street. Swarming over our maison like corpse beetles over carrion.

"Antoine!" I cry out, dropping my basket as I rush into a sitting room picked down to its bones. "What is the meaning of this? I thought you said it would only be a few pieces to tide us over! But they, they are taking *everything*!"

My husband cowers in one of the room's newly empty corners, barely able to meet my eyes.

"It is somewhat worse than I feared," he admits, giving a helpless shrug. Revulsion at his weakness burns like nettles in my throat. "Last week the duc withdrew his order, which would have gone a ways toward restoring our means. And without his commission I was stalled, unable to procure the raw material for the vicomtesse's necklace."

"How bad is it, Antoine?" I can barely bring myself to ask. "How much do we owe?"

"Well, as to the exact amount, it isn't, ah, as clear as that," he fumbles, mopping at his brow with a frilly handkerchief. *Of the very finest linen, no doubt*, I think venomously. Yet another frivolous expenditure that has paved our path to here. "I would have to revisit the ledgers, take the interest into account, and then there is the matter of the lateness penalty—"

"*How much, Antoine?*" I shriek at him like a fishwife, my hands balled into fists, nails slicing into my palms with a sharp sear of pain. "Just *tell* me how bad it is!"

He closes his eyes. "Well over twelve thousand livres,"

he whispers, biting down on the inside of his cheek. "I . . . I'm sorry, Catherine."

*Twelve thousand livres*, I repeat silently to myself, mouthing the words with numb lips. A staggering sum, a pit so deep it may as well tunnel all the way down to l'enfer. The contents of my strongbox could not even begin to fill it.

"So we have nothing." I close my eyes against a hot well of tears, my heart threatening to trample my ribs. "Less than nothing, soon. What next, Antoine? Will we . . . Will we lose the house as well?"

"I don't know," he replies, raking a hand through his rumpled hair, no longer even bothering to conceal his despair. "I've friends I might approach for a loan. Or I could see if I might transfer our debts to another moneylender."

One of the louts overhears us and pauses in his pillaging, hefting a rug more comfortably across his bulging shoulders. His eyes trawl over me speculatively, lingering on my curls and the curve of my hips.

"It needn't be as dismal as all that, you know," he remarks to Antoine, jutting his coarse chin at me. "Not while you still have her to sell. I'd wager she'd fetch a pretty penny for you, mon frère."

The breath dies in my lungs. I go cold all at once, as if the blood in my veins has chilled into a slush. Not because I cannot fathom what this jackal means, but because I can, and with terrible ease. At the fabrique, the maître ran a lively trade in women's bodies as a secondary business. While I was fortunate enough to be sold into marriage rather than a brothel, there is no guarantee that my former luck will hold.

While Antoine does not yet view me as chattel, how can I be sure that he will not change his mind?

"I am not your brother, you buffoon," my husband rails at the man, who gives a nonplussed shrug and carries on with his deplorable business. "How dare you imply something so tawdry and foul, as if I am some whoremaster? As if I would ever even think to barter away my own *wife!*"

"No need to fall into a fit about it, eh?" the man tosses over his shoulder on his way out. "I was only *saying.* So's you'd know that you have options."

Antoine continues sputtering in outrage at the man's retreating back, even as he vanishes through the door with our rug in tow.

"Catherine!" he cries, ashen-faced and beseeching as he turns to me. "You know, you *must* know that I would never . . ."

He trails away as I retrieve my basket and climb wordlessly up the stairs. I have nothing to say to him. Because while I would love to believe my husband, I know no such thing for certain.

And if I am to claw my way out of this, I will need to gamble even more boldly on myself.

## CHAPTER SIX

# The Prayer and the Proposal

That night, as I brew the philter for the Marquise de Montespan, I do something to which I am quite unaccustomed.

I pray.

Feverishly, above hands clasped so hard it bleaches my knuckles white. To whom, I am not certain. Whatever dark deities preside over Agnesot's grimoire, perhaps. Or maybe to no gods at all, but something altogether else; fallen angels burning darkly, or the prancing denizens of hell. The demons who were once my solace in the fabrique, when I comforted myself by imagining becoming one of them.

Though I doubt that any of them bother to listen, I cannot help but try. Because this philter is no longer just a potion but my hope distilled into liquid form.

A symbol of the only salvation I can imagine for myself.

Over a fortnight spins by before I hear from the marquise again.

I sit at the Pomme with Marie, drowning my woes in wine after a disappointingly thin night at the havens. Too much drink has made me a touch maudlin, treading closer to despair than I usually allow myself.

"Should worse come to worst and Antoine loses the house, you can come live with me, Cat," Marie says to me, her voice pitched low beneath the tavern's raucous hubbub, her warm hand resting on my shoulder. "It's true I practically share my tiny garret roost with the pigeons. But there is always room for you, and coin enough."

"If Antoine does not yet sell me to cover his debts," I respond darkly, taking another swallow. "Though I do not truly think he—"

I cut myself off as a cloaked figure whisks out the third chair at our table and takes a seat with us. Marie and I exchange outraged glances, and I see her hand creep down toward her boot, ready to flick out a blade. My own hand hovers above my knife belt just in case.

Then the hood is twitched back to reveal the Marquise de Montespan's fluted features, a satisfied smile hovering on her lips.

"Pardon the intrusion, mesdames," she drawls into our bemused silence. "I went searching for you at the haven first, Madame Monvoisin. But I was told that, at this hour, I might find you here instead."

She sweeps her gaze over the tavern's buckling rafters and water-splotched walls, wrinkling her nose in distaste.

"Though I confess I haven't the slightest idea why you would choose such a tasteless den of ill repute in which to while away the hours. Surely you have better choices, even in such a cesspool as the cité."

"Cesspool," Marie mutters under her breath. "Oh, that's rich, coming from a strumpet of Versailles."

Fortunately, the marquise does not hear her over the din. I glance around the room for the marquise's armed escort, should Marie think to take even more pointed umbrage; surely a grande dame would not have ventured into the cité's depths unchaperoned. Three flinty pairs of eyes meet mine from the corners of the room, laden with warning. Despite the deliberate insouciance she projects, the lady is clearly not so heedless as she seems.

"Had we known to expect the pleasure of your company, my lady," I respond a trifle archly, turning back to her, "we might have arranged for a more suitable venue."

"Oh, I know, I should have sent ahead." She waves a dismissive hand. "But I simply could not wait another moment to share the good news with you, not when I am fairly bursting with it."

She glances over at Marie, flicking up her eyebrows with pronounced distaste, as though she approves of Marie and her flamboyantly colored, oft-mended skirts no more than she does of our surroundings.

"Perhaps your . . . friend could afford us a moment alone to speak?"

At my nod, Marie rises only reluctantly, her face set

in a mask of stony fury. Once she's gone, the marquise scrapes her chair closer to mine and seizes both my hands, exuberant as a high-spirited child.

"I must tell you, it all worked beautifully," she breathes, widening her eyes at me. "Exactly as you said! I poured the philter into his wine, and not a week later I was warming his bed. Such lust, too, as I have never seen—the man positively could not get enough of me!"

"I am pleased to hear it," I respond quickly, hoping to spare myself the sordid details of her conquest even as my heart soars at my success. If the marquise is pleased with the philter's performance, that means she will soon require more—which means more coin with which to line my pockets, and to build the rampart between me and ruin.

"But it gets even better! Today he acknowledged me before all the court assembled. I am no longer just the Marquise de Montespan, you see—but Athenais de Rochechouart de Mortemart, maîtresse-en-titre to le Roi himself." She draws herself up smugly, preening, her eyes lustrous with triumph. "The official mistress of our own lord and liege."

I gape at her, shock rolling through me like great tumbling boulders. Her lover, the shining man I spied in the vision of her future—could that truly have been Louis Dieudonné, le Roi Soleil? The Sun King himself?

"Mon Dieu," I whisper, feeling the first flush of a crackling delight, as if her elation is catching as brushfire. "That . . . certainly warrants congratulations, my lady. It is quite the coup."

"To have replaced Louise de la Vallière in the king's affections, pried free her stranglehold on him? I should say it is." She squeezes my hands, blinking languorously, like a cat sated with cream. "I move into the maîtresse's apartments next week. And I owe it all to you."

"I only shed light on what was already there, my lady," I protest, but in a perfunctory fashion. I want to preserve her high spirits, keep her half mad with glee and indebted to me. "But I am very glad to know the philter won the day for you."

"But what is won must be kept, n'est-ce pas? And I have no intention of ever being ousted by some upstart as poor Louise was by me." She leans forward until her azure eyes glitter not an inch away from mine. "Not when I could have your sight to guide my every step. To ensure that my ascent continues undeterred."

"I am always here to advise and assist you," I respond, inclining my head demurely, though my mind teems with the potential of what else I might sell her. "The philter must be administered regularly, of course, to bolster His Majesty's lust and guarantee his devotion. And there are helpful spells, cantrips to ensure that his eye never strays from you—"

"But surely you can see that is only the beginning for us," she cuts me off, and I catch a sudden flash of her as I saw her in my vision. Gloriously ablaze on the ramparts, head unbowed by the weight of her extravagant almost-crown. A self-forged queen aflame with ambition. "Court is a pit of vipers beyond anything you could fathom, Madame Monvoisin. I mean to surround myself with allies, to instill those closest to me with unshakable loyalty—and for such a feat, I will require your ongoing assistance."

As my mind whirls with the implications, she favors me with a complicit smile. So suggestive and beguiling I catch a glimpse of what the king himself must see when he looks at her.

"As my very own official sorceress, bien sûr," she says, spreading her hands. "My devineresse-en-titre, so to speak. Shall we discuss the terms?"

"To begin, she will advance me a sum sufficient to save the house, so that my wastrel husband does not wind up without a home—but she won't formalize our arrangement unless I agree to live at a residence of her choosing," I explain to Marie some time later, once the marquise has taken her leave. My skin still swarms with excitement at the prospect of such salvation, my problems solved in one fell swoop.

"Apparently the cité is too disreputable for the illustrious personages she means to send my way," I continue. "Not to mention that the king's maîtresse-en-titre cannot be seen here sullying her skirts."

"Incroyable," Marie murmurs, shaking her head. "What a schemer that woman is. Be careful of her, ma belle. She may be grateful to you now, but such outsized ambition knows neither lasting loyalty nor bounds."

I frown at her, a little irritated by her lack of enthusiasm when triumph still pours so headily through my veins.

"But I thought you would be thrilled for me," I protest. "She's offering to be my patroness, and even more than that. To furnish me with a house of my own. What could be better?"

"Perhaps if she were a patroness on *your* terms, Cat," Marie replies, shaking her head. "Someone of lower rank than the marquise, and with a weaker will than yours. Not a manipulator of her ilk, who might easily grind a commoner to dust between the gears of her own stratagems."

"Do you really believe I cannot master her?" I ask, bridling that she should think me so feeble. "After my years of slaving at the fabrique, everything I endured to survive that place? You are forever saying that I always wrest things my way, by hook or by crook. Why would that not hold true with her, too?"

Marie moistens her lips, a grave expression falling over her face. "It isn't that I doubt you, ma belle. But you cannot trust someone like her. I know her type well. They are all vile backstabbers at court, underhanded and corrupt, starting with our unscrupulous brute of a king himself."

She says the last with such unwonted bitterness that I recoil a little, staring at her.

"What do you mean?" I ask her in a gentler tone. "What is it that you know of the king's corruption, Marie?"

"You know as well as I do that France has not known a moment's peace since our so-called Sun King took up the scepter," she replies, flashing me a bleak look. "Always another campaign. More rampant bloodshed and depravity, all in the name of his insatiable gloire. And what he cannot accomplish by force alone, he achieves by more insidious means. Such as the use of children for intrigue and espionage."

"Children?" I whisper back, aghast. It is difficult to conceive of our urbane king, with his renowned fondness for perfumes and ballet, sending children off to die for France. "Marie, surely not."

"Oh, yes." Her voice has fallen so low I would not have been able to make it out had the tavern not lapsed into late-night torpor around us. "And me among them. That was where I went first, you know, when les bonnes soeurs indentured you to the fabrique. To Les Pays Bas, to serve in the king's interminable Dutch war."

"What?" I ask, shocked down to the bone. "But you could not have been more than eleven years old!"

"Perhaps the king's procurer saw in me the requisite wiles, even at that tender age." She smiles, faintly and bitterly, shrugging a shoulder. "Guttersnipe orphans like me are both innocuous and cunning, ma belle. As well as dispensable. I was there for nearly two years, gathering intelligence for the crown. And the things I saw done there by our own officers, Cat, the violations visited upon the Dutch women, the butchering of their children . . ."

She shakes her head, remembered darkness swimming like ink in her eyes.

"Such a monstrous carelessness for life as I could not have conceived. No villainy that transpires in the cité could possibly compare."

"Why have you never spoken to me of this, Marie?" I ask, appalled.

"I do not speak of it to anyone," she replies with a

shudder. "Not if I wish to keep my soul intact. I still have nightmares of it, such cauchemars as you cannot imagine. But this is not about me, ma belle. What I mean to make you understand is that the king's courtiers emulate him in every aspect, follow his ruthless lead. They are no more than barbarians with beautiful faces. The lot of them."

She leans closer to me, fixing me with her eyes. "And if you choose to tread this path, they will savage you without a moment's regret should your demise ever come to suit them."

"Then what would you suggest I do instead?" I demand. "I need a way out, Marie. How else am I to keep the house for Antoine, or fend for myself?"

"Leave Antoine to his own devices, then, and come live with me," she exhorts, her face more ardent than I have ever seen it. "This is *his* mess, not yours! And it is true that we would not be wealthy, and betimes we might even struggle—but on the whole, we could be happy. I would take care of us, ma belle. You know I would."

"Of course I know, chère, and I promise I will think on it," I reply, pinching the bridge of my nose. Even if I could bring myself to abandon Antoine, I fear that were I to live with Marie things between us would change perforce. Perhaps deepen into something for which I am yet unready.

And though it shames me to admit it, I do not wish to risk poverty again. Not even the kind made merrier by my friend's company.

"The marquise is taking me to see a residence in the Villeneuve tomorrow morning, before I make my choice," I add. "Perhaps I will still decide against it."

"Perhaps," Marie says flatly, taking up her wine again. My heart sinks to see her so dimmed with disappointment, but there is nothing I can do for it, save lie outright. And I will not lie to Marie. "But if it is all the same to you, I will not hold my breath."

## CHAPTER SEVEN

# The Contract and the Hôtel

I barely manage to snatch a tattered scrap of sleep that night.

Turmoil roils just beneath my eyelids in a muddy swirl. I thrash from side to side like an animal in a trap as I consider what future path might suit me best. Though under the proposed arrangement I would be indebted to the marquise for twelve thousand livres, I would also have my own residence for the first time in my life. Yes, she will not pay me anything more until I have earned back the sum advanced; we have agreed to set the worth of each scrying session at thirty livres. But I've no doubt that once she introduces the glittering novelty of her sorceress to friends at court, I would soon secure a stream of additional income to stash away for myself.

But becoming the marquise's sorceress would mean bidding farewell to Marie, and losing our nights together in the haven of the cité. The dark sun of a world that we have made into our own domain.

Yet if I were to do as Marie urges, how could I live with abandoning Antoine in his hour of need? Feckless though he can be, he has also shown me so much kindness. Without him I might never have left the fabrique, or left it for somewhere incalculably worse. Without him, I would never even have learned to read, and Agnesot's grimoire might have remained forever locked to me.

After everything he's done for me, could I truly give up this chance to rescue him in kind?

By morning, I've yet to come to terms with myself. Sensing my disquiet, the marquise leaves me to my pensive silence after collecting me in her carriage, a lavish cream-and-gold affair drawn by two splendid snowy geldings. But when we reach the Villeneuve, a refined suburb outside the city walls, the residence she has chosen stuns me out of my introspection, replacing it with a pure, wonderstruck awe.

"*This* is the place?" I exhale, nearly pressing my nose against the carriage window like an overeager child. "Marquise, surely not."

"Just wait until you see inside," she replies, tipping me a wink.

It is a proper hôtel particulier on the Rue Beauregard, a graceful stone townhouse claiming an entire block and presiding over a pristine garden, encircled by a wrought-iron fence topped with spearhead finials. I can barely keep from gaping as the footmen help us from the carriage, escorting us to the gleaming double doors.

"You like it, then," the marquise remarks as my eyes rove hungrily all around. "I thought you might."

"How could I not?" I breathe as we cross into the soaring foyer, our heels clicking on the crimson-veined marble floor. The walls are paneled in mahogany and hung with gilt-framed Pouissins, Le Bruns, and Lorrains, so beautiful and egregiously expensive I can imagine Antoine quaking at the very sight of them. "It is astonishing!"

"Astonishingly befitting of my new devineresse-en-titre, you mean," she corrects playfully, looping her arm through mine and patting my hand. "Come, meet your staff—if you will have them, that is."

In the great hall, she's had the house's score of servants arrange themselves in two rows for us to pass between. The chatelaine dips into a curtsy at the sight of us, the rest of the staff crisply following suit, bobbing their pert heads. Even their uniforms are cut so well, embroidered with the silver and blue of the House of Montespan, that the servants themselves seem intended as adornments to the hôtel. I cannot quite wrap my mind around such a multitude of help when I've only ever had Suzette and considered myself fortunate.

From there we take the swooping double staircase upstairs, my fingers trailing over the rosewood banister's silken finish.

"Is this your property?" I ask the marquise as she leads me from room to spectacular room, all carpeted with sumptuous mulberry rugs and hung with chandeliers intricate as tiny airborne palaces. Even the wallpaper captivates me, cut velvet worked with an arabesque of bees and roses.

*Mine, mine, mine*, my heart clamors. *All this could be mine.*

"It's so lovely," I continue. "I cannot imagine why you would not live here yourself."

"Oh, no," she replies with a tinkling laugh. "This is not at all to my taste. It was one of my husband's properties, signed to me as part of my wedding gift. But I've never lived in it myself—nor do I plan to, now that I am ensconced in the maîtresse-en-titre's suite at Versailles. So you may as well enjoy it for the both of us, for so long as you serve as my divineress. Think of it as a symbol of the agreement between us—a guarantee that your services will belong primarily to me, until you earn back your debt."

I am not such a fool that I cannot imagine how easily she could whisk the ground out from beneath me, should I displease her in some way. But once I have established myself, found steady purchase with others at court, I can always renegotiate the terms. Perhaps, eventually, even buy this fairy tale of a house outright and snip myself free of her puppetmaster's strings.

My heart rises at the thought of such an independence, fluttering beneath my throat like a dove trapped inside a belfry. To be the mistress of my own homestead, the only Fate in charge of spinning out the fabric of my life.

Clotho, Lachesis, and Atropos all merged into one.

The sole weaver of my own destiny.

"But you will not attempt to influence how I ply my trade here otherwise?" I press. "As long as we agree that your needs will always be seen to first, in service to your loan?"

"Of course I would not presume to infringe upon your freedom, Madame Monvoisin. When I do not require your sight, you would be free to work your talents as you see fit, and to be compensated as per your arrangements with others."

She smiles enticingly at me, lifting her eyebrows in invitation. "Now, shall I show you the rest?"

She guides me through the expanse of the banquet room and the skylit library, through a conservatory equipped with a harpsichord, a lute, and a collection of lustrous violins. The master suite is next, and its expanse fairly strips me of breath. Antoine's and my entire home could fit within its walls with space left over to spare.

As we walk, I imagine myself here alone. Drifting through these airy corridors with my snakes slung about my shoulders, or sitting in the spacious study refurbished to meet my darker needs. On the topmost floor, the marquise and I pause before the grand Venetian window at the end of the hall. It overlooks the flawless green expanse of the garden below, the clustered rooftops of Villeneuve shimmering beyond, against a cotton-clouded sky.

Watching it all, an unexpected calm settles over me like the finest satin cloak.

After my turmoil, there is no true choice here at all, only a decision I find I've already made.

I cannot forfeit this opportunity to move up in the world, not even for Marie's sake. Not when another such may never come around again. And it is not as if I will lose her altogether, I reassure myself. Though I know the marquise would not countenance my inviting Marie here, I will still visit her as often as I can, of course, and write to her whenever I cannot come in person.

"So, what do you think?" the marquise asks, mildly enough. But I can feel the trembling needle of her need tugging at me like a compass. Though our acquaintance has been brief, I understand her well enough already to feel the fire raging just beneath her skin, to know that her desires are colossal and implacable. And this time, what she wants above all else is my skill. "Do you need more time to consider? Or will this suit?"

I draw a breath, granting myself one last chance to think. I understand the gamble that I am making here, throwing in my lot with a scheming noblewoman who does not tolerate rejection—but though Marie may be right to fear for me, I trust myself to see this through.

And I see no advantage in not playing the boldest hand I hold.

I turn to the marquise slowly and extend my hand, unable to suppress the tiny, triumphant smile that curls my lips. "Oh, yes, my lady. I do believe it will."

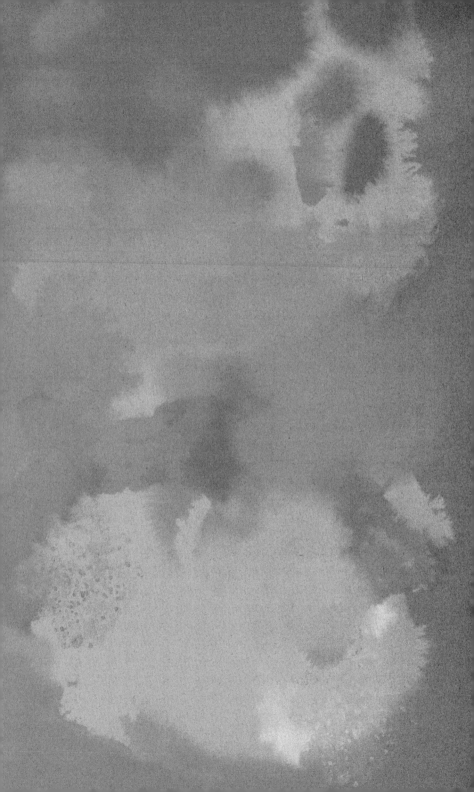

# ACT TWO: DOMINION

## CHAPTER EIGHT

# The Spirits and the Maréchale

**August 23, 1667**

"And you are *quite* sure they will not bite during the ritual?" Maréchale Madeleine de la Ferté asks me yet again, her eyes flicking warily to where Megaera surges around my left wrist. "It is only that they look rather hungry. The one around your neck has not stopped glaring at me askance since I sat."

The Maréchale de la Ferté is here at the marquise's recommendation, as one of her coveted inner circle. Which means only that the marquise finds this lady's company acceptably diverting, without excusing her from any of the jockeying for favor that the noblesse engage in as their daily fare. The maréchale is plump and mildly pretty, popular among the male courtiers and a favorite of Queen Marie-Thérèse, though I see little of her alleged charm on display tonight. She's skittish and wide-eyed as a cornered deer, her powdered ringlets quivering atop her head.

It likely does not help that she's terrified of snakes.

"They have not bitten one of my callers yet," I reply, biting back my own amusement. "I have no reason to think they will not continue to demonstrate restraint."

The maréchale blanches in the candlelight, swallowing audibly. Her eyes dart to the invitingly lit windows of my home, where the rest of her coterie are enjoying a lavish salon while they await their turn with me. As the marquise's sorceress, I do all my readings in my pavilion in the garden. Rain or wind or bracing night, I make all my callers come outside to me like supplicants, always one at a time.

It is not only that I enjoy making these spoiled aristocrats leap through hoops, though that is surely part of it. It is also that I would not be privy to half of their vile secrets, were they not assured of total privacy.

Sometimes they object to my rules, but even the most peevish of them quiet once they reach my pavilion, its pillars almost obscured by the clinging rush of ivy, the cupola limned by moonlight. I wait for them within, always swathed in black, with snakes coiled up my arms and twined over my bare shoulders. I've also stolen a page from that magician I saw in the cité, and the haunting strains of a violin emanate all around me. I make sure my violinist always stays well out of sight, playing from a grove tucked behind the pavilion where my clients cannot spy him. A busker I discovered in Montmartre, Pascal costs me next to nothing but plays like magic made sound, his harmonies burrowing beneath the skin and snagging in the soul.

I could have engaged one of my acquaintances from the cité, rife as it is with bawdy minstrels. But the marquise has made clear that she wishes my guests to witness nothing that might sully her reputation by linking her mystical divineress to Catherine Monvoisin's own seedy past in the cité. As far as the rest of the court is concerned, I have only ever been the Sorceress La Voisin: the marquise's mysterious and eldritch creature, my origin as secretive and otherworldly as my gift.

And it is true that though I have only been gone two months, my grateful husband and our house at Pont Marie, the house I saved for him, feel very far away already. Everything of that old life seems distant now, somehow tarnished and dim, drawn away from me. Like the memory of the sun, when one wakes into the black depths that mark the dead of night.

Everything but Marie, that is, whom I still steal off to see whenever I can. Marie, who still glows steadily on my horizon.

I lean forward, taking just a little pity on the maréchale. "Don't fret, madame. I assure you my girls are only here to help. Snakes are halfway creatures, you see, straddling the divide between this life and the next. Their presence draws the spirits closer to us, thereby thinning the veil. Allowing me to peer into the future for you that much more clearly."

The maréchale glances around uneasily, as if she expects to see a tiny ghoul perching on her shoulder. "There are truly spirits here with us?" she says nervously. "At this very moment?"

If there are indeed spirits here, I cannot feel them any more than she can, but that is beside the point. The same holds true for the instruments of magic scattered across the table: the scrying ball with a scorpion suspended in its center, a sinister-looking ceremonial knife that I actually use to trim my wicks, a gilded Marseille deck that I have no intention of consulting. I still rely on the clever runes from Agnesot's grimoire to help me clarify the more elusive aspects of a vision, but these more elaborate occult trappings are only a performance meant for the maréchale. I have very little need for such scrying tools. My sight only grows keener with constant practice, especially once I latch on to the hook of a client's hidden need.

But the marquise's chosen come for the spectacle as much as for a reading—for a taste of the forbidden with which to intrigue their fickle friends. They thrill at curved blades and decks and milky scrying balls, and so that is what I give to them.

I nod curtly, lifting an imperious hand to silence her. Then I let my head fall back and eyes slide closed, my lips parting as if I am gripped by some otherworldly sensation.

"By the Moon Mother Selene and Asteria of the Stars, I call upon you lingering souls to gather 'round," I intone, the phrase that Pascal knows signals a transition. A swell of music skirls around us as if from everywhere at once, both enchanting and discordant, hanging like smoke in the sweet night air. "Be welcome among us, fantômes. Seethe and teem, cluster and swarm, and know that we are grateful for your presence."

I open my eyes and reach for the maréchale's hand with both of mine. She offers it up readily enough, but barely refrains from snatching it away with a muffled squeak when Megaera and Tisiphone come coiling down my arms. Extending their heads curiously over the cup of her palm, tasting it with their tongues.

"Madame La Voisin," she gasps, squinching her eyes shut and giving an agonized squeal when Megaera ventures higher over her wrist. "Are you absolutely sure there isn't another way . . . Ah, mon Dieu, she is cold. And *slimy*."

I could swear that Megaera, who has never been slimy a day in her life, stiffens with affront before withdrawing indignantly back up my arm.

"Hush, Maréchale, please. It can be dangerous to disturb a gathering of spirits once underway," I warn as I bend over her hand. I keep my voice low and somber, verging on sepulchral, though I am sorely tempted to laugh at her distress. "And there is no other way—not if you truly want to know which of your so-called friends is plotting to oust you from the queen's favor by claiming the seat of honor to her left at the next banquet."

"*What?*" She half screeches, her eyes flying wide open, both spirits and snakes all but forgotten. "Oh, but I knew it! Tell me, is it Geneviève? Is she the adder in my bosom?"

"I'm afraid she is," I say gravely, though the hazy vision I've glimpsed so far does not actually reveal the culpable lady's face. But no matter, because I scarcely need it—not when I had Madame Geneviève Leferon in the maréchale's chair not a week ago, seeking advice on how to best supplant her friend. "Though it pains me greatly to compromise your friendship, I cannot deceive you."

I also happen to know that several other ladies wish the maréchale ill for her conquest of their husbands, along with a spurned lover who plots his own revenge against her. But since that is not the need that has brought her here tonight, I keep it tucked away for future use. After all, now that she has impaled herself upon my fishhook, the one thing I know for certain is that she will be back.

With ever more coin in hand for me to stash away.

Fuming, the maréchale chews on the inside of her lip, her doe eyes turned calculating.

"To hell with our friendship," she sneers, "if that petite salope schemes to take my place. And after all I've done for her. Such effrontery! Can you see whether she will succeed?"

I tilt my head back and forth, considering.

"Not as of yet," I allow, though in truth I have not even bothered to look. "But I do see how you might regain the upper hand, with a little help."

She nods eagerly, urging me on. "How might I do it?"

"It is an audacious solution, madame." I hesitate, as if reluctant to even share it. "One that I would never offer lightly—or at all, if I did not think you singularly bold."

*And utterly unscrupulous*, I think but do not add.

She flushes with pleasure, tossing her ringleted head. "I'm glad to know we understand each other so well already. Dis-moi, what sort of solution do you have in mind?"

I cant my head thoughtfully, lifting an eyebrow. "Madame Leferon cannot very well court the queen's favor at the next banquet if she is indisposed, can she? And I have just the thing. Not to worry, it will cause her only temporary discomfort. The sort of griping in the bowels that incapacitates but passes quickly."

I smile conspiratorially at her, as though we are partners in collusion. "Lasting just long enough to allow you to cement your rightful place."

The maréchale's eyes light like candles at the thought. "Perfect," she breathes. "How much?"

More than poor Madame Geneviève Leferon paid for the reading in which I encouraged her to attend the banquet and seek the queen's favor for herself—but less than Geneviève will have to pay for a "counterspell" to lift the enemy's "curse" that will now keep her from attending.

The counterspell I plan to sell her the next time she comes to call, and which will be a simple tisane to calm her roiling belly.

"Forty louis," I reply blithely, as if it is no great sum to ask for a tincture of castor oil and bearberry that will barely cost me a pistole to brew.

"Forty . . ." The maréchale blinks rapidly at the exorbitant number, then recovers her composure. "They do say anything worth having is worth the price, do they not? I will take it."

"Lovely." I lean back in my chair, the matter settled. "You shall have it on the morrow."

Though I would still never sell the noblesse any deadly draught, I run a brisk trade in equipping them with pricey but less lethal things. And though I peddle potions to cause unsightly boils, aphrodisiacs for unrequited lovers, and tonics for inflicting and lifting curses of my own invention, my conscience has yet to prick. Most of the noblesse are even worse than I imagined when I whispered curses into their candles, more ruthless and depraved than I could have conceived of for such a cosseted lot. Ever battering themselves against each other and thrusting blades into their own friends' backs, so desperate are they to curry favor with the king and queen. To gain entry to their sphere of influence, to win their own hearts' desires at any cost.

Their envy and ambition twists them into shallow parodies, like the pantheon of spoiled and ever-feuding Olympian gods. And if they are staunchly determined to trick and undermine each other, why should I not line my pockets with the coin they spend so readily on their own malice?

The maréchale moves to stand, then thinks the better of it and resettles into her seat.

"You know, I am hosting a fete a fortnight from now, a bal masqué in honor of my birthday," she says, lacing her hands and eyeing me speculatively over them. "Do tell me if I overstep, Madame La Voisin, but . . . perhaps you would like to attend?"

"I'm afraid I only do my readings here," I demur, shaking my head. "As I'm sure you are aware."

"Oh, no, no! I did not mean for you to come in any *professional* capacity." She casts me a fawning smile, but I can see the stratagems whirling like a cloud of midges behind her eyes. "Merely for your own amusement, if you were so inclined. As my honored guest."

Although I know that this overture serves a purpose—that she would be enhancing her own standing by hosting the maîtresse-en-titre's sorceress at a private event—I feel a simple spike of pleasure at the notion of being feted on my own account, as more than the glorified help.

As one of the wolves instead, festooned in finery, my own savagery concealed behind a courtly masque.

"It is only that I've never seen you at any of this season's fetes," she wheedles deftly, sensing my indecision. "And I thought perhaps you might enjoy an evening away from these ethereal pursuits. A night to indulge in some more earthbound fare."

I waver for another moment, wondering if I am risking my carefully cultivated aura of mystique by agreeing to attend. But I have never been to such a fete, and I find I want to go to this one rather badly.

And would it truly harm anything to spend one single night as one of them?

"Perhaps I might at that, Maréchale," I tell her. "I will think on it."

## CHAPTER NINE

# The Prohibition and the Masks

I attend the maréchale's masquerade ball as Medusa, unable to resist.

I've dispensed with my signature black, opting instead for a jade-green Grecian gown fastened over one shoulder, and a filigreed silver masque to conceal my face. An intricate jeweled headpiece rests upon my head, crafted on extremely short notice by my very own grateful husband's hands. It is a wonder, a profusion of gold and silver snakes rendered in lifelike detail, down to the notched ovals of their scales and the glinting gemstones of their eyes. My own copper curls have been shaped by my chambermaid's clever hand into serpentine coils roped through the headpiece to support its weight.

I could have worn a sturdy wig beneath it instead, like most of the other guests. I normally strive to avoid stirring the marquise's jealousy by keeping myself drab, my face unappealingly powdered in heavy white, my bright curls always covered by a shawl.

But I happen to know that the marquise is unlikely to attend tonight, as she mentioned the possibility of plans with the king himself, so I make this fete an excuse to show myself off just a bit.

As I step into the palatial ballroom, buxom shepherdesses and sultry Cleopatras whisk obliviously by me in a whirl of color, their male escorts attired as jesters and gods, or in simple Venetian domino masques. The maréchale's residence is staggeringly huge, and it is clear she has spared no expense. The ballroom has been transformed into an aviary, hung with cages of exotic birds whose cacophonous caws and trills jangle above the tide of music. A tremendous banquet table sprawls along the room's imposing length, groaning beneath a wealth of food. Glazed peacocks arrayed with their own feathers, massive breads baked into Gordian knots, tiered cakes festooned with sparkling sugared fruit. An ice sculpture dominates the center of the room: Zeus in the form of a colossal swan poised to pillage Leda.

As I accept a goblet of wine from one of the attendants, I'm overcome with longing for Marie, who will poke ruthless fun at my retelling of all this decadent frivolity the next time we are together. "Can you imagine being both so mad and so debased," I can almost hear her say, her eyes glittering with gleeful contempt, "that you're willing to spend your coin on enough ice to carve a gigantic randy *goose*?"

Though I spent a night with Marie only last week, a yearning for her and for our simpler nights in the cité caroms painfully through me. For a desperate, aching moment, I wonder if all this has been a terrible mistake. Perhaps I should never even have come to the ball.

Perhaps I do not belong here at all, marooned among these faithless libertines who know nothing of true friendship.

The maréchale descends upon me then, and plucks me from my melancholy.

"Madame La Voisin! You came after all, what magnificent fun!" she exclaims, rushing forward in a flurry of satin and perfume to swoop pecks on my cheeks. She is attired as some bird of paradise, a resplendence of feathers sewn into her scarlet gown and resting on her head. "And, mon Dieu, but you look stunning—I would not have known you, had the doormen not tipped me off! Does she not look incomparable, Geneviève?"

Madame Leferon fawns over me accordingly. Then the two link arms with me and lead me to the banquet table, chattering with each other like the fast friends they pretend to be. Still engaging in their own private little masquerade, I note wryly to myself, even as they vie to outdo each other in piling assorted delicacies on my plate.

"You must try the religieuses," Madame Leferon urges. "Madeleine's chef procured something called fruit de la passion for the filling, through some sorcery Madeleine will not reveal even upon pain of death, the wretch. The flavor is downright sublime."

"It would hardly be special if I were to tell you where I got it, you greedy thing," Madeleine retorts with a hint of sharpness to her smile. "A sorceress never reveals secrets of her craft—n'est-ce pas, Madame La Voisin?"

"It *is* singular," I say as a burst of tart sweetness spreads across my tongue, a sunny tang infused into the silky cream. "In keeping with the ball itself, Maréchale."

She glows with pride, dancing her shoulders delightedly. "I do try my best for my guests—and of course, once I thought even *you* might come, I made it my mission to outdo myself!"

Turning toward the dance floor, she tugs me with her into the fray. "Come now, you must meet everyone! They'll scarcely believe I've managed to entice you here."

Half an hour later, I escape to the powder room, my mind overstuffed with the new acquaintances, names I once knew only through Antoine's most expensive commissions. I feel as if the maréchale has introduced me to half the court, from the Vicomte de Couserans with his roving eyes to the elderly Marquise de Vasse, who plied me with breathless questions of geomantic figures, as if I might lay claim to all possible knowledge of the arcane. And once sufficient wine filled the moat I'd dug around myself, they spoke to me as if I were truly one of them. Regaling me with bawdy jokes and gossip, prevailing upon me to dance, even insisting that I call them by their Christian names.

Drawing me ever deeper into their fanged fold and tucking themselves around me, like a Venus flytrap furling slyly closed.

Worse yet, I found myself a bit taken with it all quite despite myself.

*Remember who you are, you little fool,* I instruct my candlelit reflection in the powder room mirror, peering sternly at myself. *And how far you've come to be here. Would you really risk it all just to feel as though they were your friends?*

By the time I've gathered myself enough to return to the ball, I find the ballroom much darker than I left it, smothered in an expectant silence. Even the legion of birds seems to have gone abruptly rapt, the glistening beads of their eyes fixed upon the center of the room, where the ice sculpture on the podium has been removed. The crowd chatters excitedly to one another, sneaking glances at the empty podium, as if preparing for some new spectacle.

I'm wondering what all this may be about when an arm loops through mine, and I'm engulfed in a waft of the Marquise de Montespan's heady attar-of-roses scent. She wheels me around to face her, arrayed in an azure gown that glints with some iridescent thread, a dramatic peacock masque concealing her dainty features.

"Madame La Voisin," she coos in my ear with the slightest edge to her voice. "I had heard you were about, but could not quite bring myself to believe that Madeleine had managed to wheedle you here."

"Marquise!" I exclaim, struggling to cover my surprise. "I thought you were otherwise engaged tonight."

"I was, but then Marie-Thérèse took ill with the vapors yet *again*." She gives a frustrated shrug, as if she finds the queen's frailty infinitely tiresome. "So I thought I might as well not waste the remainder of my night. And you? How did Madeleine entice you to attend?"

"She was . . . quite insistent that I come," I reply cautiously, knowing I must take care where I tread. "I hope I did not do aught amiss by agreeing, madame. I had no wish to offend one of your closer friends by turning down an invitation."

"Oh, not at all, though I *do* wish you had at least thought to mention it to me." Beneath her practiced pout, that edge sparkles in her voice again, like the glimmer of a knife blade spotted from the corner of an eye. "And since we are speaking of social calls, my dear, I would *much* prefer that you curtail your visits to the cité. Specifically to that disagreeable friend of yours, what was her name? The one I met, at that loathsome tavern in which I found you."

"Marie," I say through suddenly numb lips, my mind spinning like a whirling top. How did she even know I still visited the cité? Did the coachman report my comings and goings to her? I knew, of course, that all "my" servants were in the marquise's service, but this confirmation still comes as an unpleasant shock.

I will have to start slipping coin to the ones that matter, cultivating my own relationships with them.

"Marie, yes. As you know, my dear, you are part of my image now. A reflection of my own reputation." Her carmined lips tighten into an implacable line, and she lowers her voice. "And I cannot have you tarnishing the both of us by traipsing to the cité to mingle with riffraff at your every whim. What if you were seen there by someone not in my employ, hmm? What if it became known that the maîtresse-en-titre's famed sorceress still wallowed in that sorry muck?"

"But she is my friend, Marquise," I protest. "My oldest friend. She is . . . important to me. I can be more discreet in the future, if that is the trouble. I can—"

She draws me closer, her hand tightening around my arm so abruptly that it cuts me off, her lips hovering near my ear.

"And is our agreement not likewise important to you, Catherine?" she half whispers, her voice like a coiled whip. "Because if it is, I suggest you find another way to tend to your friendship. Send your mademoiselle Marie heartfelt missives, perhaps—but I had better not hear of you visiting her again. Do we understand each other?"

I hesitate for a moment, fuming with a quiet, blistering fury. How can she make such a demand of me, as if I am no more than one of the clipped-wing birds that line this room?

But I clamp down quickly on the rising anger before I have cause to regret myself. As my royal patroness, the marquise reserves the right to shape my conduct. And besides, just because she has my household staff still in her pocket does not mean I cannot find another way, one unbeknownst to her. I could even slip out disguised if I must, make my way to the cité concealed.

"We do, of course," I confirm, taking care to keep my tone blithe and compliant even as I simmer with revolt. "It will be as you wish, Marquise."

"Will it, though?" the marquise purrs into my ear, as though she can sense the deceit brewing beneath my surface. Her voice feels like a scalpel now, one pressed directly below my chin, where my pulse beats close beneath my skin. "Let me be abundantly clear, Catherine. Should I discover *any* defiance in this matter—and you can be sure that I would, sooner or later—I would consider our agreement null and void. Which would necessitate an immediate return of the sum advanced to you, of course. Now, I ask again, are we understood?"

I nod slowly, though my heart is a pocked pebble in my chest. The notion that I am forced to abide by this restriction makes me feel like my skin has shrunk a size too small, but what choice do I have but to agree? The independent life that I am slowly building for myself, and the very roof above Antoine's head, depend on the marquise's continuing patronage. I cannot leave Antoine not only without a home but at the mercy of the moneylender's violent reprisal.

I will abide by the marquise's command, I decide, at least for now. Until I manage to devise some safer stratagem to see Marie.

"Lovely." The marquise draws back from me, shooting me a glittering smile. "Now, look, the show is about to begin! Do enjoy the rest of your evening, won't you, Madame La Voisin?"

She squeezes my arm as though nothing is amiss between us and drifts elegantly away from me on a cloud of that cloying perfume.

As I turn to face the center of the room, all my former pleasure melting away like snow in early spring, a fresh swell of loneliness rises up within me at the thought of braving this unforgiving new life without the bulwark of my best friend.

Then a familiar figure clad in black steps onto the podium, jostling me from my thoughts.

*The magician from La Pomme Noir*, I think, catching a startled breath.

A velvet cape, sewn with silver constellations, billows behind him even in the windless room. In light of my conversation with the marquise, there is something unsettling and achingly nostalgic about his presence in this glittering place, so distant from the crumbling courtyard where I last saw him, with my fingers threaded through Marie's. As if a shadow from my old life has snipped itself loose from its owner's heels to haunt me here.

Just as silently as the last time, he transforms handfuls of feathers into a swarm of lace-winged moths that flutter above the crowd, teeming toward the chandeliers. He whisks black rabbits from his cloak before vanishing them away, twists handkerchiefs into orchid bouquets, summons a tittering lady from the crowd to bind his hands with shackles before effortlessly shedding them.

At the very end he lifts his hands to his face with a perplexed frown, running his fingers over his hairline and around his ears as if searching for some hidden seam. Then, with an anguished grimace, he seems to peel his features off to reveal a grotesque scarlet visage lurking beneath.

"Étonnant," the lady beside me breathes to her companion, fanning herself. "Gerard, have you ever witnessed such feats of la magie?"

"No, indeed," Gerard replies, sounding both captivated and a touch afraid. "If this Lesage is not truly a devil, he is at least some small god."

As wild laughter echoes from the crowd, the demon's face is peeled back to reveal Lesage's once again—followed by another, even more diabolic visage. He strips back one after the next in gruesome and gripping succession, a seemingly endless metamorphosis. Letting a litter of used faces fall to his feet like husks.

Until none of us is certain what is real, the demon or the man.

Overcome by a tingling dread, I turn on my heel and plunge back into the crowd as they begin chanting for an encore. Weaving between them, I make my way to one of the small balconies that open from the ballroom, secluded alcoves jutting out into the night. Draping my arms over the balustrade, I suck in lungfuls of night air perfumed by the jasmine that grows below. Stifling sudden tears, uncertain why the performance struck such an unsettling chord in me.

Perhaps because, beneath my serpent masque, I myself wear a checkered history of faces, and all of them beholden by necessity to different masters. The wretched foundling at the orphanage, the indentured servant at the fabrique, Antoine's window-dressing wife—and now the marquise's purchased sorceress, forbidden from seeing the one person who truly matters.

How many faces must I don and peel away before I discover a Cat that belongs only to me?

"While shock and awe are ever my goal," a low voice utters almost in my ear, scattering my thoughts like a flock of starlings startled by a fox, "I am not sure what to think of having driven you away before the show was even done."

I whirl around, my hand flying by instinct to the knife belt that no longer hangs about my waist. The magician stands behind me in his starry cloak, running a hand through the tousle of his black hair.

"And is your goal also to petrify a woman enjoying a moment alone?" I force through clenched teeth, pressing a hand to my chest. "Because if so, you are a resounding success, monsieur. Truly, bravo."

He pulls a face, then presents me with an ironic bow.

"I think I had best leave the petrification to you," he rejoins, quirking a meaningful brow at my Medusa headpiece. "Surely you must be the expert in that regard."

At this close distance, I can see that the magician is only three or four years older than myself, twenty-two or twenty-three at most. And we are nearly of a height, though he is even more powerfully built than he appears onstage. His dense black eyebrows arch dramatically above long and narrow eyes, fringed by lashes so thick I nearly envy them. Along with the bold planes of his face, they hint at what must be an Eastern heritage; Chinois, perhaps, or Japonais.

"But please, accept my apologies," he continues. "I didn't mean to startle you, only to catch you before you absconded. As a token of my contrition . . ."

With a flourish, he produces a goblet of wine from behind his back, though I could have sworn both his hands were empty. Still glowering a little, I pluck it from his fingers and take a swig, giving him a grudging nod of thanks.

"Pax, my lady?" he asks, a smile hovering over his lips. Up close there is something of the wolf to his handsome face, elegant yet a little dangerous. I can almost smell him from here, too, sharp cedar and something smokier and more herbal. Mugwort, perhaps, or maybe myrrh. "I'm Adam. Or, the magician Lesage, at your service, Madame La Voisin. Whichever you prefer."

"Adam, then," I say, turning back to the balustrade. He moves to stand beside me, his eyebrows still pitched in invitation as he slings his arms loosely over the embellished railing. "And Catherine will do. So why chase me out here, when you had the maréchale's entire retinue eating out of your hand?"

"They're a dismally dull lot, I'm afraid, once I've pocketed their coin. But you? I could not pass up a chance to meet this divineress of whom I'd heard so much, who foretells the future with the aid of spirits and snakes."

Another slice of a smile, and an appraising look that feathers over me like a touch. "Dressed all in black, I might add, and with a violinist in her employ? It all sounded, shall we say, a touch *familiar*."

"And what of it?" I snap, though my cheeks heat at the jab. "Do you perchance have a monopoly on music and the color black?"

"Please do not mistake me, madame, I'm only too happy to serve as a lowly inspiration to a sorceress of your stature," he retorts. "If imitation is indeed the highest form of flattery, how could I ever object to being mimicked by the maîtresse-en-titre's own divineress?"

I take a furious swig of the wine, my outrage only

somewhat dampened by the fact that he's not wrong. I did pilfer him, lifting my dark garb and musical backdrop directly from his playbook.

"We may have some trappings in common, I suppose. But be assured that what you only play at, I actually do," I fling back at him. "You may perform your infernal little tricks onstage, but I part the veil in earnest. And then I make their tawdry little wishes come true. How does what *you* do compare?"

"Fair enough. You might be a true oracle, and I only an illusionist barely fit to grovel at your skirts." He lifts his hands in mock surrender, his teeth snaring his lower lip as he smiles at me. "But we are both on the side of the devils, are we not? Granting these spoiled scoundrels their hearts' corrupt desires. Leading them ever closer to the pit, each in our own way."

I turn away from him, still fuming, refusing to look at him even when he leans so close his breath tickles my cheek.

"Though given what I have heard of your talents, my lady," he murmurs, "I wager you could take them far deeper into damnation. If only you cared to give your methods just a *touch* more thought."

By the time I've formulated a proper retort, I turn back only to find him vanished like a gust of wind.

It isn't until I get home that I find the flower and feather he left tucked behind my ear, though I never felt him touch me.

## CHAPTER TEN

# The Maiden and the Apple

I stew over the maddening magician for days after the ball. How dare he judge me and my methods, I fume as I sit brooding by my fire between clients, when I managed to elevate myself from a modest tradesman's wife to a royally sponsored sorceress? And worse yet, why am I dwelling on his words at all, allowing them to slide under my skin like questing needles? Can I truly control myself no better than this?

But once I regain some measure of calm, I begin to grudgingly consider that he might be right. Perhaps I *have* become too reliant on parlor tricks, instead of pushing myself to become ever cleverer and better, as he clearly has with his act. I do have a talent for nurturing evil just as he suggested, perhaps because I take such care to live by Agnesot's parting words, to guard the pulsing little venom sac in my own heart.

And though I fare well for the moment, how long can I keep the fickle noblesse interested in me before their fancy inevitably fades? They are no more than gadabouts, after all, forever chasing fads like cats hunting their own tails. At any rate, if I am to continue besting infuriating magicians who play at being the devil, then I must at least begin to think ahead.

I turn to the grimoire for inspiration.

Something tickles at me from years ago, the words Agnesot used for whatever spell she intended to cast for my freedom. I cannot quite remember what she said, but I do remember the mention of noir, as if whatever enchantment she intended to use was of the darkest nature. And I know there is a section toward the end of the grimoire titled "The Darkest Rites," which I have always steered well clear of, having no intention of meddling with something styled so foreboding.

When I flip to it that night in my study, by the wavering light of my candle, even the inscription sends an icy rill down my spine.

*If you seek that which is buried beneath the soil that lies at the very bottom of your heart, then gather what courage you may and turn the page.*

Biting my lip, I flip through the pages, a chill blooming in my belly like some wintry flower, part fear and part ineffable thrill. There are spells here to summon Lucifer himself, along with a host of other, seemingly more minor demons. And there are even spells to call upon the host of angels, though the grimoire makes clear that this is an even dicier proposition—such sacred and lofty beings apparently take far greater exception than a demon at being summoned on mortal whim.

Reading further, I discover that each of the enchantments seems to be built upon a common foundation, a base ritual the grimoire calls La Messe Noire.

The Black Mass.

I pause in my perusal, threading my fingers around my goblet of wine and taking a long, contemplative sip, unease arcing through me. While I am not sure I truly believe the devil can even be summoned—what sort of divineress could command such a force as Satan himself, and through what kind of massive magic?—Agnesot *did* vanish from the fabrique somehow. And a few years later, Antoine appeared to free me as if by magic. If indeed it works, it is not the sort of enchantment I have any desire to trifle with. Especially if it means gambling with my soul, just as Marie once feared for me.

But while I have no intention of taking such a risk as holding a mass in earnest, the spells do give me a delicious idea.

A smile spreading over my lips, I consider what Adam said to me at the ball—speaking of us both as pied pipers of a sort, playing an infernal song, dancing the already depraved noblesse ever closer to hell. Why not indulge their taste for danger by taking a step further, offering access to the devil himself?

And if my ritual happens to be an outright fake, well, they will certainly never know the difference.

I wait until the night of the next full moon to host my first "Messe Noire."

By the time my handful of invitees files in, hooded and dressed in black at my request, my library has been meticulously transformed into a sorceress's opulent lair. I've lit bushels of candles everywhere and rolled the carpet back to paint the parquet floor with runes—most of my own invention, and a few legitimate, drawn from the more sinister-looking but innocuous sigils listed in the grimoire. Largest is the menacing pentagram in the middle of the room, a candle set at each of its points, an altar at its heart. The skylight directly overhead illuminates the altar with the full moon's silvery pour. The room roils with curls of incense smoke, enough to steep into every page of the books that line the walls above like brooding sentinels.

I've also scattered rose petals and raven feathers all about, my own little private joke. A sly thumbing of my nose at Adam himself, who stands among my gathered guests. I had to invite him, of course, to witness my new handiwork. To show him I can draw whatever inspiration I like from him, and grow it into something far darker and more tantalizing than his own act.

The rest of the guests I carefully selected from the marquise's inner circle, inviting only those I know to be debauched and wanton beyond any redemption. While most of the noblesse at least play at piety, these few are among the very worst the court has to offer. A handful of the most jaded and profligate, those who would readily sell their own mothers in pursuit of the next gilded excitement.

When I offered them the chance to whisper their desires in the devil's waiting ear, they could not have agreed any faster.

"Welcome, my guests," I intone, dipping my head so that my hood casts a shadow over my growing smile. The candle I hold in both hands throws a wicked light up toward my mouth like a dragon's kiss. Alecto coils languidly around my neck, completing the effect.

"Thank you for trusting me enough to join me here in this corner I've carved out for us and hidden from the eye of notre Dieu. So that we may, together, court a very different kind of light. The kind shed by a darker star."

I whisk the damask cloth off the altar table with a dramatic flourish, drawing a sharp gasp from the attendees as I reveal the nude form of the courtesan I've hired for tonight.

"Tonight, the pure vessel of this maiden's body will serve as our living altar," I continue, and I swear Camille's sensuous mouth curls just a whit, amused by the allusion to purity and maidenhood. "The centerpiece of an arcane ritual of worship ancient as the grave. Our offering to Lucifer Morningstar, banished from heaven and reigning king of hell. Hallowed be his shadowed name."

My guests shift from foot to foot with a whispering of robes, still captivated but now a touch unnerved. They all attend entirely of their own volition, of course, but nothing could have prepared them for this darkness I've curated for their entertainment.

Nor could they have anticipated the splendor of Camille.

She lies perfectly still, just as I have instructed. Moonlight sluices over her fine skin like some forbidden sacrament, limning the contours of her body with an inviting silver glaze. Her dark tresses pool over the tabletop and cascade to the floor, shining in the firelight and twining like ivy around the table legs. She is every bit as lovely as the sleeping beauty from the tale. The sight of her stirs even me, who arranged her there.

I take a pause, drawing a breath to quell the faint flutter in my belly. While I aim to stoke my guests' own lust, I cannot afford any distractions tonight myself.

Not when I am to serve as their sacrilegious prêtresse.

"Are you ready for this worship?" I demand, raking them with an austere gaze. "Do you stand willing, with bloody hearts beating in your hands?"

"We are ready," the marquise pronounces on the guests' behalf. She exchanges sparkling little looks with the maréchale and the sly Monsieur Philbert, one of the king's most favored court musicians, all three incandescent with excitement. The lecherous Vicomte de Couserans is here as well, alongside the king's own Master of the Wardrobe, the hatchet-faced and vain Marquis de Cessac. I had considered asking my attendees to come masked, but now I'm glad that I did not. They could never betray one another's presence here without revealing their own participation, and this way they can freely catch each other's eyes, mutually savor the experience.

"Then join me in this prayer to our shadow sire," I go on. "In which we call on Lucifer by his many names. Mephistopheles, Belial, Asmodeus, Legion. Prince of darkness and daystar of the damned."

Their voices merge with mine as I lead them through the prayer, a simple call-and-response I devised only this morning. It is ridiculous, of course, pure invention.

And yet, watching their rapt faces, I see they believe me anyway. It makes me feel brazen and powerful, a gout of fire searing through my veins. As if I myself am the shrewd and seductive evil they think to enjoin.

"Are you ready to pay obeisance?" I demand. "To offer up a draught of your own spirit before you partake of the dread lord himself?"

The guests murmur that they are, though I can feel their tension spike until the room fairly vibrates with it. *They are nearly where I want them*, I think as satisfaction waxes within me, full and round as the risen moon.

Now to take them even more firmly by the hand.

"To fuel this prayer, there must be pain," I inform them, approaching the altar and setting my candle down, then taking up an apple and a wine-filled copper chalice from beneath. I take care to keep each movement languid and hypnotic, purposely captivating. Just as I would if I were charming snakes.

"After all, gaining the shadow sire's regard always demands a sacrifice."

I set the chalice down above Camille's heart. Her pale hands drift up like little ghosts to curl around its stem, keeping it in place. Then I take the candle back up, walking slowly around the altar with it raised above her body, tilting it to drip forth a steady stream of wax. She swallows a gasp as each droplet strikes her skin, though I have negotiated all of this with her in advance. What I may do during the ritual, what she will accept from the guests. For all that she is paid handsomely, I would never ask her to endure anything other than what she might happily invite herself.

Once the wax begins to harden, I set the apple, a crimson so dark and gleaming it looks nearly black, into the dip of Camille's navel. It rises and falls, trembling a little with her every breath.

Though I have planned all of this down to the last detail, I am struck by how she must appear to my rapt guests. Speckled with wax and with the chalice clasped between her breasts, a forbidden apple cradled on her belly.

A fallen Eve in repose, flawless and indolent.

I sense the weight of Adam's eyes on me, glancing up to find them glinting like spun coins from the shadows pooling in the corner of the room. His lips curled with admiration, he tips me a sardonic little nod, as if to say, *Well played.*

Pleased by his reaction, I look back to my guests. Dropping my voice to a whisper, I beckon them forward with a curl of my hand.

"Come forth," I invite them with a smile like light shining off a blade. "For he requires your sacrifice as well."

They creep forward single file, wary yet drunk on danger, torn between enchantment and trepidation. I reach first for the marquise, who was bold enough to venture closest. When she gives me her hand, I flick out a knife from the folds of my cloak, mutter some nonsense syllables over it, and slice shallowly into her palm.

To her credit, she barely hisses in a breath as I hold her hand above the chalice and squeeze a few drops of her blood into the wine.

"Merci, madame," I murmur to her, folding her fingers closed over her palm. "Rest assured, your willingness will not go unrewarded."

She inclines her head to me, a silken smile playing on her lips before she steps away. The rest of them follow suit much more easily in her footsteps, coming forward biddable as lambs. Almost as if eager to be lanced. And though I do not show it, it gives me a vicious pleasure to cut them, to leave them with my mark.

This brief slice of pain is the least of what they deserve, for all their betrayals and travesties.

Once they've all been bled, I take the shining apple from Camille's belly and the chalice from her hands. Then I pass both to the guests, inviting them to nibble and sip, as a twisted inverse of Holy Communion. I've laced the wine with damiana, and glazed the apple with sweetened bishop's cap, both powerful aphrodisiacs.

To ensure they will go home all aglow, intoxicated with the veiled wonders of this night.

"Now that you have partaken of the Morningstar, I invite you to entreat him," I say, setting a small pot of pigeon's blood and a quill on the floor beside the altar. "Write him your wishes, with this maiden as your parchment and this blood as your ink. Then seal your desire with a ceremonial gesture of your choosing. A holy defilement, if you will, rather than a sacrament."

I sink to my knees behind the altar, to let this last part

unfold beneath my watchful eye. Though all of them have been told what is allowed and what proscribed, I remember that Marie once called them beautiful barbarians. My role now is to make certain that they indulge without transgressing too far.

The marquise approaches first again, kneeling to carefully write her wish along Camille's thigh, nibbling on her lip in thought. She chooses to seal it with a gentle kiss pressed to Camille's hip, running her palm lightly down the length of the girl's leg.

The gesture takes me aback a bit, surprises me with its boldness. It isn't what I would have expected of the marquise. But it is a good reminder that no one is quite as they appear.

And that even these overindulged savages cannot always be predicted.

Less than an hour later the ritual is done, leaving Camille a cream-and-crimson scroll of wishes. I lead the guests through a closing chant before dismissing them with suitably solemn farewells. Then I transcribe the wishes into my journal, taking careful stock of each before I send Camille off to bathe.

For how better to play these nobles' wicked dreams to my advantage than by collecting and studying them?

When a knock sounds at my study door, I'm still deeply engrossed. "Dieu merci, what is it, Simone?" I ask a trifle impatiently without looking up, assuming that only the chatelaine would think to disturb me at this hour. "The hour is late, and I'm rather occupied at the moment."

"Not Simone, I'm afraid, but I *do* promise to be brief," Adam responds, his voice lilting with humor. Startled, my eyes fly up to see him draped against the doorjamb, a hunter's smile hovering on his lips. "Might I come in?"

"I suppose you may," I say with a cool composure I do not feel. I flip my journal closed and set it to the side, leveling a gaze at him. "What are you still doing here, Adam? How did you get back in?"

"Forgot my cloak," he replies with a wink that implies he did no such thing. "I'm forever misplacing the blasted thing. Or is it that I never brought it in the first place? *Impossible* to know. Whatever the case, I managed to prevail upon one of the more amenable of your strapping young footmen out there to allow me to retrieve it."

He pushes off from the doorframe and strolls into the study, still smiling. "And you'll forgive my presumption, but I found I couldn't take my leave a second time without paying you my compliments."

I press my lips together, resolving to have a stern word with whichever footman had let him back in. Though I find that I am rather pleased by his return, almost as if a part of me had hoped against reason that he might linger after the rest of them had left.

"Wine, perhaps?" I ask, rising from the desk, my heart fluttering like a sparrow against my ribs. "I noticed you did not care to take my communion at the end."

His wolf's smile widens at the mock solemnity in my tone. "Of course not. Not without knowing what . . . choice enhancements you might have thought to add. But I'll happily take some with you now."

I move to the walnut sidebar and pour us both a glass of pale Bourgogne wine. His warm fingers linger on mine a touch too long when I hand him the goblet, and he tips his head wryly as he raises it in a toast.

"To your ingenuity, my lady," he proposes. "And a truly masterful performance. I'm especially pleased to find you took my advice on artful devilry to heart."

"And how do you know I did not have all this planned long before we even met?" I demand, even as I clink my glass to his and allow myself a smile. "Or do you always take credit for others' success?"

"Only when it's due." He sets his glass down on the sidebar, tilting his head quizzically at the sight of Alecto, who is still at her usual perch around my neck. "She is beautiful, your little friend. Might I say hello to her?"

I nod, making an effort to stay still as he traces a finger down Alecto's sinuous length with unsettling slowness. She lifts her head curiously at his touch, tongue flickering.

"She likes you," I inform him, trying to keep my voice steady, though in truth, I am a little rattled by his nearness. "You should be flattered. Alecto is quite discerning as to the company she keeps."

"Alecto!" His eyes widen with delight. "The Endless? You named your snake after one of the Erinyes? I find myself both bewitched and alarmed."

I start at that, surprised that he not only recognizes the name but even knows what the Furies are called in the Greek. "I have all three, actually—though Megaera and

Tisiphone are in their vivarium tonight. They are not quite so tractable in public as their sister."

He nods a little abstractedly, still stroking Alecto's scales. "And why the choice of name? Though I suppose it's of a piece with a Medusa masque."

"I do have a weakness for Greek mythology," I admit. "Apollodorus's *Bibliotecha* was one of the first books I read for pleasure. And the Erinyes are infernal goddesses of vengeance. I suppose the notion appeals to me in some way."

"Vengeance on men, and those who have sworn false oaths," he murmurs, surprising me all the more. His fingertips drift from the snake to my own skin, eyes flicking up to gauge my response. When I do not move away, he continues delicately tracing up my throat. "Ever more intriguing, my lady."

"Why do you keep calling me that?" I murmur back, a little hoarsely. Besides Marie, no one—certainly no man—has ever touched me like this before. The weight of his attention feels both heady and disconcerting. "You know I am no highborn dame."

"Because you are so clearly formidable, even without any title." He leans forward to brush a searing kiss under my chin, seemingly fearless of the snake that curls not far from his lips. "And therefore much, much worthier of respect than most born to the blood."

When he lifts his head, eyes latching to mine, my lips part to meet his kiss.

His mouth is deft and scorching, his hand sure at my back, the other rising to wrap around my nape. He tastes sweet beneath the wine, of nutmeg and mint, the callus of his palm a warm scrape against my neck. The feel of him is intoxicating, enticing, and unfamiliar. The shape of his desire tantalizing in its strangeness, rougher and more urgent than kissing Marie has ever been.

Almost a little dangerous, somehow—but in a way I find appeals to me.

At the thought of Marie, I feel the slightest pang of guilt, as if I am breaking her trust by sharing a kiss with someone else when I am not even permitted to see her. But there was never any promise made between us, no mention of fidelity. And though I have not heard from her since she wrote to tell me that she understood why I must keep away, I believe she would not begrudge me this closeness now.

Adam pulls back slightly, as if he can feel the current of hesitation running beneath my skin.

"A problem, my lady?" he asks, his voice still low and uneven. He pulls the springing curls by my face through his fingers, drawing them out to their full lengths. "Some uncertainty, perhaps? It is late, as you said. And I would not wish to overstay my welcome."

"No," I reply, leaning forward to whisper the rest against his lips. "I was only thinking that I . . . that I want you to stay."

CHAPTER ELEVEN

# The Invitation and the Rift

Though my days are pleasantly haunted by the flickering memory of our night together, painted in candlelight, I am also so preoccupied with my study of the noblesse's wishes that I manage not to dwell exclusively on Adam for the following fortnight.

Until his invitation lands on my escritoire.

"'I hope you can forgive the abominable delay in my communication, my lady—at least enough to join me for another evening of sublime diversion,'" I read aloud, my lips curving at his brazenness. His penmanship is very like him, too, both whimsical and deliberate. "'A special fete devised with you in mind.'"

I tap the paper against my pursed lips, considering. Is becoming more entangled with him wise when I should be focused instead on my work, on ensuring that my star continues in its steady rise?

But I *want* to see Adam. And I've earned a respite, I reassure myself as I begin to pen my response, having scarcely taken a day of rest since the Black Mass. My sight is in more demand than ever, and deciphering my list of wishes takes up countless hours. Some of my guests were annoyingly cryptic in their prayers, perhaps assuming Lucifer could glimpse into their hearts even without the clearest guidance. And some were likely merely being discreet, veiling their desires from their peers' prying eyes. It takes a finicky combination of scrying and educated guesswork to discern the truth of them.

So far, I've managed to surmise that Monsieur Philbert is raging at his mistress, wishing some dread vengeance on her for having thrown him over. Meanwhile, the Vicomte de Couserans merely longs for more excitement, whether it be in the form of a fresh lover or a novel business venture. And the Marquis de Cessac covets his brother's beautiful wife with a troublingly overzealous ardor.

Only the Marquise de Montespan remains single-minded as ever, dogged in her one desire, yearning only to sink her claws ever more deeply into the king.

Petty and downright vicious as their wishes are, I find plenty of opportunities, spaces into which I might insert myself via talismans, potions, and spells. Still, I'm thrilled at the prospect of a night away from the headache of it all.

Especially, I consider as my chambermaid tucks the final whalebone pin into my upswept hair the following evening, if it is a night spent in Adam's company.

When my carriage rattles through the city's gates, dusk has drawn over Paris like a damask curtain. Summer's languor has yielded to autumn with unaccustomed haste, setting the city's foliage ablaze with the turning. The air tastes sweet and chilly with the promise of the coming frost, and my breath fogs in ghostly plumes against the window glass. As we roll along the promenade of the Cours-la-Reine, I marvel at the fiery, dying splendor of its four rows of regal elms.

Being back inside the city walls tugs at me painfully, as if this incrementally greater nearness to Marie only enhances the dull yet ever-present ache of missing her. It has been over a month now since I have seen her in person, and nearly three weeks since she wrote to me last. I can barely fathom that I will be spending this coming winter without her warmth, and yet this is where I find myself.

Then my breath halts altogether when I spot a familiar figure hastening across the promenade, her pennant of dark hair whipping in the wind. As if I have conjured her there with the sheer force of my yearning.

"Stop!" I call to my coachman, my heart kicking up. I track Marie's weaving progress through the pedestrians, afraid to let her leave my sight. "Do you hear me, stop *now!*"

I fling myself out of the carriage almost before it's rolled to a full halt, rushing after her. I know my coachman is still the marquise's man, but I have taken to augmenting his salary with my own coin—enough that I can buy his silence for at least this one encounter.

When I grip her shoulder, Marie wheels around to face me, her teeth all but bared, a stiletto materializing in each hand. Shock whips back and forth between us like a jagged rod of lightning as we take each other in.

"Catherine?" she says incredulously, her eyes narrowing even as she lowers her knives. "What are *you* doing here?"

I ignore the question, searching her face.

"What's happened to you?" I half whisper, setting my hands on her frail shoulders. Where she was once slim, my best friend is now painfully gaunt, her bones standing stark beneath her skin. She's clearly been eating neither often nor well. Her lips are tinged dark blue with chill, and the whites of her eyes murky as puddle water, bleary from lack of sleep. "You look . . ."

"Terrible," she finishes flatly, blowing a wayward strand of hair out of her mouth. "How observant of you. Whereas you look quite splendid, a proper lady."

Recoiling a little at the unexpected sharpness of her tone, I jerk my chin back to the carriage.

"Why don't you come talk with me?" I offer. "I can take you wherever you're headed, save you the walk. Steal a little time together, just this once."

"Oh, how generous of you." She sheaths her stilettos, casting my waiting carriage a withering look even as her shoulders quake with cold under my hands. Her cloak is threadbare, worn nearly transparent from overuse. "But you know, it being such a lovely bracing night, I really think I'd rather walk."

"Marie!" I exclaim, consternation sweeping over me at her acerbic demeanor, this almost-cruelty that I've never seen from her before; at least, not wielded against me. I reach for her thin arm as she turns away. "I understand that you are . . . angry with me, perhaps, for keeping away. But I *told* you, I explained why it was necessary. And you wrote to me that you understood!"

"And I do, Catherine." She huffs out a faint husk of a laugh laced with bitterness. "I understand altogether better than I wish."

*I should have known*, I think with a sinking heart, *from the brevity of her last note, that all was not right between us.* And yet I did not question her, press her on it.

Perhaps I simply did not wish to know the depth of her distress.

"I understand that when push truly came to shove, you chose *this* life"—here, she gestures scathingly at my fine brocade skirts, the plush ermine lining of my cloak—"over me. Without so much as a backward glance."

"You know it was not like that!" I protest, though guilt gnaws sharply at me in response to the accusation. "I, I wrote you every week! Is *this* why you haven't written back, because you were cross with me? But you know that the marquise demanded that I not—"

"And you did not exactly fight her, did you, Catherine?" Marie breaks in, her eyes glittering with a well of sudden, furious tears. "When she directed you to jump, you leapt dutifully at her bidding. As if leaving me behind barely even pained you."

"*Of course* it pained me! *Of course* it did!"

She gives a listless half-shrug, looking away from me. "Not enough, it would seem."

Perhaps she is right, at least in part. For all that I have missed her every day, perhaps I acquiesced to the marquise's demands more readily than I should have, for fear of being thrust out of my promising new life and banished back to the cité. To the specter of poverty and squalor ever looming forbiddingly over my head.

As if now that I have become accustomed to so much more, that old life—the one Marie still inhabits—has become the worst fate that I could imagine for myself.

I wish desperately to draw her into my arms, but there is little Marie puts more stock by than her pride. And I can see that I have wounded it badly, along with her secretly tender heart.

I lick my dry lips instead, attempting to gather myself. "Please, Marie, give me only a few minutes. I keep a spare cloak in the carriage as well. If you like, you need only stay until you've warmed your bones."

She chews her lip, her face still simmering with hurt, but it is the promise of warmth that finally sways her. She gives a grudging nod and follows me inside, shrugging me off brusquely when I move to help her up. After I've ordered the coachman to strike ahead once more, I throw the cloak over her shoulders and take her hands into my lap, chafing them briskly as I've done so many times before. Out of the two of us, I have always run much hotter, though her hands have never been quite this icy or frail.

"Thanks," she says, stiff as a stranger, eyeing me askance. "It *is* damnably cold. Normally I would not mind bidding all that summer stench and scorch adieu. But this year, well . . . this winter promises to be rather worse than most."

"Why?" I ask, squeezing her hands. "What has you so run down?"

"The vagaries of life, ma belle," she retorts with a wry twist of her lips. "Or have you quite forgotten how pressing those can be?"

"It must be more than that," I say quietly, giving her a level look. "The Marie Bosse I know is more than equal to such predicaments."

"The Marie Bosse you know has never been nearly penniless, nor hunted by the king's men," she spits, turning to stare blackly out the window. "Have you truly become so sheltered that you have heard nothing of the recent police raids on the cité?"

"Raids?" I reply blankly. "Beyond the Palais Royal, why would the king even concern himself with Île de la cité?"

"It is not the Île on the whole, but the cité itself that offends him," she replies, withdrawing her hands from mine. She tilts her temple against the window, fingernails tapping a nervous tattoo against the glass. "The cité's welter of magicians and sorcerers, that is. We criminals and so-called charlatans who deal in something so vulgar as magic. His Majesty means to stamp us out."

I lean back into the cushions, awash in sudden understanding. From what I've heard from his courtiers, the Sun King prizes logic and reason over anything that smacks of the arcane. The new Royal Academy of Sciences enjoys his august patronage, and he has equipped its observatory with a telescope so powerful it can surveil the stars themselves. Rumor even has it that when one of the royal menagerie's elephants died, Louis not only donated it to the academy for dissection but insisted on being present for the procedure, so fascinated was he with the physicians' expertise.

Of course a king who so esteems science and disdains superstition would wish to grind the cité's havens under his heel. Even as his own maîtresse-en-titre keeps a sorceress and his courtiers flock to my Black Mass. I know from the marquise that the king only indulges his beloved mistress's darker games to keep her content, even as her tastes run against his own grain. But what it amounts to, in the end, is the same disparity that always defines the gaping schism between the poor and the rich.

As ever, the rules imposed upon the lowborn do not apply to the noblesse.

"Quelle pagaille," I murmur, shaking my head. "What a terrible mess."

"It is much worse than a mess," Marie responds bleakly. "Not only is he tossing us into Vincennes and the Conciergerie upon mere suspicion of wrongdoing, he is stealing our livelihood. We are mostly too busy evading his patrols to properly ply our trade. I've barely been able to see even my regulars, not when everything is so deuced uncertain."

"Do you need money?" I ask, reaching for my coin purse. "I could—"

"No." She cuts me off with a slicing gesture, her tone hardening. "Or rather, I do, but not from you, Catherine. Not when I no longer even know what we are to each other."

I drop my eyes and roll my tongue along the inside of my cheek, burning with some ambiguous shame. I suppose I do not know what we are to each other, either. And I certainly do not know how I am to bridge this new rift between us, without sacrificing everything that I have gained.

As if she can sense my turmoil, her face turns a touch more gentle. With a wistful ghost of our old fondness, she leans into the space between us to tip a finger under my chin.

"Is this truly the life you wish, ma belle?" she asks softly. "Everything you've told me of the noblesse, their schemes and plots against each other . . . do you really want to build up your life so entwined with them, ever pandering to their endless treachery? I know you worry for Antoine, but he would find his own way even if the marquise demanded a return of her sum. Men like him, they always do, when their hides are on the line. You could still come back to the cité, if you wanted. You could come back to *me*."

"Oh, Marie," I whisper, tears leaping into my eyes even as I avert them, unable to withstand the intensity of her gaze. "You are my . . . the dearest friend I've ever known. But—"

"'Friend,'" she echoes with a bitter shake of her head. "How long will you cling to this tired fiction? Why do I even bother to try, when you are so unwilling to admit how much more lies between us besides friendship?"

I take a deep breath, uncertain how to respond. "Perhaps you are right. Perhaps I *am* afraid. But even if we set us aside, it is not only concern for Antoine that keeps me here. Life with the marquise . . . it gives me *room*, Marie. Room to become someone I could never have been before. Someone strong. Someone free."

She closes her eyes for a long moment, shaking her head slowly. "Can you not see how such a freedom will consume you, Catherine? If you can even call it that in the end?"

"But I am only doing what I must," I argue. "Surely you of all people can understand as much, after all you've done to survive."

She shakes her head ruefully, thumping the carriage's roof to signal the coachman to stop.

"Except that I would never willingly rid myself of you, ma belle," she says. "No matter the cost of keeping you. But that is you, is it not? By hook or by crook, ma belle always gets her way."

And with a wounded glance that runs me through more neatly than her stilettos ever could, she alights from the carriage and disappears into the night. Leaving behind only a resounding silence, and the lingering scent of citron and sandalwood.

It could not have ended any other way, I tell myself, though my chest feels like a cavity, a bloody abyss stripped of something vital.

*And at least*, I think for some small measure of comfort, *she has my fine cloak to keep her warm.*

## CHAPTER TWELVE

# The Mirror and the Devil

I am in a black mood when I reach Adam's abode, still brooding over my encounter with Marie. The magician lives on the Rue Saint-Jacques in a half-timbered town-house sagging tiredly against its more upstanding neighbors. But when I rap the tarnished knocker against the flimsy door, a petite and well-groomed maidservant opens it to greet me with a smile.

"Welcome, Madame La Voisin," she says with a smooth dip of her head, gesturing me in. "Monsieur Lesage is expecting you. And the others have already arrived."

"The others?" I echo, bemused, as I step beside her into the foyer's dim interior. The walls are papered in somber maroon, and the gloom so dense with dust the candelabra's watery light barely manages to dilute its murk. "But I thought it was to be just the two of us tonight?"

Her tidy face creases with such chagrin on my behalf that my foul mood uncurls and expands, gaining in vigor. Though Adam called this evening a "fete" in his invitation, I'd thought that only an arch term for an intimate rendez-vous between the two of us.

Clearly I have mistaken his intentions.

"I am afraid not, madame," she says regretfully, taking my cloak and offering me a black hooded cape in exchange. "My apologies for the confusion."

"It's hardly your fault," I mutter, stifling the urge to snap at her as I sling the cape over my arm. Though ten-drils of suspicion stir inside me like ivy creepers, whatever is truly afoot here has nothing to do with her. "And what am I to do with this?"

"Put it on, please," she instructs as she leads me up the carpeted stairs to the second floor. Our footfalls release breaths of dust with each step, its motes whirling through the feeble halos cast by each flickering sconce.

Then she opens another door, nodding me in, and sud-denly everything becomes much clearer to me.

The room beyond could be a run-down replica of my sorceress's lair on the night of the Black Mass, a reflec-tion viewed in the surface of a muck-riddled pond. Artfully sloppy runes deface the splintered hardwood floor, includ-ing a pentagram so slick and glistening it may have been painted with fresh blood. Though Adam is nowhere to be seen, a wooden full-length-mirror frame set with black baize instead of glass stands at the pentagram's head. What use, I wonder with foreboding, could he possibly find for something like that? At least he has not aped my living altar. His is merely a table scattered with candles and occult artifacts, nothing of any particular note.

And there is no fragrant incense, no feathers and flowers here. Where I strove for polish and decadence, Adam has embraced seaminess and grit.

Perhaps he thought it might instill his stolen ritual with authenticity.

*So this is what he has been devising while he stayed away*, I think with a mounting fury. A Black Mass to rival my own. That he would thieve my idea from me, after the night we spent together, rives me through with rage, along with a scalding mortification. Is this why he wanted me at all? So that he might avail himself of more of my secrets, pry them loose from my lips upon my own pillow?

How stupid of me, how terribly foolish and naive, to invite him not only to my Messe Noire but also into my bed.

But then, I wonder, my thoughts doubling back upon themselves, why summon me here at all to witness this traitorous turnabout? Why call this a fete devised for me?

"Madame La Voisin!" a delighted voice purrs into my ear. I turn with a start to find my very own patroness standing among the hooded guests clustered against the room's back wall. The marquise beams at me, porcelain-cheeked and perfect as Aphrodite against the black of her borrowed hood. She leans forward to brush a greeting kiss over my cheek. "This is all so delightfully sordid, is it not? And what a marvelous surprise to find you here. I would not have expected you to attend a rival sorcerer's Messe Noire."

"A rival . . . sorcerer . . ." I sputter, so beset by outrage I can barely control myself. I swallow with an effort, my hands curling into tight fists by my sides. The painful slice of my nails into my palms brings a welcome burst of clarity. "He is no *sorcerer*, Marquise. Only a simple magician, a tawdry illusionist. If he has presented himself as anything grander to you, then I'm afraid he has tricked you here under false pretenses."

"Oh, hardly." She flicks one shoulder in a heedless shrug. "I confess I came out of sheer curiosity. What can this Lesage possibly do, I wondered, that my own divineress—ostensibly the very finest of her age—could not manage better?"

I read between the lines, divining the true meaning of the cold and pragmatic twinkle in her eyes. While my standing may still be safe with her, she sees no harm in taking the measure of my competition, drawing her comparisons. Determining if Lesage might perchance suit her even better than I do.

It makes all the sense in the world, in the heartless way native to the aristocracy.

I take covert stock of the rest of the room, gauging Adam's audience. Amid a scattering of faces I do not recognize, I spot the Vicomte de Couserans, who tips me a wink when I meet his eye, along with the marquise's usual entourage of Madame Leferon and the maréchale.

Then, heralded by a swell of invisible violins, Adam appears beside the mirror between one breath and the next. As if conjuring himself out of thin air.

"Welcome, all you gathered," he booms, spreading his hands with a flourish, his eyes aglitter with a ferocious mirth. He's clad all in black, as ever, though beneath his cape he sports no waistcoat or shirt. Above his pantalon, his sinewy torso is adorned with blood-red sigils, candlelight gilding the flow of muscle and the neat taper of his waist. "I thank you for gracing my home with your presence. Now, shall we court our demonic liege together?"

The marquise titters beside me, then heaves an admiring sigh.

"I suppose he does not even need a living altar, does he?" she whispers to me behind her hand. "Not when he might as well be an offering himself."

As the ritual begins, I see why Adam chooses not to speak when he performs his magic shows. Charming as he is in private, in public he does not possess anything close to my poetic flair. Though his ceremony is in close mimicry of mine, his prayers sound simple and slapdash, pallid reconstructions of my own.

And yet it galls me to admit that it all still works quite well, because what the magician lacks in substance, he makes up for in form. Though he steers clear of obvious tricks, the glassless mirror at the altar's head does all the work for him. It produces stunning images, from roiling darkness to gray smoke to licking flames, followed by outlandish tableaux both lush and obscene.

The most extravagant of these evokes Eden after the fall, filled with smoldering embers and withered trees, their branches heavy not with apples but with snakes.

As if he is affording all of us a glimpse through some profane window, a stolen peek into perdition. A porthole into hell.

Then there is the subtext only I can read, a sly tongue-in-cheek mockery. The way he's taken back everything I stole from him and remade it into something almost better. But even as it makes my blood boil like tallow, I find I cannot help but admire the enterprising mind behind it all. When he looks my way, cocking his head almost as if in question, his eyes gleam with something both more complex and benign than the malice I expected to see. Something much more interesting than mere triumph at having outwitted me.

He wants me to appreciate this performance, I realize with shock, a little of my umbrage fading; he seeks my admiration. Which means that his invitation, while deceptive, was not intended as an insult. Because he does not see me as an enemy—but rather, as a skilled opponent who has borrowed from him in the past. An adversary whose respect he wishes to win.

I could learn from him, I realize, from his keen scalpel of a mind and dispassionate cunning.

And once I have learned, I could be the one to best him.

When he reaches the ritual's climax, Adam instructs us all to kneel. "Let us look upon the face of our dread lord," he intones, "and bask in his regard. There is no longer any need to merely hope that your prayers will reach his ears. Not when you can look the daystar directly in the eye."

"No," the marquise breathes beside me as we both sink to our knees, sounding genuinely unnerved. "Surely that cannot be possible."

I think of Adam's gruesome demons' masks at the maréchale's bal masqué, and his dancing skeleton in the courtyard of the Pomme.

"He *is* a renowned illusionist, Marquise," I whisper back. "Who knows what further deceptions he has in store."

Once he has us on our knees, Adam stands beside the mirror and sweeps his arms up slowly, as if in wordless command. A series of gasps sound from the crowd as a demonic visage coalesces in the mirror, lurid and scarlet and somehow all aglow, a storm cloud of black hair whipping around its frightful face. It yawns its mouth open in a silent roar, exposing a serpent's flicking tongue and dripping fangs. It is of a piece with the infernal landscapes that came before it, yet somehow more substantial, infinitely worse to behold.

From the collection of ragged breaths and wide eyes all around me, I can tell just how deeply it has struck home.

*Another illusion*, I think irritably, wincing as splinters dig into my knees. This diabolic apparition can be nothing but an image somehow cast onto the baize, as in a shadow play. Though I cannot think of how he achieves such depth and vibrancy of color. Worse yet is how eagerly his guests— including *my* marquise—lap it all up like starving strays. Their wonder is expansive and genuine, and I can barely fault them for it. His staging is immaculate, the marvel of his mirror all the greater when set against the dilapidation of the surrounding space.

It only reinforces my resolve to learn from him, then to best him at his own game, to win this feral little contest between us.

Because he cannot have this life I've fought for tooth and claw, wrested into being by the force of my own will. I will not be upstaged when I have been so clever and worked so hard for all of it.

Especially not when it has cost me Marie.

After the ritual, Adam departs from my example by hosting an actual late-night fete. While the guests are occupied with chattering to each other of everything that has passed, his violinists strike up a merrier song.

As servers file fleetly into the room, bearing platters of wine, cheese, and fruit, I circulate among the attending noblesse in an attempt to salvage the evening in my favor.

"Alors, what were your impressions, Madame La Voisin?" the Vicomte de Couserans asks me, his eyes drifting appreciatively down my neck and the exposed swell of my bosom. I curse Adam inwardly for having misled me into wearing a more revealing gown than I would have chosen, had I known some of my clients would be here. "I found Lesage's ceremony exceptionally chilling."

"And I!" the marquise gushes, giving an ecstatic little shudder. "Heavens, that *face*! I swear it shall follow me directly into my dreams. Was it truly le Diable, do you think? I imagine it can't have been anything else."

"Very doubtful, my lady," I say, taking heed to mask my turmoil. "Of course, I cannot say for certain, but it is worth remembering that Lesage is only an illusionist. Not a sorcerer, and certainly no dark priest. All this was not so different from his magic act. More a dangerous mockery than anything else, of a ritual that should only ever be undertaken with the proper respect."

The two lapse into pensive silence for a moment, mulling this over. *Perhaps this is how I might sway them back toward me*, I think with a flare of hope. By convincing them that there is a protocol to dallying with the devil. A certain way these things must be done.

In other words, *my* way.

"But the images in the mirror!" the vicomte insists, his ruddy cheeks blotching even further. I remember his wish, the craving for excitement in any form. Of course he would want to believe in something so thrilling as having seen the devil's face. "Not only that countenance, but the fire, and those stunning panoramas! I cannot imagine how any of it could have been feigned. But you, madame, are you not acquainted with Lesage? Do you have any notion of how it was done?"

"I've no idea, I'm afraid," I reply, shrugging as if Adam's secrets hardly matter. "We do know each other, but it is as they say. Magicians are loath to reveal their tricks."

"Well, perhaps you will entice him into some disclosure yet," the marquise suggests coyly, fingering the silken ends of a ringlet and tipping her head toward the back of the room. "He seems . . . rather partial to you."

I glance over to where Adam holds court with several of the other nobles while gazing my way, eyebrows lifted in invitation. Making my excuses to the marquise and the vicomte, I wander toward him. He extricates himself from his admirers at my approach, leading me lightly by the elbow toward the impromptu dance floor, where a few couples drift in a slow pavane like lily pads caught in a lazy current.

"Well?" he asks as he whirls me around. "How did I do? I am all but dying to hear your thoughts."

"My thoughts are that you are a scoundrel and a rake," I say under my breath, keeping my tone studiously placid and my expression smooth. "Neither of which comes as any great surprise."

"My, such harsh words!" That wolf's smile again, curling the corners of his mouth. "Come now, my lady, all pique aside. Were you not pleased by the performance? I did so hope you might enjoy it."

I struggle with myself for a moment, torn between aggravation and curiosity.

"How was the illusion done?" I demand. "And let us not prevaricate. That was no more the devil himself than it is the devil who reads their wishes by my hearth."

He purses his lips into a tantalizing moue, tilting his head back and forth as if deciding what to divulge. When I start to pull away from him, he makes an apologetic noise and tugs me delicately closer.

"Stay with me tonight," he murmurs into my ear. "After they've all gone. Stay with me, and tell me that the next Messe will find us standing together, as black priestess and her priest. If you agree, I will do one better than tell you—I will show you how it was done."

"*That* is what you wish?" I ask, both taken aback and, despite myself, a little gratified. "A partnership with me? That is why you invited me here under such brazen false pretenses?"

"Of course," he says blithely, as if it should have been clear to me from the start. "Is it not the obvious next step? With forces joined, would we not command immeasurably more influence?"

I stare consideringly into his eyes, so dark they look almost black in the room's low light. There is merit to his suggestion. What could we achieve if we merged our respective powers instead of continuing our struggle to upstage each other? With our stars yoked together, what blazing constellation might we scrawl across the heavens?

Together, what might we become?

"We could *own* them, Catherine," Adam says fiercely, just above a whisper, sensing the soar of my temptation. The first time he has used my Christian name. "All of them, up to le Roi Soleil himself. Louis may be enthralled by the novelties of science now—but when faced with advisers such as the two of us, with your scrying gift and my legerdemain? Nothing would be beyond our reach. Not even the space just behind the throne."

*Such power*, I think dreamily, swept up by his vision of us as shadow regents, weaving our dark stratagems from the catacombs. And the vast influence and wealth that might be amassed in this fashion, the staggering freedom that would come with it.

Surely no one else would be my master then.

When I shake my head, it is reluctantly, and with a tinge of genuine regret.

"To stand beside you, I would have to trust you with my future," I say with an almost rueful smile. "And under-handed as you have been tonight, how could I trust you with anything of mine? No, I'm afraid we are better suited as we are."

"Perhaps you are right," he says, shedding some of that banked intensity and slipping back into his easy smile. "Or perhaps you will take some time to reconsider? Because I am not going anywhere, my lady. And while I do not consider us enemies now, is that not what we are destined to become, if we do not choose to thwart fate by becoming friends instead?"

With a kiss brushed over my knuckles, he releases me and melts back into the fray.

## CHAPTER THIRTEEN

# The Ingenue and
# the Newcomer

I linger at the fete far longer than I'd like, reluctant to leave Adam to his own devices. Should something else transpire, some other crafty piece of drama, I cannot afford to be left in the dark.

At the same time, my stately oracle's masque begins to chafe. The fete has devolved into a sloppy bacchanal, and I grow heartily sick of making conversation with soused aristocrats. The vicomte alone has attempted to paw me thrice. Should there be a fourth time, I will be sorely tempted to fling my wine into his face, social niceties and my livelihood be damned.

My patience fraying, I retreat to the sidebar for a moment to gather myself.

"Are you quite all right?" the young woman beside me asks, in a voice so light and sweet it barely carries over the festive ruckus. "Pardon the presumption, but you do not entirely look as if you are enjoying yourself."

Though the question comes across as somewhat impertinent, the tone itself is not. When I turn to look at her, I find that she is perhaps seventeen, comely and well attired, but clearly not highborn.

"I hope that was not too forward," she says timidly, shrinking a little under my openly appraising regard. "I am only asking because I wish to leave, myself, but would not want to offend our host."

"I rather doubt you would," I reply sourly, glancing over at Adam, who is sampling a bunch of grapes dangling from the Vicomte de Couseran's hand. "He seems far too busy cavorting with his more esteemed guests to even notice. If you do not mind my asking, how did you come to be here at all? Are you a friend of Adam's?"

"Oh, no," she says with a fetching flush, her skin dramatically pale for someone with such dark eyes and hair. "I saw a show of his only last week, and then he bought me some wine after. When he invited me to a fete, I was so flattered, and I thought . . ."

She bites her lower lip, sighing a little. "In truth, I am not sure what I thought. But, mon Dieu, I did not expect anything like this!"

"You mean he did not warn you the devil would also be stopping by?" I ask dryly, sipping my wine, half wishing to laugh at our shared predicament. "How very thoughtless of him."

The girl giggles so adorably it teases a real smile from me. She really is so refreshing in comparison to the overdone fops and cloying grand dames that take up all my time. Perhaps, in a different time or place, we might have become friends.

"At least I'm not the only simpleton taken unawares, non?" she mutters, then claps a mortified hand over her mouth. "Not that *you* are a simpleton, of course, I did not mean to—"

"I did not think you meant to say so," I reassure her, giving her shoulder a light squeeze. "Tell me, what is your name?"

"Oh, how rude of me—I am Mademoiselle Claude de Vins des Oeillets," she adds, dipping into a curtsy. "No one of any particular note, I'm afraid. My parents are both actors of some renown, but the family art of artifice seems to have ended with them. I am certainly no great comedienne."

"In my experience, there are far worse afflictions than a lack of artifice," I reply, making her smile again. "Take it from me. You are entirely charmante just as you are."

"Thank you," she says, bobbing another endearing, unnecessary curtsy. "And are you a friend of Adam's?"

"Something like that. Though I would call us more colleagues than friends. I'm the Sorceress La Voisin, in service to the Marquise de Montespan."

"Truly?" Her rosy mouth drops open, eyes flying wide. "You are the maîtresse-en-titre's divineress? But you, you are so *young*! It must be très glamereux, being in such a grand lady's employ."

"Would you perhaps like to find out?" I ask her, a wisp of an idea taking shape. "If you are interested, something might be arranged."

I know the marquise recently lost a trusted companion who doubled as her lady's maid, and has been woebegone over the loss. I'm sure she would be quite as taken with the novelty of this girl's artlessness as I am.

And given the way the wind is blowing, it would not be unwise to begin protecting myself. There would be worse things than having someone in the marquise's household firmly in my debt.

"What?" the girl breathes, as if not daring to believe her luck. "You think the maîtresse-en-titre may have some need of *me*?"

"Stranger things have happened, chère," I say, taking her by the arm. "Come, and I will tell you what I'm thinking."

On the morrow, I wake better disposed. Before I left the fete, I made the introductions between Mademoiselle des Oeillets and the marquise, and just as I anticipated, my patroness was instantly taken with the girl. Enough to accept her on the spot as a replacement for her lost lady's maid.

Now all I must do is continue to cultivate my friendship with Mademoiselle des Oeillets, and, gently but insistently, never let her forget to whom she owes the elevation in her rank.

And there is more wind to fill the sails of my restored mood. Tonight, I have a reading scheduled for someone new, a noblewoman who sought me out on her own rather than yet another of the marquise's stale sycophants. The novelty of a session with a stranger has yet to lose its savor, and as she seats herself in my pavilion, I stir eagerly in my chair.

"Thank you for seeing me on such short notice," she says, adjusting her voluminous velvet manteau over her legs and flashing me a wan flicker of a smile, vanishing almost as soon as it appears. "Illustrious as your roster is, I thought I might have to wait weeks if not months to meet with you."

"I make it a point to set time aside for newcomers," I tell her, inclining my head graciously. "Were I to read only for those whom I know well, it might render my powers sluggish and stale."

Her lips twitch at the mention of my powers, curling a little as if in skepticism. Something about the expression renders her face, large-eyed and dainty as a madonna's, vaguely familiar. I squint at her for a moment, trying to pinpoint the source of this odd sense of recognition. Perhaps it is no more than her stylish aspect; surely a thousand well-bred women sport such tight curls, rouged cheeks, and velvet beauty marks speckling heavily powdered skin.

Even more oddly, she watches me with a bewildered crease between her own brows, as if I might be familiar to her, too.

"But enough about me, madame," I say a bit uneasily, thrown off by her keen attention. "Shall we begin?"

She nods, though I can still feel her assessing eyes as I bend over her hands. A vision washes over me almost immediately, nearly painful in its force, yanked brutally forth by the ferocity of her need.

"Two men on either side of you," I whisper, a little dizzy with the onslaught of the sight. It pounds in my skull like a pendulum swinging from side to side. The vision crystallizes before me in the form of an otherworldly chessboard, in which she appears as a queen flanked by both a bishop and a rook. "One, you are shackled to by the ring on your hand. The other, you long for, just as he yearns for you."

I glance up to see her eyes widen with surprise, then narrow with satisfaction.

"Good," she says shortly. "Good, so far. And what else?"

"The bishop," I say hoarsely, the words sour in my mouth. I watch as the piece chivies the queen ruthlessly across the board, badgering her back and forth, never allowing her a moment's rest. "Your husband. He . . . he uses you ill."

"That he does," she says with a terrible equanimity. As though this abuse has come to be simply a matter of course for her.

"And the other man . . ." I begin, trying to see beyond the vision's symbolism. "Not only your lover, but an artist. His art is how you first fell in love."

"The painter my own husband commissioned to paint my likeness, yes. And he is everything my husband is not," she bites off with a shake of her head so furious it near unseats her wig. "Penniless yet rich in talent. So gentle, and unfathomably kind. A man the likes of which I did not even think existed."

In my vision, the queen begins to shed a glow onto the dreamscape board, emanating a dreadful crackle of light like a thunderhead. Then she rears back and cracks into the bishop, sending him spinning off the board, which rives itself in two beneath the force of her quaking rage. But the solitary rook remains, safe by the queen's side.

"And you wish your husband dead so you might be free of your torment—and free to wed this other man instead." I sit back, letting the remnants of the vision slip away as I release her hands. "But since the law gives you no recourse, you have come to me for help."

She nods ardently, eager eyes fastening to mine. There is a new light to them now, a sort of certainty. Something like recognition.

"They speak of your potions with such veneration at Versailles, you know," she says, her voice taking on a wheedling tone. "I've heard rumor that the marquise even credits your love philters with having won her the king's affections. And I thought, if you could manage something so grand and all-encompassing as love . . ."

"That I should not blink at a spot of murder," I finish wryly, shaking my head. "I am sorry to disappoint you, but you have come knocking at the wrong door, madame. I am no widow-maker. Not even when it comes to heavy-fisted louts."

She blinks at me, taken aback by the staunchness of my refusal. Then a small, strange smile overtakes her face, sparking an unnerving glimmer in her eyes.

"Not even at the request of an old friend, Madame La Voisin?" she says with deceptive lightness, tilting her head. "Not even then?"

"What are you saying?" I narrow my eyes, scrutinizing her in the pavilion's flickering light, unease nudging in my belly. That eerie familiarity beckons to me again, crooking its finger at me from the shadows. "What friend?"

"Come, Catherine." She leans forward, letting the candle-light bathe her face. "Have so many years passed since the fabrique that you truly do not recognize me?"

At the mention of the fabrique, my heart thrashes like a snared rabbit, fit to escape the confines of my chest. When I still say nothing, she shakes her head with mock disappointment, pushing her pointed sleeves up to her elbows.

"Here," she says flatly, stretching her arms across the table for my inspection. "Perhaps this will help."

My lungs suddenly shrunken with fear, I look down to find that the insides of her arms are silvery with scars. A gallery of little burns exactly like my own.

Where both of us were scalded by droplets of tallow spitting from a cauldron too vigorously stirred.

"Eugenie!" I breathe, my eyes flying up to her face—which seems to waver and then resolve, hardening like wax into the memory of the girl I knew at the fabrique. Pretty, sharp-tongued Eugenie, who once tended to the cauldron beside my own. "Is it— Could it truly be you?"

"I am afraid so," she retorts, pulling back her arms and crossing them over her chest. "I was not sure of you, either, at first, but I could not mistake that hair for long. Little Catherine, grown up to be nothing less than the maîtresse-en-titre's divineress. You really have come up in the world, just as that bedamned Agnesot said you would."

"And *you* wished for a husband!" I blurt out, remembering her mockery and taunts, her challenging scorn. "When Agnesot offered you a wish to prove her powers. A wealthy husband, so you need never toil in the fabrique again."

"They do say to be careful what you wish for," she says darkly, setting her teeth. "Especially when spurning a divineress. She certainly made a fool of me in the end. Because when I said I wished to wed a wealthy man like the maître, rest assured I did not actually mean Prudhomme himself."

"Maître Prudhomme," I whisper through numb lips, suddenly struggling to breathe. "*That* is whom you wed?"

"Trust me, I did not become the royal candler's wife of my own choosing." Her eyes burn, dancing with the candle's reflected flame. "He took, shall we say, a special shine to me."

I shake my head, jittery with panic, a terrible weakness seeping into my limbs. Like the remembered feeling of being helpless beneath a pinning weight, the burn of a bullwhip scored across my back. "What . . . what do you mean?"

"Catherine, please." She pins me in place with an unwontedly tender look, a dreadful sort of gentleness that leaves me with nowhere to hide. Where could I even hope to conceal myself, from a girl who once dwelled alongside me in hell? "You may not have met with such a fate yourself, but you must have known—or at the very least suspected—what happened to those of us he summoned away from the floor."

I bite down on the insides of my cheeks until I taste the iron tang of blood, fighting a tide of tears so inexorable I fear it might sweep me away.

"I'm so sorry," I whisper through trembling lips, though I can feel the stirring of some great and vicious fury beating inside me like bat wings, both leathery and clawed.

Eugenie leans forward, propping her elbows on the table and fixing me with an unflinching stare.

"You are not the one who should be sorry, Catherine," she whispers, her face setting in a bright mask of rage. Crimson splotches burn high on her cheeks, visible even through the thickly obscuring powder. "We were all damned in that fabrique, one way or another. Either tormented by the overseers, or doomed to become my foul husband's playthings."

"But it must have been terrible for you. So . . . *so* much worse."

"Worse is that he chose to keep me," she spits out. "Why, I could not say; perhaps Agnesot would know. But I *do* know that he is a monster who does not deserve to live. And that is why I ask that you help me kill him."

## CHAPTER FOURTEEN

# The Recipe and the Alchemist

Once Eugenie leaves, I retire to bed with my snakes. Usually it gives me comfort to have them coiled around me, but tonight I cannot even conceive of sleep.

I feel as if I burn from within with stifled memories, swept up in a flood of scorching tallow that ravages all the defenses I have so fastidiously built. Over the years I have surrounded myself with instruments of darkness, from the pet Furies slung around my neck to the occult curiosities I collected. I enjoyed them for their own sake, too, but there was always more to it than that. A secret hope that it would all amount to some protection, a shielding rampart to guard me from the remembered horrors of the past.

An effort to convince myself that I would never again be so trapped, nor so vulnerable. That I would never live through such a misery again.

But now that I know others suffered even worse evils there than befell me, none of my efforts matter so much as a whit. The monster Prudhomme still walks the earth, more demon than any I could pretend to conjure. And though I have never been a murderer, I know what I must do. His death would not be true murder but rightful justice; the kind no one else will ever grant us.

The kind no one ever grants unwanted and forsaken girls.

Sometime past three, my bed comes to resemble less a place of respite and more an instrument of torture. Abandoning the thought of sleep, I rise and drape my dressing gown over my shoulders. By the leaping light of a candle clutched in my unsteady hand, I drift to my study to pore over a section of the grimoire that, before tonight, I have left untouched.

Agnesot's recipes for poisons.

I flip through them, shuddering a little at their repellent ingredients, rejecting one poison as too obvious, another as too painless. Finally, my finger stills halfway down the fifth page.

"'Aqua tofana,'" I read to myself. "'A fearsome and fleet poison, bringing about a quick yet agonizing death without leaving any trace. Take two buds from the nightshade flower, an executed convict's powdered finger bones, a handful of a virgin's locks, three feathers from a black albatross . . .'"

The rest of the entry reads as if it were half recipe, half spell. There is a lengthy incantation to be spoken over the brewing potions, runes to be drawn into its bubbling surfaces. The entire process is risky and time-consuming, unforgiving of missteps and taking well over a week to complete. But it is nothing I cannot handle with the grimoire's careful instruction and my own steely temperament.

However, the ingredients themselves are both grotesque and arcane, and I will require help procuring them. What I need, I decide just before the sun comes crawling over the horizon like some fat-bellied yellow spider, is a proper alchemist.

The kind one finds in the cité.

I crept out of the house in the freezing hours just after first light and made my furtive way to the cité.

At such an early hour, I doubted I would be spotted by anyone in the marquise's employ. But still I took every precaution, including taking a hired coach and swathing myself in a heavy cloak with the hood drawn over my face. Should my patroness hear of my foray here anyway, my pretense will cleave close to the truth: that I required rare ingredients for the love philters I still regularly brew for her, which I have not yet managed to procure anywhere else.

I remembered the name of the alchemist Marie preferred to deal with, from whom she purchased the tinctures she peddled to her own clients. Once I arrived in the cité, it only took a few well-placed questions at several of my former haunts to find my way to the alchemist Blessis's workshop, tucked into an alleyway off the Rue de Glatigny. I rapped lightly on his weathered door, and when it swung open with a wheezing creak, I presented myself to the man within as a colleague of Mademoiselle Bosse.

Aside from his gaudy alchemist's robes, richly embroidered with the discipline's traditional white, black, and vermillion, Blessis is a small and innocuous man with a reedy voice.

"Do come in, the air has such a snapping bite to it today," he says with a curt half bow, waving me over his threshold. "A friend of Mademoiselle Bosse is always welcome here."

I incline my head, my throat tightening with the knowledge that at this moment, Marie likely does not consider me any sort of friend.

As he bolts the heavy door behind us, I wrinkle my nose against the odd assault of odors that mingle within the workshop. The room smells both heavenly and rank, of fragrant herbs like meadowsweet and some acrid musk like a tomcat's stench. Though he is arguably more dangerous than the alleged charlatans the Sun King means to stamp out, as a practitioner of science Blessis appears to have no need to hide the trappings of his trade.

Or perhaps he poses as a simple apothecary to the uninitiated—and though trading in medicinal herbs does form part of his trade, even the most naive might balk at the contents of his shelves.

They are stacked with bell jars of wildly varying sizes, bright liquids glimmering in some, others holding dried sprigs of plants or greasy powders. A few contain such oddities as live and crawling beetles, the pearls of tiny teeth, and iridescent feathers tied together at the shaft like unlikely bouquets. The trestle worktable in the center supports a collection of beakers, flasks, and some finicky contraption that I assume is used to measure weight. An armillary sphere sits beside it, golden and elaborate, winking in the light like a complex jewel.

"And what can I help you with, madame?" Blessis asks, standing decorously by the hearth with his hands clasped behind his back. A cast-iron kettle burbles behind him, emitting a greenish smoke I pinpoint as the source of that offensive smell. "Arcane ingredients for spellwork? Herbs for a physick? I assume your interest does not lie with the transmutation of base metals."

"No, indeed," I say, wandering over to the table to flick the armillary sphere into motion with a fingertip. It spins beautifully, the celestial rings whirling around the earth in a shimmering golden blur. "Here, I've brought a list of what I need."

"So you are attempting aqua tofana, then," he says, his sparse gray eyebrows shooting up as he peruses my list. "One of the rarest and deadliest of the occult poisons—and devilishly difficult to make. I have never known anyone to try their hand at it. Unless I am mistaking your intentions?"

I hesitate for a moment, leery of admitting to planning something so lethal.

He flicks me a mildly exasperated look. "Come, now. What else might you mean to do with this particular assortment of magically endowed items and herbs? Do forgive my bluntness, but it is a necessary part of my profession's creed. We value discretion, but cannot afford to court confusion."

"You are not mistaken," I finally admit. His matter-of-fact tone sends a flush of misgiving rolling through me like a thunderclap, from the pit of my stomach up to my tingling scalp. Now that I am actually here, what I aim to accomplish suddenly feels all too gruesomely real. No hazily vengeful fever dream, but a cold reality only inches beyond my grasp.

And now that I am here, can I truly go through with it?

Can I make myself into a murderess?

He scrutinizes me for a long moment, perhaps appraising my commitment. When I meet his stare as steadily as I can, he cedes a nod and leads me to the back of the room, where a whole section of the shelved wall hinges inward at his touch. A hidden door so seamlessly concealed that I would never have spotted it.

*So the mantle of science does not fully protect him, then*, I think. *Even an alchemist must practice certain things concealed.*

The door swings into a long and narrow room that smells even more forbidding than the antechamber, metallic and sharp as recently spilled blood, with an incongruously pretty note of almond. There are no armillary spheres here, nothing so whimsical behind the counter that Blessis skirts around. Only the milky gleam of jars and green stoppered bottles stacked on shorter shelves, peering like blind eyes from the low ceiling to the floor.

"Why aqua tofana?" he muses, his eyes roaming the shelves. "When there are so many easier poisons to choose from? Arsenic, for instance, is ready in a snap, and mimics the progression of naturally debilitating disease. One need not even be a divineress to brew it."

"But arsenic leaves a telltale trace, if one knows to look for it. Whereas aqua tofana leaves the corpse entirely unscathed."

I do not add that aqua tofana causes terrible pain, as well as paralysis of the body without any clouding of the mind. I want Prudhomme to feel not just agony but utter helplessness in the hour of his death, just as we all felt powerless in his cruel thrall.

Though it is true that a lengthier poisoning might be somewhat safer, I know from Eugenie that Prudhomme has become prone to gout and fits; sudden death would not seem so remarkable in his case. And I do not want her to suffer her marriage for any longer than she must.

"I see," Blessis mutters abstractedly, skittering his fingers up and down the shelves. His fingertips are cracked as old leather and discolored, likely from a lifetime of handling corrosive substances. "And it is very painful, too, is it not? You mean to devastate."

A wave of vertigo comes crashing over me, another dreadful deluge of misgiving even worse than the one that came before. I take a halting half step toward the counter, bracing against it with my fingertips. *What in hell are you doing, Catherine*, I rail at myself, *meddling with matters such as this?* This is not the simple mischief I've become accustomed to making, but full-blown murder. And not the murder of some commoner, but that of the royal candlemaker, an artisan so wealthy and influential he sometimes dines privately with the king.

All my turmoil is shot through with an even deeper vein of doubt, like an apple tunneled by a worm. Who am I to steal another's life, even if that life belongs to one such as Prudhomme?

"Are you quite well?" the alchemist asks with surprising solicitude. "I could fetch you a tonic if you like. Something to calm the nerves."

"No, no, I am fine." I wave a hand at him, though I am still taking desperate little breaths. "I only . . . feel a little ill. It will pass in a moment."

Blessis watches me warily, unconvinced, tugging at his lip in thought.

"Are you quite certain you wish to do this, madame?" he asks, fixing me with an incisive stare. "Murder by poison may not be quite so bloody as that done by garrote or knife, but in some ways it is far, far worse."

"This is a strange and backwards way to peddle your wares, monsieur," I half laugh, in a feeble stab at humor. "Should you not instead be attempting to convince me to buy?"

He does not take the bait, his grave mien only sobering further. "What you do with what I sell you is entirely your business—but what you intend to undertake is not for the faint of heart. Once you have committed, there is no turning back."

His probing serves to crystallize the wavering core of my intent. I stand now at a crossroads, caught in a moment of choosing—am I still that girl from the fabrique, chained and powerless? Or am I La Voisin, the sorceress, a willful Fate and Fury in my own right, ruthless and single-minded in whatever act I choose to undertake?

All I know is that I cannot abide being this weakling the alchemist imagines me to be. Waffling pathetically over the murder of a truly monstrous man.

My indecision vanishes like a puff of breath dissipating in frosty air, and with it my dizzy spell. I abruptly feel like some icy blaze, roaring with all the blistering force of a deep-winter wind. As if I have been distilled, or whittled down, to a purer, more concentrated version of myself.

I straighten up from the counter and lift my chin, crossing my arms loosely over my chest.

"I am far from faint of heart, monsieur," I tell him crisply, each word as cold and unyielding as a diamond on my tongue. "Nor am I undecided. Now, let us discuss price."

CHAPTER FIFTEEN

# The Poison and
# the Partnership

Making the aqua tofana is the hardest thing I have ever done.

I make my excuses to the marquise ahead of time, telling her that my blood is upon me, too painful and ill-omened to allow for any productive scrying sessions. The rest of my clients are given less specific excuses for my temporary seclusion; all the better, as it will only serve to enhance my mystique. Let them think I have withdrawn in order to commune with whatever eldritch forces they believe underlie my sight.

Let them believe whatever they wish, as long as they leave me alone for this time I need, free from all distraction.

For the first four days, I read and reread the entry for aqua tofana until I know it nearly by heart, and follow all the painstaking instructions for preparing the ingredients. This involves ornate exercises like soaking the belladonna and virgin's hair in water that has held a gibbous moon's reflection, then drying them over a fire stoked by hazel wood felled and gathered by my own hand. A tall order for a city dweller, but one I managed all the same.

Once I instruct the chatelaine to have food left outside my door and refrain from otherwise disturbing me, I am ready to properly begin.

I tend to the cauldron for three seemingly endless days and nights, keeping it at the same precise temperature, stirring and chanting and inscribing the bubbling surface with hundreds of complex runes. Sweat dribbles down my face and stings my eyes, my fingers trembling from the effort of such precision. There are brief intervals of stability during which I rush to relieve myself, splash water on my scorching face, and cram some food into my mouth before I must begin again. Not nearly enough time for sleep, so I run on sheer dread energy and infusions of strong black tea.

Should my attention flag even for a moment, should I skip a single step, the substance will yield not a poison powder but a deathly smoke able to kill me with a breath.

It is at once so tedious and terrifying that I am transported back to the fabrique, firelight from remembered braziers licking at the edges of my vision, my shoulders tensed against a bullwhip's sting. By the time the substance has reduced into an odorless powder—which Eugenie will mix with Prudhomme's cosmetics, so that it will sink into his blood through his skin—I am so exhausted that I feel almost as if the making has drawn something vital from me.

Shaved off a sliver of my own soul to incorporate into itself.

*And perhaps it has*, I think, falling into bed immediately after Eugenie has collected the powder, leaving a heavy purse in its place.

But it is worth it, to know exactly how Prudhomme will leave this earth, with crystalline awareness, and in fearsome pain. Inflicted by my own and Eugenie's hand.

The only thing that I can hope for further is that he finds his way directly into hell.

For the next few weeks, my clients can speak of nothing but the royal candlemaker's untimely death.

"Dead between one day to the next, as if struck down by notre Dieu's own lightning!" the marquise remarks to me during a session, narrow-eyed. "Though with everything I have seen of late, perhaps it *was* the devil's handiwork . . ."

"I hear his widow is beside herself, absolutely woestruck," Madame Leferon twitters later, hands clasped to her bosom. "Such a devoted, pretty thing. I daresay she won't be mired long in her widow's weeds before another suitor snaps her up."

"Was it his heart, do you think?" the Duc de Nevers questions, brow wrinkled with a vague curiosity. "Surely it must have been, to cut him down so fast. And he always *was* such an unhealthy man."

Though they ply each other heedlessly with love philters and dastardly draughts, somehow none of them think to consider poison in this case. As if one of their own could never have succumbed to such an ignominious fate.

I stay silent throughout it all, my lips curved in an impenetrable smile. My placid surface masking the crashing victory that breaks within my heart in wave after stormy wave. The bane of my youth is gone, the mythical monster of my past vanquished. Eugenie's and my justice done.

Agnesot would be so proud of me, and of the legacy I have become.

And I feel more powerful and unfettered than I ever have; colossal in size, almost larger than mortal life. As though I have summoned one of the true Furies and then swallowed her whole, unhinged my jaw to suck all her power into myself. Now that I have taken matters into my own hands once, what is there to stop me from doing it again? Especially when so many of the vipers in the Sun King's court are far more deserving of death than even Prudhomme.

It occurs to me that if I might be paid to help their enemies kill them off—as Eugenie insisted on paying me, a far greater sum than I would have thought to ask of her—I can not only administer the justice sorely lacking at court, but ensure the sort of livelihood for myself that will eventually cut me loose even from the marquise.

The kind of elevation that will finally set me free.

"Do not mistake me, Catherine," Adam says, steepling his fingers beneath his chin. We have just finished a sumptuous dinner that I had catered for us at his home, as an ostensible peace offering. "It isn't that I am not delighted by your changed heart, but you do not exactly strike me as a fly-by-night. The opposite, in fact. So tell me, what am I to make of this reversal in your desire to work with me?"

"You were right," I say simply, dabbing at my mouth and setting my napkin aside. "And I was wrong, and short-sighted, to boot. I am not such a stubborn fool that I cannot admit as much."

A lazy smile spreads over his fine-cut mouth.

"And I am not so modest to pretend that it does not please me to hear it." He runs his lips thoughtfully over his knuckles. "What brought on this realization?"

"It is just as you said." I shrug, spreading my hands. "We are each formidable in our own right. But together, we should be unstoppable, a force the likes of which this city has not seen. So let us cease dissembling and share freely with each other. Lay all our cards on the table, as it were."

One black eyebrow flicks curiously up, like a raven taking flight. "Meaning?"

"Meaning we use my sight and your tricks to select our most strategic and profitable noble marks," I clarify. "You show me how your magic is done, and I share my visions with you—then we decide, together, how to turn it all to our mutual advantage."

"Forgive me if I speak out of turn," he says dryly, taking a swig of wine, "but what you are proposing is not entirely fair, not when the risk falls squarely upon me. While I cannot hope to steal your gift, you can certainly divest me of my tricks. How am I to trust that you will not do just that?"

"I am a divineress, Adam, not an illusionist. Seeking to become one would take far more time and trouble than it is worth. And if we were to pool our talents, why would I bother with stealing your tricks at all?"

"Oh, because you have done as much before?" he hazards with a wry grin.

I incline my head, as if to say, *Touché*.

"I can see why you would hesitate; I would, too, were I in your place. But I am not trying to gull you, Adam. As a token of my trust, an assurance of the openness I hope to foster between us, I would offer you some information as collateral."

Intrigue flares in his eyes like sparks falling from a struck flint. He twitches his long and tapered fingers, beckoning me on. "By all means."

"The royal candlemaker, Prudhomme. You've heard of his death, I presume?"

"Mon Dieu, how could I not? The vicomte and his entourage grow tiresome with their constant carping on it. Much like your marquise, I'm sure." He rolls his eyes in collegial exasperation, and I do the same, though it still galls me that he only gained the Vicomte de Couserans as a patron by stealing his favor away from me. "What of it?"

"He did not die of any obscure natural cause, nor of any of the satanic balderdash they're spouting at court." I watch him, unblinking and austere. "He died because I helped kill him."

Adam smiles broadly at that, as though I must be jesting. But his mirth soon fades at the cool equanimity on my face.

"You . . . helped kill him," he says slowly, as if turning the words around in his mouth like a sweet. Tasting them for truth. "And why would you do such a thing, Catherine?"

"His wife sought my help in ridding herself of her abuser, and paid handsomely for it." I leave out Prudhomme's link to me, Eugenie's and my shared history. Just because I recognize the worth of a partnership with Adam does not mean I care to trust him with my vulnerability. "Handsomely enough that I supplied her with a very clever poison. The sort only a divineress could make."

"I see." He watches me avidly, poised between admiration and a slightly horrified awe. "How terrible, and rather marvelous. Quite the piquant secret to share with me, indeed."

Beyond its sensationalism, the obvious shock value of my admission, this secret is not so valuable as he thinks—which is why I chose to offer it. Should Adam turn on me down the line and seek to hang me with this knowledge, it will be long after interest in Prudhomme's death has died, his body interred, and Eugenie united with her painter and far too content to ever speak out against me. Not that she would, anyway, as the poison was administered by her own hand; I never set foot anywhere near Prudhomme. There is no proof, no evidence linking me with the murder—especially since I plan to make no mention to Adam of Blessis.

Still, any confession is a powerful offering, and I can see that it sways him.

"Would you have accepted anything less as barter?" I lace my hands together, smiling at him over them when he shakes his head. "I thought not."

He watches me for a long moment of frank deliberation, his dark gaze gliding between my eyes.

"A well-earned death, I imagine," he finally says. "I performed my show for him once at his home, several months ago. The man was a brute to his wife, a bastard of the vilest sort. Whatever death you and his widow saw fit to give him was likely less than he deserved."

Something like glee uncurls itself inside me, tickling at my ribs. This is exactly what I had at once expected and hoped to hear from him.

"And no one else knows of this?" he continues.

"No one. Save for my client, of course. Obviously Prudhomme's widow would never tell another soul." I lift my eyebrows in question. "So, what do you think?"

"I think I would hear more." He leans back in his chair, tilting his head. "Tell me, how exactly do you envision our partnership? Because I would have been content with acquiring ever more powerful benefactors for the two of us. But it seems you have set your sights even higher, with more sinister aims."

I nod. "Clients will only pay so much for the sort of services we have thus far been providing—we will hitch up against dead ends much sooner than we'd like. But what if we begin to seek out select clients with darker demands, like Eugenie Prudhomme, only even more influential and wealthier, the sort we want in our debt?"

"And are you so fearless that you do not fear to hang for murder?"

I lean back in the chair and shake my head, a smile tugging at my lips. "No, I do not fear the noose—because if we are careful and clever, we will never find one around our necks. I will brew the poisons for them, to whatever effect they wish, but you and I will never administer them ourselves. The dosing itself, the act of murder, must always be committed by their own hands."

"Brilliant," he murmurs, his eyes shining with admiration. "Shared culpability removes the incentive to turn against us. And how shall we decide upon our noble marks?"

"We already have our first leads," I reply, spreading my hands. "Those who've attended our Messes Noires, those willing even to entreat the devil. Those who have already divulged their darkest wishes to me. I already know of at least three who dearly desire someone's death."

"I assume you do not intend to offer our services to *everyone* at court with murderous inclinations," he remarks with a quirked eyebrow. "For we should find ourselves overwhelmed within a fortnight, and in gaol not soon after, shared culpability be damned. There are droves of would-be murderers in the Sun King's den, many of them fool enough to boast of their diabolic pursuits to their friends."

"Of course not *all* of them," I say, taking up my wine for another sip. "Or even most. Only the ones we deem dependably discreet, capable of taking such a secret to the grave. And most importantly—to me, at least—the ones who wish to murder someone of equally villainous ilk. Because I will not be party to killing innocents, Adam. That is where I draw my line."

"Then we are of a mind," he says, favoring me with another of those lupine smiles, sharp as teeth glinting from the brush. "We will make quite the pairing, you and I.

Sorceress and magician, infernal priestess and priest. The unholiest of alliances."

I laugh, my heart swooping a bit in exhilaration. I realize, to some surprise, that I am looking forward to this collaboration not only for how far it might take me, but also for its own sake. I know exactly why I wish to do this; for the coin and influence, and the freedom both will eventually secure me. But also for the justice I can see done, by meting out punishments the decadent blackguards of Louis's court would otherwise never have met.

But I am still not at all certain what drives Adam's own ambitions—something I would very much like to understand.

"So, we are agreed, then?" I ask him, taking up my goblet in toast.

"We are agreed." He clinks his wine against mine, holding my eyes even as we take our drinks. "A ta santé, Catherine."

"And now that we are partners, will you tell me about the skeleton and the demon's face?" I burst out before I can contain myself. "The ones you conjured in your act. How was it done? Mirrors, accomplices in costume? I have racked my brain over it, and am still no closer to understanding."

He shakes his head, amused by my enthusiasm. "No accomplices. Much like you, I prefer to rely exclusively on myself."

"Until now, that is," I correct.

"Until now." He rises from the table and holds out a hand. "And what I will show you, no one else has ever seen."

## CHAPTER SIXTEEN

## The Devilmaker and the Mark

Adam's magician's atelier is in the attic, the ceiling steeply canted from the pitch of the mansard roof. Unlike the rest of his tumbledown home, there is no dilapidation here; the air is kept scrupulously clear of dust, and all the wood has been stripped and buffed smooth. A large cage sits in one corner, holding ravens with their heads under their wings. My eye lands on the wall of masks hanging from hooks—a series of the diabolic visages I remember from the maréchale's bal, along with uncanny, flattened replicas of Adam's own face, unnerving in their eyeless stares.

"Magnifique," I murmur, drifting closer to run them between my fingers. Each is even more stunningly detailed when viewed up close, the features painted onto silk so thin it must be nearly sheer beneath the paint. The likeness to Adam is exceptional. "What intricate work."

"And see how they fit, one over the other," he explains, layering them and then lifting them over his face to show me. "I paint them using a mold of my own face, to account for the distortion caused by my features beneath. My nose, my lips, even the projection of my brow—it all affects the verisimilitude."

"So when you intend to pull this trick, you begin the performance already masked," I say, putting the pieces together, marveling at the ingenuity. "And from the distance at which the audience stands, no one is any the wiser. Damnably clever."

"Thank you, my lady," he replies with a little half bow. "I like to think so. And if such trifles impress you, I suspect you will like my lanterna magica even more."

He leads me to a worktable in the corner, beside one of the dormer windows. An odd contraption sits upon it: a mahogany box with a protruding brass cylinder affixed to its front.

"Behold," he says grandly with an ironic flourish, though I can see genuine excitement and even a touch of self-consciousness in his eyes. It lends him a surprising and sweetly boyish air. "The magic lantern. Or as I prefer to call it, my devilmaker. It's a Dutchman's invention, one I came across and purchased during my . . . time abroad."

I glance at him curiously at this halting mention of travel, but he does not elaborate. Smiling, he lights a candle from the table and hinges open a door in the contraption's wooden body to reveal the contents within. Peering inside, I see a concave piece of glass set into the center, a transparent slide slotted in front of it. Adam tucks the lit candle stump behind the glass, then jerks his chin toward the black velvet screen we'd passed on our way into the room, strung up by the door.

"Take a look," he says with a wink. "You might spot a familiar face. Or, rather, the absence of one."

I turn around to look over my shoulder, my heart hitching up and then lodging at the base of my throat. Adam's magic lantern casts a haunting image onto the velvet backdrop—the leering skeleton from his act at the Pomme, though its outlines are crisper and more static without the smoke. Now it is more obviously a picture, a one-dimensional projection, not a revenant summoned from beyond the grave.

"Mon Dieu," I say under my breath, glancing between the skeleton and Adam, utterly enthralled. "It is so well rendered! Though not quite so terrifying without your artificial fog."

"Indeed," he agrees, tipping his head. "The smoke is crucial to presenting the illusion—and to obscuring the black screens I use as a backdrop for the projection."

"And the dancing . . . How do you make it move?"

"A simple mechanism," he explains, gesturing me close to the device. I peer inside along with him, and he shows me the clever clockwork that rotates the slide back and forth, alternating between a series of images. "You see how different depictions of the skeleton are painted onto the slide? To foster the illusion of movement, one must only set the mechanism into motion. I wind it exactly like a watch, set to begin at a certain moment in the act."

"How clever," I breathe, glancing at him for permission before I reach in to touch the delicate gears and threads that surround the slide. "And the slides, where do you obtain them?"

"Oh, I do not obtain them," he replies, grinning with evident pride. "I paint them myself."

He removes a walnut chest from one of the drawers beneath the worktable, lifting the lid to reveal glass slides stacked like playing cards. He riffles through them delicately before selecting one, plucking it out and offering it to me. I peer at its surface, a tiny landscape of withered trees hung with snakes—the fallen Eden from his Messe Noir, rendered in exquisitely miniature detail.

"They are so little and perfect," I say softly, awestruck by the artistry. "Downright breathtaking. Why do magic at all, when you have a talent such as this?"

"If I could paint my way to power, I've yet to discover how," he says, baring his teeth in an approximation of a smile, charmless in comparison to his usual beguiling grins. "Who are the painters who gain renown in Louis's court? White men to the last, waxen as withered lilies. Do you expect their well-heeled patrons might be inclined to welcome me into their ranks?"

"But you have the Vicomte de Couserans's patronage now," I point out.

"Only because he believes I practice a low art like the occult, deemed appropriate for the likes of me. In the Sun King's court, what could be considered a baser skill than magic?"

There is a rancor to Adam's voice, a bitterness even beyond that warranted by the arbitrary cruelties of the beau monde's glittering world.

"You hate them, too, don't you?" I remark with sudden understanding. "The noblesse. Perhaps even more than I do."

"I do, because why should they have it all?" he demands, his voice dropping to a whisper. "Glory, luxury, even infamy. When they've earned it through neither talent nor perseverance, but only through a fortunate accident of birth. I deserve wealth and renown more than the lot of them—and I mean to have it, Catherine. And if I must struggle and claw my way to what should be mine, then so be it. People like us . . . we are never promised clean hands. Not if we wish to leave any sort of mark."

For a moment I can feel the wellspring of his throbbing need, the force that propels him forward. It kicks loose a fragment of a vision—an image of a woman's lovely face, her eyes long and narrow as Adam's but an even truer black, with a frank luster to them like freshwater pearls.

Then her smooth cheeks grow purple and mottled, her eyes blowing open wide and horrified even as her mouth gapes in a scream.

The meaning of this snippet is clear to me; this woman met her death by murder. And though I cannot grasp exactly what befell her, I think, with a sweeping sadness, that I understand who she might have been.

"What is it?" Adam says sharply, jerking me out of my reverie. A thread of tension pulls taut between us again. He stares suspiciously at me, his face tightening with sudden mistrust. "Why are you looking at me so, Catherine?"

His eyes flick between mine, leery and searching—as if he suspects what I was doing, and without his consent. But

I know better than to admit to such an intrusion, even if unintentional, when our partnership is still so new.

"I am only thinking," I say instead, "how much all those heathens at Versailles deserve to be knocked down a peg."

His forbidding mien loosens at that, softening into something more inviting.

"I could not agree more," he says, setting the slide aside to reach for my hands and thread our fingers loosely together. When he speaks again, we have drawn so close, nearly mouth to mouth, that I can feel his next words carried on the heat of his breath. "And who better to cut them down than you and I?"

Adam and I decide to make Louis Guihelm de Castelnau, the Marquis de Cessac and the king's own Master of the Wardrobe, our first mark.

Four days later, the marquis sits across from me in the pavilion, having responded to my urgent summons with agreeable alacrity. I wrote to him only that morning that I'd had a vision, sent to me by our shared master—presuming he could read between the lines enough to surmise whom I meant, without me committing to paper any outright mention of the devil—and that I needed to speak with him forthwith.

Now the chill September breeze stirs his elaborate russet wig, one of his ludicrous affectations. Only the king himself boasts a more boisterous head of hair, though his curls are said to be au naturel. The marquis grits his teeth against the prickle of cold, chilled even under his rich port-wine velvet.

"While I am eager to hear what you might have to share with me, madame, might I ask that we retire inside? It is becoming blasted frigid, even this early into fall."

"Of course, if that is what you wish, messire. But out here, I can ensure privacy." I sweep out a hand to gesture at the still garden around us, the last of the roses bobbing their heads in rhythm with the wind. I have dispensed with Pascal's music for tonight, wishing to underscore the need for both discretion and urgency. "Whereas inside, as they say, even the walls have ears."

Interest sparks in his shrewd, pale eyes. "And what you have to tell me . . . it is of a very delicate nature?"

"Exceedingly delicate." I take a deep breath, as if to calm myself, and drop my tone urgently low. "As I said, I have been visited by a vision. As his devoted servant, sometimes the daystar communicates this way with me. And I saw you, messire . . . and not just you, but your brother. And his very charming wife, Gisele."

The marquis sucks in air, his palms flattening on the table, eyes roving between mine. I can see the frantic turning of the gears behind his eyes as he considers what I've said. While the wish he professed during my first Messe was to steal away his brother's wife, it was written in such oblique fashion that its essence only became clear after hours of my scrying and some subtle research on Adam's part, discreet delving into the marquis's private life.

Now he wonders how I could possibly know what he had meant without having truly been visited by the devil. I can see the precise moment he dismisses any doubts he may yet have held about my powers, any lingering skepticism quelled.

"And what . . . what did you see?" he asks, his voice a rusty croak.

"I saw how you yearn for her, messire, and how very unhappy she is with your brother. Were he not there, there is no reason to think her affection would not fall on you. Does she not steal glances at you when his attention is otherwise occupied? Has she not always been unusually kind in your exchanges?"

"Yes, perhaps—but the scoundrel does stand between us," the marquis mutters. "Though he *knew* I favored her long before he did. I would not even put it past him to have married her largely out of spite for me."

The animosity between the brothers is a well-documented affair. Moreover, the younger de Castelnau's reputation for malfeasance is so prominent, even in the cesspool of the court, that few of the noblesse have managed to acquire quite so many enemies as he has. The man has made a blood sport of challenging lesser noblemen to duels over minor offenses, and then dispatching them. Adam confirms that even the Vicomte de Couserans loathes the younger de Castelnau, and the vicomte is so otherwise blase that he rarely bothers with vitriol.

In other words, the vicomte's brother is a victim well suited to our needs.

"But what if he were to be removed?" I ask, fixing the marquis with a somber gaze.

". . . removed?" He blinks at me, brow knitting with confusion. "Madame, what do you mean to say?"

I spread my hands, as though the answer should be obvious to him. "That Lucifer himself is inclined to grant your wish, using the both of us as instruments. Much nobler and worthier men than your brother meet their end before their time, messire. Through mishap and accident."

"Are you suggesting *murder*, Madame La Voisin?" His voice dips so low and circumspect, as if shocked by my suggestion, that I might even be alarmed if I could not feel his true response—the need festering beneath his skin like something long buried yet still living.

"*I* am not suggesting anything," I clarify delicately. "*You* are the one who drank the devil's wine and ate of his apple, messire. *You* are the one who set this into motion with your entreaty. I am only relaying what I saw, and what our master conveyed to me. Whether or not you choose to accept his dark blessing is entirely up to you."

The marquis mulls this over, caution warring with that writhing hydra of need that lives within him. With a flush of pleasure, I see that Adam and I have chosen well. Not only is the marquis motivated and amenable, but he is exactly the sort of mark we wish to cultivate; a noble so highly placed he has occasional access to the king himself.

It takes him even less time than I had expected to come to terms with fratricide. The alluring prospect of a widowed Gisele, waiting for him on the other side of his decision, likely helps.

"And if I did?" he asks, teeth worrying at his lower lip. "What must I do?"

"First, an oath upon your soul to Lucifer himself: that you will never speak of this again to anyone, lest he reap your soul before your time, and you spend eternity roasting in perdition's flames for your betrayal." I can see from the flare of true fear in his eyes that the gravity of the oath has sunk home. "Then, a payment to me, for the preparation of the poison. And for the rituals I will undertake to ensure our master's continuing favor, to see this endeavor safely through."

When I name the sum, he nearly staggers bodily in his chair.

"But, madame, you . . . you cannot be serious," he stammers, blinking at me. "That is . . . that is a quarter of my yearly allotment from His Majesty, that is—"

"That is what it costs," I say, cutting him off. "Not only is the substance itself comprised of rare ingredients and difficult to make, but you must understand, messire, that each time I court our dread lord's attention, I risk the very substance of my own soul. And he is a fickle master, as you must surely know. We must always be certain to appease him."

"I suppose that stands to reason," he murmurs. "And what will happen to my brother?"

"The poison you shall slip into his drinks at each royal banquet will drive him out of his wits over the course of a month, before finally killing him. It will appear as though he has been stricken with a sudden malady of the mind, one so potent that it eventually overwhelmed even his body."

I am not planning on using aqua tofana this time, as it would be terribly unwise to cause two identical deaths within such a short span. And the marquis does not need his brother dispatched with any particular haste. No, secret du crapaud would do well instead—Toad's Secret, another of the occult poisons from the grimoire. Much less demanding to prepare, and in some ways even more heinous in its effect.

A fitting end to such a bloodthirsty bane as de Castelnau.

The marquis nods, undisturbed by the notion of inflicting such suffering on his brother—just as Adam and I had expected.

"He has more than earned it, has he not?" the marquis says under his breath, echoing my own thoughts, anticipatory triumph sparking in his pewter eyes. "Detestable as he has been all his life. No wonder even the devil can see as much. I do wish to proceed, madame. I wish to proceed *now*."

## CHAPTER SEVENTEEN

# The Bacchanals and the Ultimatum

The marquis's brother dies in less than a month, before the leaves have even completed their turn. The secret du crapaud drove him so utterly out of his mind that he simply walked off his own balcony in the dead of night, desperate to escape the hallucinations that had flocked to plague him.

It could not have ended better for us, giving rise to not even a whiff of foul play.

In the meantime, Adam and I have reworked our joint Messe Noire into a decadently gruesome spectacle far beyond what either of us could have achieved alone. Adam supplies a phantasmagoria of illusions with his devilmaker, while I invent lavish new rituals and procure ever more exotic snakes. We host them in my home twice a month, at both the full moon and the dark of the moon, in a banquet hall I've lined with vivariums for my more venomous additions. Each Messe devolves into a lurid bacchanal more outlandish and debauched than the last—dancing with the devil, Adam calls it—while Adam and I hold ourselves regally above the fray.

Sitting side by side on black cast-iron thrones I've had custom built for us, both crowned with curling antler's horns.

The reigning king and queen of our own finely orchestrated hell.

At each subsequent Messe, we allow guests to bring a companion of their choosing, someone they deem both trustworthy and worthy of the devil's favor. And the Marquise de Montespan, taken by the glamor of our partnership and the twisted opulence of the new Messe, continues to introduce us to her closest cronies—ever widening the pool of suitable marks.

After our success with the Marquis de Cessac, we select the Comte de Gassily and the Duchesse de Vivonne as our next targets. The comte's vicious uncle and the duchesse's cheating and violent husband are soon sent shuffling off this mortal coil, courtesy of a bouquet infused with venom, and candied truffles imbued with deathly substances. There is no outcry at either of their deaths, no talk of skulduggery or poison. Only the same breathless gossip that followed in the wake of Prudhomme's death.

Perhaps, elsewhere, there might be more serious mention of wrongdoing. But it is to our advantage that court is such a dangerous place. So lousy with intrigue, and overrun with duels, fortuitous "accidents," and even the occasional disappearance, that a few more deaths do not seem to inspire any overarching dread.

"What of Monsieur Philbert next?" Adam asks as we laze in my canopied bed two months after our first Messe together, Megaera draped over the two of us. "He who so ardently longs to murder his former mistress? We should give it a few weeks, so as to not arouse undue suspicion. But after that, he would do quite well."

"I do not trust Monsieur Philbert any more than I would a parrot," I reply, leaning into his touch as he combs his fingers through my curls. "The man favors his liquor a great deal more than he should, and it leaves him garrulous. Not to mention that, besides tiring of her married lover, Philbert's young mistress has done nothing wrong. Certainly nothing that should doom her to a horrid death."

"But Philbert is one of the king's best loved troubadours," Adam argues with a cocked eyebrow. "Phenomenally wealthy, well positioned . . . think about it. We could do worse than having him in our thrall, Catherine."

"*No*, Adam," I retort, somewhat more sharply than I intended. "I won't have any hand in killing that girl. And please, do not ask me again. My answer will not change."

"Very well. Consider the subject dead." He breathes a mildly exasperated breath, drawing away from me. Sometimes I feel as if even my scant scruples irritate him. As if, left to his own devices, Adam might be much less discerning in whom he saw fit to help kill, should the end result be favorable for him.

I must not be quite so ruthless in my marrow, as sometimes my conscience nags even when it comes to the irreparable scoundrels we have agreed to kill. But each time this happens, I must remind myself that I am no quaking girl, but a Fate and Fury in my own right, an arbiter of justice. A divineress who holds her own life's reins.

"And what of the marquise?" Adam asks, parting me from my thoughts. "It seems an age since you've spoken of her."

"She attends our Messes religiously, does she not? Forever imploring Satan to keep the king well in her clawed grasp."

"But as I recall, you used to scry for her nearly every other day. Have you had a session with her lately, besides keeping her well stocked in philters? You know how she adores your visions, Catherine. All that pandering to her growing glory, 'queen in all but name,' and so forth."

"According to Mademoiselle Claude, the marquise has been plenty busy defending her territory against interlopers," I reply, rolling my eyes at the marquise's folly. "Both real and imagined. She mistrusts every woman who trades so much as a glance with the king, as if they are all brazen wantons scheming to catch his eye."

My good-natured little plant has kept me well apprised on the marquise's household, though she clearly believes that the information she relays to me is only idle gossip shared between friends. Mademoiselle de Oeillets still speaks of the glamorous marquise in starstruck tones, as if she is fortunate merely to exist in her midst.

"The king's own Cerberus, that one," I continue. "Prettier than a three-headed dog, perhaps. But no less ferocious when it comes to guarding his attentions."

"And she has not sought your help in fending her challengers off?" He hitches himself higher against the headboard, furrowing his brow. "I'd think in her paranoia she would be hanging on you night and day, desperate for your counsel."

"Oh, she has been quite insistent the past week or so." I take up Megaera and settle her comfortably around my shoulders. "But what with our other projects, I haven't been able to spare the time. She can wait until next week, for once."

"You should tread very carefully with her, Cat," Adam cautions, trepidation creeping into his tone. "She is your patroness. And a known viper, even in the tangled nest that is the court. No good will come of putting her off."

I feel my own muscles tighten in response, at his unconscious echo of Marie's words so many months ago. *What a schemer that woman is,* Marie said to me then. *Be careful of her, ma belle. She may be grateful to you now, but such outsized ambition knows neither lasting loyalty nor bounds.*

Though the ache of Marie's absence never dissipates, sometimes it cuts the keenest when I am at odds with Adam. Though we have thrown our lots in together, become both lovers and partners in our dark endeavor, anything between us is built only on the promise of mutual benefit. Adam may be my confidant, but I am under no illusion that he is either my protector or a friend. Should the tide ever turn against us, he would abandon me in an instant if it meant saving his own precious skin.

I cannot hold this selfishness against him; not when I guard my own interests just the same, and understand exactly where I stand with him. While we each admire the other's talents and dedication, there is nothing between us that even hints of love.

Adam will never—could never—be what Marie once was to me.

"But you barely even see the vicomte," I argue, exasperated. "When did *you* last have a session with him?"

"It is not the same," he counters. "The vicomte merely likes the glamour of having a sorcerer in his keeping—he has little need of actual divination. But you, Cat; not only are you indebted to her, you are here at her express pleasure. And if she takes against you . . ."

"I can handle her, Adam," I say, more confidently than I feel. "I have thus far, have I not?"

"What we are doing together is much bigger than anything either of us has tried on before," he presses. "Should the marquise become displeased with you, who knows what she might do? You know as well as I do, Cat, that we cannot afford to anger her."

"I will make sure to see her soon, then," I reassure him, nuzzling my cheek against Megaera's coils to stifle my growing unease. "I promise it will all be well."

Though I take Adam's advice to heart, the marquise does not give me the opportunity to rectify my mistake.

A day later she blows in unannounced, as if carried by the wings of an ill wind. When I come to meet her in my salon, she is icily resplendent in blue silk sewn with shard-like diamonds, her fine neck looped with pearls like frozen milk. As I sit across from her, I see that my offering of elderflower cordial and lavender petits fours has been left pointedly untouched.

"Good afternoon, Marquise," I say, masking my unease with courtesy. "A pleasure to see you as always. How have you been faring since our last Messe?"

She ignores my greeting, trailing a frosty look around the room's gaufrage velvet walls.

"Tell me, Catherine," she says in a tone like a lash. "Whose lovely drawing room is this that we are sitting in?"

"Yours, my lady," I reply, swallowing down a swell of trepidation. It seems I have indeed made a dangerous misstep; perhaps an even worse one than Adam feared. "Or mine, I suppose, by your leave."

"Exactly," she spits at me, her eyes slitting like a baited wildcat's. "By *my* leave. You occupy this place, and your position in society, *only* by my leave. This being the case, how is it that you no longer seem to find the time to attend to your patroness's needs?"

"My apologies, Marquise," I say, bowing my head so she cannot see the revolt brewing in my eyes. "It is only that this has been . . . such a tumultuous season at court. The many friends you have sent my way have consumed a great deal of my time."

"Oh, spare me," she says. "Would you truly pretend to have been busy in my service, when you and Lesage have been passing the time between your Messes by assiduously poisoning half the court?"

The words all but turn me to a pillar of stone, so petrifyingly matter-of-fact is her tone. It is nowhere near half the court, of course, only four so far. But that is more than enough to spell my utter ruin, should she choose to wield this knowledge as a weapon against me.

I stare at her mutely, tongue-tied, forcing myself not to wring my hands in my skirts.

"Come, Catherine, did you truly think that word of it would not reach me eventually?" she exclaims, scathing incredulity dripping from every word like venom. "The Duchesse de Vivonne—loose-tongued lush that she has become, upon being liberated from her late husband—implied to me that the duc's death was no accident. The silly twit did not elaborate, ostensibly not wishing to wind up in the Bastille. But she *did* let slip your name, likely assuming I would already know of my own divineress's exploits. I imagine Lesage is mixed up in this as well, now that you two are thick as thieves."

I swallow hard, my blood coursing with ice. Part of the reason we had selected the Duchesse de Vivonne at all was that she was so self-contained, so rigorously controlled that she barely even imbibed at the fetes following our Messes. It had not occurred to either of us that being freed from her husband's oppression might alter the very fabric of her character.

"Then I thought to myself, hmm, have there not been quite a few unexpected noble deaths of late?" The marquise tips a finger to her chin, pleased with herself like a cur that has treed a cat. "Perhaps more than one might expect would arise from the natural order of things?"

"I . . ." I begin, my mouth rank with the taste of iron. "Marquise, it is not . . ."

"Please, do not bore us both with tiresome professions of innocence," she says, waving her hand. "I've no intention of seeing you hang for your hand in this—not when you are far more use to me alive."

She leans forward, resting her palms on her thighs and fixing me with a flinty glare. I curse myself inwardly, for what, I am not even sure. For not having been more careful, though I am not certain how I could have been so. For, at the very least, having underestimated my patroness's fearful intelligence.

Athenais may be many unpleasant things, but she has never been anyone's fool.

"As long as you do a better job of remembering your place, that is," she adds. "Might I remind you that it was I who installed you here, plucked you from that stinking quagmire in the Seine and made you into my sorceress? And our agreement is what it has always been—that you see to *me* before you occupy yourself with anything else. Do we understand each other?"

"We do," I respond woodenly, my heart settling like a crushing boulder in my chest. She has no proof of my involvement in any of the murders, of course, given the occult origin of my poisons. But what proof would the maîtresse-en-titre even need to plant a seed of doubt, when she has the king's own ear? "Again, I beg pardon for my neglect, my lady. It was unintentional. I . . . I shall resolve to do better by you."

"I know you will," she says easily, her ire vanished in an instant now that she has me pinned, speared in place like a butterfly behind glass. "And you shall start by removing that simpering twit Claude de Vins des Oeillets from my sight."

"You wish your new lady's maid gone from your household?" I ask, perplexed by the sudden change of pace. "Surely I can find another position for her, but why?"

"I do not want her merely *gone*," she responds witheringly, as if I am an abject simpleton. "I want her dead. She sashays like a strumpet in front of Louis when he comes to visit me, seeking to ensnare him. To win his favor in my place."

"She does?" I ask, utterly disbelieving. "But she is such a sweet girl, so naive! And she credits you so highly. She idolizes you, even, styles herself after you in every way."

"I suppose it might not be wholly calculated on her part," the marquise concedes, shrugging, as if intentions do not matter a whit. "But either way, the fact remains that she has caught his eye. He says nothing of it, but I am not blind to how his eyes follow her about the room, like a dog tracking a bitch in heat. I will not have it, Catherine. Not when I have worked so hard to make him mine."

"What about a love philter instead?" I attempt desperately, my entire being quailing at the notion of causing that darling girl's death. "A new one, something more potent than what we have used for His Majesty thus far. I have a recipe for a remarkable Italian concoction of cantharides that—"

"No," she says, slicing a hand through the air. "There is nothing for it but her death. And she must sicken first, in a way that compromises her fair looks. I will compensate you for the poison's preparation, of course, as this goes beyond the scope of our original arrangement."

"Compensation is not the issue, Marquise," I say tightly.

"Then what is?" She tilts her head curiously to the side. "It is not as if I am asking for anything beyond the pale. Is murder not your latest business endeavor?"

"I do not make a habit of targeting the innocent, Marquise," I reply, gritting my teeth.

"A murderess with scruples, how absolutely charming!" she crows, clasping her hands in mock rapture in front of her chest. "But I'm afraid you shall have to make an exception for your patroness. Whatever you have been using for poison, it is clearly both unusual and quite cleverly made to not have aroused any suspicion. A pattern I should wish to continue in this case."

"And if I do not agree? Claude and I . . . you must know that we are friends."

Though her smile does not falter, a dangerous glitter sparkles in her eyes, like light glinting off icicles dangling from an eave.

"If you do not, I shall have to reconsider your worth to me, Catherine," she says, soft yet barbed with malice. "Perhaps I will even discover a newfound need to see you face justice for your crimes. And even if there should be no proof, well, you would still be jailed while an inquiry was carried out. How do you think it would suit you, languishing for months in Vincennes?"

My entire body suffuses with a stinging rush of adrenaline, as though I have been brushed with poison ivy from within. She would do it in a heartbeat, I know beyond the inkling of a doubt. Claude's death is a test of my loyalty, my continued willingness to put the marquise first, just as much as it is her true desire to see an imagined rival dead.

I hate her so much, loathe her so thoroughly it beggars belief. And should I fail her, she will not hesitate to throw me to the wolves.

"And so?" she prompts. "Do we understand each other in this as well?"

"We do," I say, though it costs me dearly to look her calmly in the eye when I wish to fly at her instead, rake my nails down her smug face. "Of course we do, my lady."

"Lovely!" She beams at me, clear-eyed as a cherub, unaccountably beautiful for a creature so evilly made. A basilisk wearing Aphrodite's transcendent face. "I knew someone so clever as you could be counted upon to see sense."

# ACT THREE: PANDEMONIUM

## CHAPTER EIGHTEEN

# The Summons and the Prophecy

**December 2, 1667**

After a debilitating decline, Mademoiselle Claude de Vins des Oeillets dies before the first snow.

And I fall headlong into a dreadful agony of remorse.

Perhaps I might have borne it better had I not been forced to witness the sweet girl's demise, but Claude had truly considered me a friend, enough to seek the comfort of my presence during her final ravaged days, when the poison had leached the color from her bright cheeks and stolen the luster from her hair. And I did not have the heart to refuse her requests to see me, not when I was the cause of her suffering.

The least I deserved was to see what I had done to her.

"How could I do it?" I bemoan to Adam as we walk the winding path through my sparkling garden, buried under the weight of newly fallen snow. "How could I have thought to pair such an innocent with a hyena like the marquise? And then agree to poison her with something so unforgiving?"

"You had no choice, Cat," Adam soothes briskly, tucking my hand into his elbow. "There is no use in berating yourself over it. Had you refused Athenais, she would have had us both clapped in brodequins. That harridan cannot stand being denied."

"Perhaps we belong in brodequins," I retort, turning bitter eyes up to the leaden sky, swollen with more impending snow. "Perhaps Claude's life was worth more than both of ours combined."

"I cannot speak for you, ma chère, but I value my life more than some stranger's, no matter how sweetly disposi-tioned," Adam responds with a touch of impatience. He does not approve of my prolonged melancholy, not when, in his estimation, I chose the only rational path available to me. "You know that the marquise would have disposed of her even without our help. And there is always a price to pay for a triumph such as ours. I should pay it gladly a thou-sand times over, if it means making something of myself."

*And am I equally willing to sacrifice others for my benefit?* I wonder bleakly, my eyes still cast up. While I have recon-ciled myself with the necessity of meting out well-earned deaths to the reprobates at court, am I just as ready to cull the innocent when it suits my purposes?

And if I am, does that not make me into a villainess far worse than the marquise?

The gimlet sky stares grimly back at me like some forbidding god, offering no reply.

I might have wallowed in my misery for weeks or even months to come—that is, had Adam and I not been summoned to Versailles to perform a Messe Noire for the king himself.

"This royal summons is her handiwork, mark my words," I repeat to Adam as we rattle like peas in my carriage, along the rutted road that wends through the snowbound countryside and culminates in Versailles. "It smacks of the marquise. What do you suppose her design might be?"

"From what you have told me of her, I expect she means to tantalize the king," Adam responds.

He is much less troubled than I am by this turn of events, so excited he can barely sit still. He drums his elegant fingers impatiently along his thighs, vigor snapping in his eyes. Unlike me, this summons has only ignited his ambitions.

"Perhaps she can sense him tiring of her, and she seeks to revitalize their spark with a taste of the forbidden," he suggests. "And what better curiosity to present him with than Satan's own priestess and priest?"

"But do you not think she might be setting some kind of snare for us?" I ask, my chest tight with disquiet. "The king is a self-proclaimed devotee of the sciences. What interest could he *possibly* have in a Devil's Mass? Remember, he even had his police storm the cité's havens back in the fall. Why would he allow something of this ilk under his own roof?"

"Perhaps he is only indulging his maîtresse," Adam offers with a shrug. "Stranger things have been done in the name of love. Or he may even be approaching this with a skeptic's eye, the better to debunk our claims of devilish communion."

"I expect the consequences of failing to divert him would be steep in either case," I mutter to myself. "A fine predicament."

"Dieu merci, Cat, what does it matter why he calls for us?" Adam demands with a hint of sharpness. "Is this not what we have been waiting for—an opportunity to ensnare the king himself, to make him our audience? How are we to garner his good graces if we never even perform for him?"

I nibble on my knuckle, unconvinced.

"Perhaps," I say uncertainly. "Though you are right in any case; it is not as if we could have told him no."

"Are you still comfortable with what we discussed?" Adam asks, fixing me with an intent gaze. "My devilmaker will serve us well, but the pièce de résistance must depend on you."

"Do not worry about me," I say shortly, turning to the window.

"But, Cat, you are *certain* you will be able to do it?" he demands. For the first time, his composed aspect betrays a hint of anxiety. Perhaps that is what his frenetic animation truly is, nerves masquerading as zeal. "I know the tension will run high, but—"

"It will run higher still if you do not cease pestering

me," I snap, rounding on him. "I *said* I could do it, and I will. Now let us concentrate on making this an evening His Majesty will not soon forget."

Adam opens his mouth as though he wishes to add something else, then thinks better of further provoking my ire. He is right; we both know that tonight's success largely depends on me. There is nothing to be gained by thinning my nerve before we even arrive.

We lapse instead into a tense silence, each lost to our own thoughts. It is just past the early winter sunset when our carriage draws through Versailles's soaring gates.

The gold leaves are wrought into fantastical shapes; curling fleurs-de-lis, overflowing cornucopias, Apollo's masks, and entwined *L*'s honoring the king's Christian name. They make me feel as though we are entering not just the château's marbled cour d'honneur, but le paradis itself.

I had thought myself prepared for the sight of the château, after all the stories I have heard of its delights. I know its extraordinary gardens contain more than a thousand sparkling fountains, and a cruciform canal large enough to host a sailing ship flotilla. And the marquise has rhapsodized over its pleasures to me many times, telling me of torchlit picnics in the parks beneath bursting fireworks, gondola trips on the canals by night, and even nocturnal theaters held in the orangery, with its miniature trees and pillars of lapis lazuli.

But I could not have conceived of Versailles's colossal expanse, nor of its snow-limned splendor.

Under a sky still flushed from recent sunset, the château glows like a tremendous jewel. The sun's last, lingering rays light the facade's golden embellishments with an almost holy fire, and a candle flickers in each of its countless windows. Doubtless fragrant beeswax to the last, as the Sun King surely does not skimp when it comes to his own light. How much such an extravagance must have cost, I cannot begin to fathom. It is wondrous beyond all words, this château the size of a small city. An otherworldly palace fit more for god than king.

"Pour l'amour du ciel, it is amazing," I whisper to Adam, half undone by wonder. "Notre Dieu himself would not be ashamed to make it his home."

"Is our king not divine, then?" Adam responds wryly. "Such blasphemy, Cat. Consider his name: Louis Dieudonné, the God-given. A gift to France from le Dieu himself."

When we alight, we are escorted inside by guards liveried in the House of Bourbon's royal blue and white. There is no fanfare to our arrival; quite the opposite, as it would not do to have rumor spread of Adam's and my presence here. This Messe Noire will be a secret one, as befits a Christian king. I barely have time to drink in the palatial marvels—towering columns, frescoed ceilings, mosaics of starbursts inlaid into the gleaming marble floors—before we are rushed through the crowd of courtiers and common supplicants milling around the halls. More than a thousand nobles make Versailles their home, and the palace is open to the public, too, allowing even the lowborn to catch a glimpse of their lord and liege.

We are shown to a room small and simple by the château's standards. Which means only that the floor is not marble but a shining caramel parquet, and that the statues of seraphim peering reproachfully from their alcoves are not quite as tall as me.

"This will do quite well," Adam says quietly to me, running an appraising eye over the room. "It will require a slightly different angle, but to excellent effect."

I nod curtly, chill tendrils of foreboding creeping up around my chest, afraid that speaking will only betray my anxiety. I desperately wish I could have brought my snakes; I feel nearly naked without at least Alecto around my neck.

But we have performed alongside each other enough times now, and tangled together in my bed, that Adam has grown as sensitive as a weathervane to the gusts of my emotions. He ventures closer and gently uncrosses my arms, waiting to see if I will resist. When I do not, he pulls me flush against him, cheek to cheek.

"You are always spectacular, my diabolic priestess," he whispers, a smile hiding in his voice. "But tonight you will be incomparable—a dark star to put Lucifer himself to shame."

I bite my lip, stirred by his support; tenderness between us is not our wont. But before I can respond, servants come bustling in with our accoutrements.

"You have two hours until your esteemed visitor arrives," the most officious of them tells us with a meaningful look, avoiding outright mention of the king. "Be sure that your preparations are complete by then."

And then there is no further time to fret.

When the servants withdraw, Adam and I fling ourselves into a whirlwind of activity. While Adam tends to the devilmaker and prepares his other tricks, I get down on my hands and knees to set out candles, paint the floor with runes, and arrange the provided claw-foot table as our altar centerpiece. I also tuck macabre curiosities into every corner of the room: little bouquets of black hollyhock and raven feathers tied with scarlet ribbon, clusters of sharp avian skulls, and my obsidian scrying bowls filled with red wine and pigeon blood.

Usually we would also have my snakes and at least one ceremonial knife, but we were ordered to bring nothing that might be construed as a threat. And though we were not forbidden the use of scents, we forgo incense as well. We cannot have our reasoned king growing giddy, perhaps fearing that we mean to poison him. The Sun King has enough enemies that his taster not only samples all his food but also rubs the king's silverware and royal toothpick on bread, in case the utensils themselves are somehow befouled. It is a testament to Athenais's unswerving dedication that she ever managed to dose his wine at all.

When the appointed hour strikes, we stand waiting in our hooded robes, Adam poised and empty-handed, me with a flickering candle clasped between my sweaty palms. My breath nearly stutters when the gilded door swings open.

But it reveals only a slight young herald, whose eyes flare wide as he takes in the room's dark delights. He clears his throat, struggling mightily to master himself.

"Bow before Louis, ah, Louis XIV," he stammers, sweat pearling on his brow. I imagine it must be nerve-racking to introduce a king under the best of times, much less to a magician and a sorceress. "Par la grâce de Dieu, roi de France et de Navarre. And his maîtresse-en-titre, Francoise-Athenais de Rochechouart de Mortemart, Marquise de Montespan."

Adam and I exchange a meaningful glance—so this was indeed Athenais's handiwork—before the pair glide into the darkened room. As Adam bows beside me, I drop into a curtsy so deep that by the time I rise, the king has already been seated on the gold-leaf armchair that is to serve in place of a throne. The marquise sits beside him on a lower and much simpler seat, and the king's two stone-faced captains of the guard stand at their backs.

The king himself wears no crown, nor any of the splendid garments he is known to favor. Both he and the marquise are in hooded black, for discretion as well as ceremony. Yet even without any royal raiment, there is no mistaking Louis. Beneath his hood, his famed curls tumble dark and abundant, framing a face so fine-boned and elegant it is no wonder he has broken such a wealth of hearts. With his hands laced loosely in his lap, his eyes bolt the both of us in place like flung javelins.

And though only I can see it, the Sun King radiates an extraordinary burnished glow, the likes of which my sight has never shown me outside the confines of a vision.

It reminds me of when I first saw his silhouette, the outline of his gloire blazing in the marquise's misty future; though that glimpse could never compare to witnessing him in the flesh. The aura of his power sears through me like liquid lightning, singeing every nerve. I have performed our Messes for nobles of every stripe and color, but this is no mere vicomte, no louche marquis.

This is le Roi Soleil himself, Louis XIV, reigning scion of the Bourbon dynasty.

Despite his solar emblem and allegiance to the god Apollo, this king is nothing so simple as the sun. He is both sun and moon at once, the eclipse that blots the heavens out. A beacon of burning darkness set against a ravening light.

And I find myself desperately short of breath at what I aim to do for him tonight.

He flicks his fingers at us, idly imperious. "Proceed," he says in a knelling voice that makes even the single word sound like an edict.

"Of course, Your Majesty," Adam says, inclining his head. "But before we begin, let us see whether the augurs remain auspicious."

The king nods impatiently, surveying us with heavy-lidded eyes verging perilously on boredom. I get the sense that he anticipates only another overwrought diversion he must sit through, one more sordid spectacle that he is willing to endure for his maîtresse's sake.

As if she can divine as much herself, the marquise reaches over and clasps his hand.

"Just wait, mon bien-aimé," she coos to him, brushing her lips over his cheek. "The sorceress La Voisin is my personal divineress, well versed in matters of the arcane. And Lesage is her magician consort."

When the king's gaze rakes over me, I nearly feel its fiery brush across my skin. "No doubt I will be suitably impressed by their . . . skills," he says, his dry tone belying the sentiment.

Something about his flippancy, this preemptive dismissal, grates at me. My stage fright all but forgotten, I set my teeth and lift my eyes to his.

"No doubt you will, Your Highness," I echo, the ringing authority of my tone startling a frown from him. "Prêtre Lesage, let us consult the Morningstar's will."

Adam nods solemnly, though I catch the twitching of a muscle in his jaw, the wicked cast of his lips as he restrains a dangerous grin. No doubt he is just as irked as I am at being treated like some inept jester, when we are both performers of unparalleled ilk.

And neither of us came here to disappoint or bore a king.

"Bend your eye to us, O Lucifer," Adam booms, stepping forward and spreading his hands. "And reveal your will in these blackest blossoms, these darkest of all blooms."

As he speaks, he whisks a wild bouquet from nowhere, an extravagant posy of black dahlia and hellebore that seems much too huge to have been concealed. Before the king and the marquise can even register the shock of it, he flings the flowers above his head—where they disperse, transforming into bats with chittering voices and flapping wings.

"He is with us!" I intone with a touch of manic glee, loud enough to register over the king's cry of shock and the marquise's delighted squeals. "The dread lord has shown his presence here!"

The bats flap about the room's domed ceiling, circling and diving, before swooping down to roost in the dark recesses that house the marble seraphim. The king watches their progress slack-jawed, clearly confounded but still unafraid. I let out a breath, sending silent thanks to whatever watches over me that Adam managed to get them properly trained.

"Join me, Your Highness, in this prayer to our shadow sire," I say, hearkening back to one of my favorite openings. "In which we call on the prince of darkness by his many names. Mephistopheles, Belial, Asmodeus, Legion. Le Diable, and daystar of the damned."

I lead us through a poetic prayer I penned just for this occasion, though unlike the marquise, the king does not indulge me by echoing the words. Then I turn to face Adam, who takes the candle from my hands and draws me close. We share a very deliberate kiss, slow and lingering, and I know just how beautiful we look together—mouth to parted mouth, black hair to red, his hand beneath my chin. We have practiced this in the mirror, honed the sacrilege of our candlelit communion.

Adam and the demon goddess Lilith in place of Eve, stealing a moment under the forbidden tree.

"Dread lord and shadow sire, we offer you our flesh," I say against Adam's mouth. "Along with our blood, and the darkest of our passions. We offer you all the storms that pass our lips."

I turn away from Adam, breaking the kiss. Then, slowly and with care, I lift my hands to the robe's hem and slide it off my shoulders, letting it whisper to the floor.

The stunned silence that falls across the room is unlike anything I have ever felt.

I stand before the king, naked and unflinching. Poised as one of the marble seraphim despite the frantic thrashing of my heart. A stolen glance at the marquise shows me the flash of her narrowed eyes, her gritted teeth. I know I am incurring a tremendous risk by provoking her thus, appearing in my full youth and beauty before the king.

But should our gambit succeed, any danger will have been worth it.

I can see the shock scrawled across the Sun King's features as Adam takes me by the hand, leading me to the altar at a stately pace. I lie down upon it with aching slowness, uncoiling my limbs along its length with a snake's languorous grace.

"Tonight, Your Highness, I offer you my body," I say, tipping my head back so that my curls flow off the table and pool along the floor. "As a sacred, living altar. As Lucifer's own avatar. As the Sorceress La Voisin, Priestess of Snakes."

At that, Adam fetches one of the scrying bowls and tips its contents over my body, bathing me in a scarlet sluice of wine and pigeon blood. When he withdraws into the deep darkness beyond the candlelit altar, I count the prearranged number of seconds under my breath, giving him time enough to prepare his part. Then I arch my back against the table and fling out a beckoning hand.

"Would you come to me, le Roi Soleil?" I call out. "Would you come and see your glorious future dancing in my eyes?"

The silence stretches for long enough that I wonder if he will not deign to come, if setting me out as bait has failed. I wait for him with bated breath, the room's chill air stippling gooseflesh onto my wet skin.

Then I hear the click of the king's high-heeled shoes on the parquet, and a moment later his face hovers into view above. His skin is so pale and smooth, his lashes swooping against his cheeks like a little boy's. With all his grace and grandeur, it is so easy to forget that our Sun King is only twenty-four years old.

"What would you have me hear, La Voisin?" he whispers, thoroughly rapt, yet still unafraid. One of his curls slips loose and tickles my cheek, shedding a floating trace of his renowned perfume. Lavender and ambergris, coriander and marjoram, along with subtle hints of some musk I cannot name. "You strange and lovely siren of the damned?"

Just then, Adam's lanterna magica flares into life high above us, carefully obscured behind the strung-up damask screen that conceals both him and the device. It bathes me in a lurid crimson glow, casting an image of the devil's visage over my features, superimposing it across my face. It also projects pictures of painted snakes that writhe along my limbs, lent the clever illusion of movement by Adam's own design.

As the king's face contorts into a rictus of pure fear, I reach up and clasp his cheeks between my bloodied hands.

This is, by far, the most dangerous of all our stratagems; one does not lay so much as a finger upon the king without his consent. Though I cannot afford to break our gaze by looking, I hear his captains crying out, the clattering racket of their swift approach.

"No!" he calls out sharply, waving them off. "Noailles, Rochefort, stay back! She is not causing me any harm, and I will not have her interrupted!"

The relief that tramples through me is so tremendous it is a wonder that I do not come unraveled. I struggle to compose myself, not speaking until the king's captains have withdrawn. Then I gently tug the king's face down closer to my own, and lean into the sight harder than I have ever dared.

Fiery images streak across my mind's eye like a brace of comets, blazing fragments speeding by so quickly I can barely capture them. I see death and rampant warfare and the murderous gleam of bayonets; an ever-churning cascade of coin, glittering inside a soaring vault; the clever glass and bristling instruments of an observatory swimming in a sea of stars. It is so easy to scry for this king when nothing I have ever felt could match the roaring force of his need.

He feels like some beast's gaping maw, insatiable in his desire to amass ever more gloire. To cement his legacy, to stamp the likeness of his face upon the kingdom like a blistering brand.

"L'etat, c'est moi" is more than just his motto; "I am the nation" is the creed by which he lives.

But Louis XIV is more than just leaping flames, the all-consuming inferno of his desires. He is also terribly afraid, of dying young and of being forgotten.

"Louis Dieudonné," I whisper so that only he may hear. "Even the Morningstar himself cowers before your ferocious light. You need not fear an early death, nor any violent end. Instead you will hitch France to the bright star of your soul, and bring her to such heights as she has never known. For three score and ten, your rule will cast a shadow over neighboring lands and even across the seas. History will know your name as the monarch who would not be denied."

The king hisses through his teeth, a great, ravening grin splitting his face. "Tell me more, sorcière jolie," he commands, reaching up to grip my wrists. "Whether or not Satan truly feeds your gift, I would hear more of your sweet blasphemy."

So I speak and speak until I am dizzy and breathless, listing a grand litany of achievements I barely even understand. I push myself harder than I have ever done, feeling desperately powerful and strange. As though his future is an entire ocean I have somehow scooped up between my hands.

Le Roi Soleil demands ever more from me, until I have spoken myself hoarse. The only thing I leave out is the dismal torment of his end, the gangrene that he will succumb to well into his old age, when he has finally exhausted the last dregs of his mighty will.

By then, my vision has begun darkening at the edges, curling inward like a burning scroll. I am so tired I give in almost gratefully, my hands leaving scarlet trails as they slip from His Majesty's cheeks.

I can hear Adam's voice calling to me as if from across a great expanse, but I do not even bother to struggle against the onslaught of unconsciousness.

Now that I have done this great work for us, the least Adam can do is close out the ceremony himself.

CHAPTER NINETEEN

# The Mother and the Duchesse

Due to the unsavory nature of our magic, Adam and I are not granted permission to spend the night at Versailles despite my fainting spell. It is just as well; we would not have enjoyed its splendor anyway, utterly spent as we both are.

Instead we celebrate on the ride back home, passing a flagon of the château's exquisite wine back and forth between us. Though I am beyond exhausted, a triumphant satisfaction drips sweetly through my veins like some slow sap.

"Did you see how he could not get enough of me?" I crow to Adam, tossing back a mouthful before passing the flagon back to him. "I thought he might keep us there forever, to hear his future spun like a story rather than living it at all. Like some greedy child listening to a fairy tale."

Adam casts me a cut-glass grin, lifting the wine in an ironic toast.

"You heard what he called it, your 'sweet blasphemy,'" he mocks, giving the words the king's refined intonation. "I daresay he could not have liked hearing it more. And how did he style you again? Pretty witch, siren of the damned?"

"Sorcière jolie, yes. It was a fine idea you had, to use me as the altar." I wince a little at the memory of the marquise's face. "Though I hope the marquise does not take against me now, thinking he means to have me. Did you see the way she looked at me when I disrobed?"

Adam shakes his head decisively. "I would not worry. I watched her closely afterward, while you had him under your spell. She was fairly beside herself, all umbrage forgotten, delighted to see him enjoying her thoughtful gift."

"And you!" I smile at him, unabashed in my admiration. "The flowers and the bats! They will be chasing them about the room for weeks. I can still barely fathom how you did it, and I saw you prepare."

A furious trembling overtakes me then, without any warning—the overexertion of my sight finally catching up to me.

Though we are protected from the freezing cold outside, the air inside the carriage seems to take on a bitter chill. Seeing my teeth begin to chatter, Adam swings over to sit by me, draping his cloak over my shoulders and tugging me close.

"You should try to sleep, Cat," he says into the top of my head, his breath blissfully warm against my scalp. "I cannot imagine your fatigue, after spinning such fictions for him for so long."

"They w-were not f-fictions," I reply through clicking teeth, nestling into the crook of his neck. "Every word of it was true. H-he will truly be remembered as France's most majestic king."

He is silent for so long that I grow warm enough to become drowsy, thinking he must have fallen asleep himself. When he finally speaks, it nearly startles me.

"How unfortunate," he says, bitterness curdling his quiet tone. "I had rather hoped to see his court fractured in my time."

I stir against him, lifting my heavy head. "I did not know you took such exception to the court. Are we not angling to become the king's dark counselors together?"

"We are, to be sure, but I would prefer both. The noblesse are a tangle of heartless vipers, good for nothing other than being milked—as I mean to do with our Louis."

"Not that I do not agree, because you know I do," I say. "But it sounds as though you have some particular bone to pick with the peers of the realm. Beyond what you have told me."

He swallows hard, his throat bobbing with the motion.

"My father was a duc, you know," he says in an unwontedly somber tone. "And my mother a chambermaid who caught his eye. He was quite taken with her, from what I recall before she died."

"I am sorry to hear you lost her. What happened?"

"An 'accident,'" he replies with a wry devastation that makes my heart hitch up against my ribs. I have never heard him sound so human before, so nearly vulnerable. "The story was that she fell into the lake on the estate and drowned. But she was a robust swimmer, and she never would have swum at night alone. Not without me by her side."

"Adam," I begin, not knowing what to say. The snatch of vision I saw when we first began our work together floats up before me again, in the form of the black-haired woman's lovely face. And that he is a noble's son from the wrong side of the blanket explains so many things; the scope of his learning, his unstudied arrogance. "That is . . . that must have been truly terrible for you."

"It was the worst heartbreak of my life," he says softly, gathering me closer. "Maman was such a sunshine. There was no proof of any malefaction, of course, but of course that's what it was. The duchesse could not stand having my mother under her roof—especially once I grew old enough for my father to show in my face. For him to begin taking an interest in me."

"And was the duchesse punished for her crime?"

"Come now, Cat, you know better than that," he scoffs, barking out a scornful laugh. "When I caused a ruckus, the duchesse had me sentenced to the galleys for an invented crime. My father did not even bother to fight for me, not when she was mother to his legitimate son. It took me years to claw my way back to France's shores."

I breathe for a moment, trying to grasp the stunning extent of this betrayal. No wonder Adam has no compunction when it comes to poisoning the noblesse.

"We will make them pay, Adam." The words fly loose before I can properly consider them, but I find that I mean what I say. "Your father and stepmother both. Your half brother, too, if you wish."

"Of course we shall," he says, his voice snapping with a quiet fervor. "Once we ascend to our rightful place, all these degenerates will dance upon our strings like marionettes."

I tip my head back against his shoulder, moved that he should choose to share so much of himself with me.

"Thank you for trusting me," I whisper. "You did not have to tell me any of that."

"If I cannot trust my prêtresse with my blackest secrets," he murmurs into my hair, "then whom could I hope to trust?"

I lapse into silence, unable to think of a reply. I suspect this is the closest either of us will ever come to any true feeling for each other. Though there is no love between us, at least there is this: the embracing of our mutual darkness, the love of shadow that we share.

The reflections of ourselves that we each see in the other's eyes.

## CHAPTER TWENTY

# The Lieutenant and
# the Prisoner

I barely have time to bask in our success at Versailles before Gabriel-Nicolas de la Reynie comes to call on me.

"It is the lieutenant general of the Paris police for you, madame," my chatelaine informs me when she comes to fetch me from my study, three days after my return from Versailles. Though Simone is typically the epitome of composure, immaculate as the household that she runs, today she looks distinctly rattled. "He is rather insistent that you make the time for him."

"Tell him I will be with him in just a moment," I say weakly, trying to master my dismay, though I abruptly feel like a rabbit with a fox nosing a snout down its warren. "And see if he should like anything to eat or drink while he waits."

Simone shakes her head, nervously licking her thin lips. "He has already declined refreshments, madame. He says to tell you that this is not, alas, a social call."

*What does he know*, I think wildly as I rise, *when there are so many things for which I might be caught?* But if he came here to arrest me, would he not already have done so?

When Simone withdraws, I toss back a brimming glass of wine before I go attend to the lieutenant general, hoping it might curb the tempest brewing in my chest. I take my time traversing the halls, and when I reach the salon I am almost back in control.

"Monsieur de la Reynie," I say smoothly, offering him a cool but courteous smile. Presenting a demeanor of slight inconvenience, as though he has parted me from some crucial task. "I am pleased to make your acquaintance. To what do I owe your visit?"

La Reynie surveils me from under beetled eyebrows, his fleshy mouth twisting with some vague displeasure. He perches uncomfortably on my delicate love seat, as though it might give way at any second beneath his weight. With his bold features and officer's coat, he looks disconcertingly hawkish and masculine against the salon's ladylike décor. As if a peregrine falcon has come to roost among all the cream-and-rose brocatelle. He sports a dark riot of hair that rivals the Sun King's own curling mane—I have a fleeting, nonsensical thought that the Marquis de Cessac would be envious of its natural splendor—and the late-morning sunlight slanting through the window shines off his golden epaulets. At least he has doffed his imposing feathered cap.

"Madame La Voisin," he says with a curt nod. "My apologies in coming unannounced. But per the king's own command, my investigation into l'affaire des poisons could not wait."

*The affair of the poisons.* So Adam's and my exploits have somehow emerged from the shadows and into the light, enough to acquire an actual name.

My head tolls as if a clapper has been struck against my skull, and it is only the icy composure I have cultivated for so many months that keeps my knees from turning to water.

"I'm afraid this is the first I have heard of any such affair," I say briskly, clasping my hands behind my back to still their sudden trembling. "Might I ask you to explain?"

The lieutenant general's piercing glare shifts between my eyes, a touch perplexed, as though he senses that my stillness masks something untoward.

"You have heard nothing of it?" he queries, as if finding this curious. "Four members of the court have met an untimely end in the last two months alone. There is . . . some suspicion of the use of pernicious substances. I should think that given your somewhat unique position, word of such foul play would surely have reached your ears."

"The marquise keeps me busy," I reply shortly, though inwardly I am quaking. How could this have happened, when we were so very careful to leave no trace behind?

But I remember how Blessis recognized the ingredients for aqua tofana, even without having ever made any himself; a reminder that the poisons I have been relying on exist even beyond the pages of Agnesot's grimoire. Rare as they are, perhaps one of the king's more shrewd and open-minded advisers recognized their effects.

And if the cunning marquise was able to divine that something untoward was taking place, perhaps I should not be quite so surprised that it might occur to the law as well.

"Too busy to spend my time on idle rumor," I add, biting down on the inside of my cheek to keep my teeth from chattering.

"Oh, it is rather more than idle rumor now," La Reynie replies, puffing out his chest. "The king has appointed me commissioner and rapporteur to the newly created Chambre Ardente, to investigate and try any individuals found to have been implicated in the affair."

Chambre Ardente—the "burning chamber." I can almost feel a hungry tongue of fire licking at my toes.

"And has . . ." I clear my throat to force the faltering words out. "Has anyone been implicated thus far?"

"Oh, yes." An unsettling expression, somewhere between professional satisfaction and a more intimate sort of malice, drifts across La Reynie's face. "We have a suspected poisoner in custody at Vincennes at this very moment, but our efforts to draw out a confession have been unsuccessful. The king suggested that you might be of help. He believes you have some . . . insight, a certain innate wisdom that might be of use to us."

From the sour skepticism in his voice, it is evident La Reynie does not share the king's confidence in my abilities. At the thought that I am not a suspect—to the contrary, I am to serve on the side of the authorities—my trepidation lifts, to be replaced by an almost hysterical elation.

What an utter absurdity, to be summoned to weigh in on someone else's guilt for my own crimes.

And something in me gives a strange and joyful flicker that the king did not even mention Adam's name, nor call upon him to consult with the police. No, the golden weight of Louis's regard clearly rests solely on me.

"Bien sûr," I say, spreading my hands. "I am at your service, Lieutenant General. What would you have me do?"

"Accompany me to the fortress, if you please," he says, hefting his bulk cumbersomely from the love seat. "It would be best if we went now."

The fortress of Vincennes sits to the city's east, near the lush forest of the Bois de Vincennes, almost an hour's carriage ride away from the Villeneuve. Despite the golden pour of sunshine over its towers and battlements, which hint of its stately past as the royal family's ancestral home, the grimness of its stone exterior leaves no doubt as to its dire purpose now.

And if its outsides are forbidding, the dungeon proper is far, far worse.

As I trail La Reynie through the rank passageways that tunnel beneath the château, I feel as though I am traipsing through some nightmarish terrain. Sepulchral voices wail from each barred cell, and the cold, dank air crowds into my nose, reeking of rotting wood and sweating stone. I keep my eyes averted from the rusting spikes of the bars, having no wish to witness the misery of those trapped behind them.

But for the grace of notre Dieu, or whatever more diabolic deity watches over me instead, I could very well be chained up here myself.

"No place for a woman, to be sure," La Reynie remarks, though his easy tone indicates he is unfazed by the captives' distress. "Which makes what follows an even more thankless task."

Before I can ask him what he means, he draws to a halt in front of a corner cell. "Bosse," he orders briskly. "Come forth, will you, and let us see your treacherous face."

I nearly choke on my own suddenly deadened tongue, feeling as though a blade has pierced my gut at the mention of Marie's name.

But it cannot compare to the devastation that tears through me at the sight of her face, when she shambles out of the darkness and closer to the light shed by La Reynie's torch, wrapping her frail hands around the bars. Her wrists are chafed to bleeding from the manacles clapped around them, their long chains looping back to the crumbling walls. She wears some coarse gray scrap barely long enough to cover her thin legs, and her beautiful dark hair has tangled into a wooly snarl, littered with shafts of the dirty straw that line her cell.

And she has been beaten almost beyond recognition, the flesh around the slits of her eyes taut and glossy as a split plum.

"What do you want *now*, you misbegotten putain de batard?" she spits at La Reynie, not yet noticing me behind him. "Do you not tire of hearing my thoughts on your maman?"

I nearly double over at the injustice of our respective lots—her consigned to this barbaric place, and me free on the other side of the bars. The worst of what she feared for me has come to pass, and yet it has been inflicted on her instead. I can think of no greater punishment for myself than to have damned her in this way. And though I rack my brain, I cannot even fathom why she should be in here at all.

Though she must be in an agony of pain, I am slightly heartened to see that her eyes still glint with their usual clarity. As her glare locks with mine, burning with banked intensity, I can almost hear an echo of her unspoken command:

*If you value either of our lives, do not dare to recognize me.*

"And who is this . . . this unfortunate?" I ask, barely containing the quaver in my voice.

"Mademoiselle Marie Bosse," he replies, instilling "mademoiselle" with an acidic twist. "A minor grifter and fortune-teller who plies her illicit trade in the cité. Her name was already known to us from the raids on the occult havens; we suspect she may be the mastermind behind the spate of recent noble deaths."

"A lowly grifter from the cité, to have orchestrated the murders of those in the highest ranks?" I ask, pitching my voice high with incredulity. "You would understand such things better than I, of course. But I'm afraid it sounds rather far-fetched."

"I would agree—save for Bosse's connection to the alchemist Blessis. He is credited with knowledge of some of the occult substances thought to have been involved in the deaths. And when we conducted an investigation into his affairs, Bosse emerged as his foremost known accomplice."

"And is this Blessis here in gaol himself?" I ask, dreading the possibility. Though I have had a cordial business relationship with the alchemist, I have no reason to believe he would not yield my name if his own life were at stake.

"No, he seems to have fled the city already." La Reynie's tone is bitter with frustration. "We can find neither hide nor hair of him. And thus far, Bosse has been remarkably obstinate in admitting to her own malfeasance."

"Because I am *innocent*, you corrupt sous-merde!" Marie growls through chapped lips, spitting at his boots. "A concept with which you seem woefully unfamiliar."

I bite my lip, hideously torn between wild laughter and tears. Of course she would preserve her high spirits even in this abject place. I have seen nothing that can rattle the core of steel that undergirds Marie.

"That being the case," La Reynie continues, as if Marie has not spoken, though I can see the dangerous tightening around his mouth, "the king suggested that we enlist your help, Madame La Voisin. Perhaps you can see something in her that might be of use to us."

"Of course I will try," I say glibly, inclining my head. "As the king commands."

"Go ahead, then," he says, waving his hand vaguely toward the bars. "Do . . . whatever it is you must."

"May I touch M— The prisoner?" I ask, stumbling over the last word as I nearly say her name. "Physical contact enhances the sight."

"Yes, but be careful of her nails. This one has the claws and feral nature of a rabid alley cat." He eyes Marie askance, his sharply flared nostrils widening even farther. "And take heed, Bosse. Should you be tempted to harm a hair on Madame La Voisin's head, not even a testament of your innocence from our Lord God himself will save you."

Marie shifts her eyes balefully to me.

"I promise not to bite, my lady," she says witheringly. Though I am nearly certain the loathing in her eyes is intended not for me but La Reynie, it makes me quail all the same. I deserve her hatred twice over, for leaving her behind and then landing her in this predicament. "Upon my honor."

Before La Reynie can change his mind, I draw closer to the bars and slide my hands around her icy fingers, trying to instill her clammy flesh with my own heat. I peer intently into the brown depths of her eyes, partially in an act of concentration for La Reynie's sake, but mostly to impress upon her my commitment to freeing her.

Though I do not dare mouth anything, I make a silent vow. *I will do anything it takes to set you free*, I promise silently. *I will not let you die in here, even if it means that I must face death for my crimes myself.*

From the incremental softening in her face, I gather that she understands.

"This young woman is innocent," I declare, releasing Marie's hands and stepping back, massaging my temples to indicate the effort I have expended. "There is no taint of guilt whatsoever on her soul. She has nothing to do with any of your murders."

I turn to La Reynie, leveling him with an austere look. "In fact, if there is any crime here at all, it is the travesty of the violence that you have visited upon her. And if I do not soon hear news of her release, I will be sure to divulge your methods to the king, the next time he summons me for my counsel."

I know that goading him this way is dreadfully unwise; it does not take the sight to bespy the violence churning in this man's depths. But furious as I am, I cannot help myself.

"She will not be released until the chambre has declared her innocent," he grinds out, blood leaching from his lips. His mouth trembles from the force with which he clenches his teeth. "Especially as she is a criminal nonetheless, a hardened swindler whose very trade is bilking her betters out of their coin. But I, in turn, will be certain to pass on your *very great* concern for her well-being to the king."

The heavy-handed subtext—that Marie and I are cut from the same deceptive cloth—hangs in the air between us like some acrid smoke. I stare at him defiantly, bitterly amused at how close to the truth he treads. Turning on his heel and storming ahead, La Reynie barely bothers to wait as he leads me out through the reeking maze of the halls.

And as I follow him out of this abhorrent underworld unfit for Hades himself, I am certain only of two things.

One is that I must ensure Marie's freedom at any cost.

The other is that I have made an enemy of Gabriel-Nicolas de la Reynie.

## CHAPTER TWENTY ONE

# The Threat and the Divination

I can barely live with myself, knowing that Marie molders in the dungeon in my place, at the mercy of that detestable man.

While Adam is terrified that Marie will cede our names under pain of further torture, I know better than to doubt my friend's steely resolve. And without Blessis to interrogate, or any other concrete proof at hand, surely the Chambre Ardente's investigation will die out soon enough, burn itself to ash and cinders like a fiery serpent eating its own tail.

In the meantime, we cannot afford to have our names and "poison" spoken in the same breath. Though Adam had previously drawn up schematics to construct more devil-makers and expand our offerings, we decide to suspend all our upcoming Messes at least until the smoke has cleared, confining ourselves only to private sessions with existing clients.

The rest of my time I spend devising wild stratagems to break Marie out of the gaol.

"But what about your devilmaker?" I harangue Adam one evening, chewing on my knuckles. "We could cast some sort of illusion, convince the guards that the fortress has been breached by demons. And then take advantage of the ensuing chaos to somehow spring her loose!"

"And how do you propose we get inside at all, much less smuggle in the devilmaker and my other tools?" he asks reasonably, by now well accustomed to defusing my hysterical plots. "Even if such a gambit were to succeed, what then? Perhaps one of the guards might oblige us by handing over the key we need to open her cell? Or do you intend to stay hidden there yourself, and saw your friend out with a nail file over the course of several months?"

"Then what do *you* suggest?" I fling back at him. "Besides more excuses to sit idle and do nothing? Do not pretend that you even care if Marie sees the light of day again!"

Adam comes to his feet and rakes both hands through his hair, darting me an exasperated glance.

"I do not pretend to care about her at all," he retorts coolly. "But I *do* care for you—enough, at least, that I would lend my help if I could safely do so, and if I thought it might do any good. But all of your schemes wind up with us imprisoned, or worse. And I will not agree to sentence myself to death to assuage your own guilt."

"Because you are a *coward*," I spit at him.

He heaves a long-suffering sigh, impatience sweeping across his face. "No, Catherine. Because I am not a fool, certainly not enough to meddle in whatever it is that lies between the two of you. So do us both a favor, and do not persist in dragging me into it."

With that, he stalks out the door, refusing to engage with me any further.

Once he's gone, I lock myself away in my chambers with my snakes and sink into a sullen fury, enraged by my own impotence. What use is my vaunted sight or my well-honed wiles if neither of them can serve me now that I need them more desperately than ever?

Perhaps I would lose myself entirely to this hopeless lassitude, were the marquise suddenly not in such constant need of me. Though I can barely stand the sight of her face, she besieges me almost every day for new philters with which to ply the king, demanding that I scry incessantly for her.

"What do you see?" she asks me each time, in a desperate sort of fervor. "Tell me, am I still upon the battlements? Do I still wear my almost-crown?"

"Of course you do, my lady," I reassure her, though the truth is that I see no such things—and I have not for a while. The marquise's destiny increasingly forks away from the king's, twisting from the light and into an ashy darkness I suspect is some tragedy of her own. "You are still with him, and so very beautiful."

"*Beautiful,*" she spits bitterly. "Am I, still? For I am almost five and twenty, you know. Soon he will turn away from me, repulsed by my advancing age. Replace me with another, some rosy little apple with unlined skin, not yet shriveling on the vine."

"This is not true," I protest, although in truth, it likely is. The marquise is nothing like old, of course, and still amply lovely. But there is always someone younger to be had, and nothing so fickle as noblemen's taste, when they deem it time to abandon and replace their mistresses. Had the marquise not killed poor Claude, she would likely have been ousted from the king's bed already. I indulge her only because I am beholden, though I am sick to death of reassuring her that she is the fairest in all the land.

And there is something increasingly savage about her need to cling to Louis's flagging affections, when it is clearly well past time to let him go.

The next time she calls on me, she storms back and forth across my study in a sweep of damask skirts like some demented hurricane.

"Truly he is no better than a rutting dog, for all the fidelity and regard he has for me," she forces through clenched teeth, lifting her goblet to her lips. Though it is barely afternoon, she has already quaffed two glasses of my finest burgundy wine, and seems disinclined to stop.

"No matter that I have gone to such lengths on his behalf, showered him with such unrivaled gifts as a Messe Noire and your prophecies. No, it is as if he cannot be bothered to control his own baser impulses."

I barely manage to hold my tongue, sorely tempted to remind her that the king has been faithless from the very start, given that she displaced both Louise de la Vallière and the queen herself to win his favor.

"And that is the trouble, you see," she ruminates,

twisting her curls around her fingers so tightly, it bleaches her knuckles white. "Even if I were to have you poison every simp that crossed his path, he would still find another one to woo. Even if it meant that he must make do with a pig farmer's most ill-favored daughter. The relentless pursuit of debauchery is one of his foremost skills."

"Perhaps it is time, then," I suggest delicately, aware that I am treading on extremely brittle ice, "to consider breaking with the king?"

"Relinquish him, you mean?" She blinks at me with such shock and incredulity that I may as well have sprouted horns. "Of my own volition? Dieu merci, Catherine, surely you must be jesting. Are you so cruel as to suggest that I should simply resign myself to seeing him content in another's arms?"

"Then what would you have me do, Marquise?" I ask, struggling to maintain my equanimity rather than giving in to sheer frustration. "There are always new philters we might try, of course. Different formulations."

"Oh, hang your spells," she spits, flicking a dismissive hand. "They are clearly no longer enough. No, if the philters have finally failed us, then I have all but lost him. I suspect he already yearns for that flighty twit Anne de Rohan, the Princesse de Soubise. Which leaves me with only one thing left to do."

I shrink back against my chair, dreading this precipitous new turn. "And what might that be, Marquise?"

She hesitates for a moment, shifting her jaw from side to side, her eyes both wild and distant with some furious deliberation. Then she turns to me like a demon come to roaring life, a dreadful clarity of resolve blazing upon her face.

"He must die himself," she pronounces. "If I am forced to live without him, then at least I will have been the last to know his love."

I gape at her, stupefied, thinking I must surely have misheard her.

"You wish to . . . to kill the *king*?" I manage to eke out, my voice emerging an undignified squeak. I feel a vertiginous drop deep in my bowels, as if I am somehow falling through my seat. "But, Marquise, you cannot mean it. That is not only murder you are proposing, but the very worst sort of treason!"

"It is also self-preservation," she says softly, sinking into a damask armchair as if all the weight has left her body now that her decision has been made. "Having known the ardor of his love, the searing glory of it, in his absence I would be left with nothing but cold and ash. I may yet recover from his death—but never from his betrayal. It would spell my own cruel end."

"We all recover from such losses, at one time or another," I offer as gently as I can, desperate to find some way to bend her back toward reason. "Even the most shattered heart still knows how to mend."

"Even if that were true, how am I to stand seeing another bask in all that comes with being his maîtresse?" she demands, throwing up her hands. "After a fashion, France herself was mine while I was with him. How will I return to being only myself again?"

Unhinged as she is, there is some bright pearl of truth

nestled deep in the slick flesh of her madness. Having witnessed the king's dazzling aura for myself, I can understand why she should fear the coming deprivation.

Losing the love of such a gilded, God-touched king must surely be akin to being struck blind after having reveled in the most heavenly color.

And to be stripped of everything she had become, by virtue of being by his side? His love has turned her into something of a demigoddess, a temporary queen. I can almost see how the prospect of losing her status, of shrinking back into the space she previously occupied, might be sufficient to fracture her mind.

That I should understand a madwoman's motivations so well terrifies me most of all.

"I know this is a tragedy for you," I try again, shaking my head as if to clear it of such preposterous notions. "Truly, I do. But please, consider your future. Should we ever be found out, we would both pay the price with our own heads. And the risk is greater now than it ever was; the king has already established a commission headed by La Reynie to investigate the other poisonings. Surely nothing passes his royal lips that has not been vetted."

"Then I expect you will simply need to be more adept and devious than ever," she says with maddening complacency, as if I have already agreed to help her. "Certainly you have had the requisite practice, wouldn't you say?"

I grit my teeth at the needling reminder of what she holds over my head. "This is different. This is the *king*. We would almost certainly be caught."

"Even so, I trust that you will find a way to administer the poisons and to evade suspicion." She shrugs, pursing her lips. "You will, because you are nothing if not enterprising. And you will because you must."

"If you mean to blackmail me again, I assure you any such attempt will fail," I counter, far more assertively than I feel, my hands clawing into the chair's wooden arms. "The king will take no heed of your accusations now that you are no longer in his favor, especially as there is no proof of my involvement. I know as much from La Reynie himself."

"No proof?" She feigns surprise, then lifts an elegant eyebrow almost indulgently, like a mother amused by a precocious child. "Have you forgotten poor, sweet Claude's demise so soon? I kept every single vial you provided me with, you know. They still smell quite strongly of whatever vile substance it is you used to ruin her."

I barely manage to keep from dragging a despairing hand over my face, cursing myself for being an utter fool. Of course she would have preserved the means to blackmail me even further, when she has already done so once armed only with supposition.

"And how would you implicate me in her death without also implicating yourself?" I challenge her, grasping for straws.

"You are my divineress, are you not? I would say you gave them to me under the guise of a healthful elixir, that you murdered Claude for your own loathsome ends." She leans back, steepling her hands in front of her chest. "I imagine Louis would not be best pleased to hear it; he was much distraught over her passing. And after that spectacular Messe, surely he knows that you are Satan's wench."

She has me cornered, and she well knows it, especially now that I have earned the enmity of La Reynie. All she would need to do is whisper my name to the lieutenant general to have him clap me in chains.

I dangle, caught and helpless, trapped like a half-gnawed fly in Athenais's odious web.

And though everything in me bridles at the notion of agreeing, of becoming complicit in a plot to kill a king, I can see nothing for it but to at least pretend to acquiesce.

"All right, my lady," I bite off. "You have won, as you always do. It will take time, but I will devise some stratagem. An untraceable way to give you what you wish."

"My clever Catherine." She smiles, madness still sparkling in her azure eyes like sunlight breaking upon the peaks of a storm-tossed sea. Smug as a cat that has glutted on too much cream. "You do always come around. And do not tarry too long, please. My patience is already in tatters, and is only fraying further."

*She is exactly right*, I think once she is gone and I have racked my brain for hours, trawling for an answer to no avail. I must indeed become more adept and devious than ever before. And if my own cunning fails to light my way, then perhaps I might use my sight as an oar.

To bail myself out of this predicament before the waters close over my head.

Though I have come a long way since my days of fruitless tinkering with Agnesot's grimoire, I have never truly succeeded in scrying for myself.

And though my need is immense, caught as I am between Athenais and La Reynie like a ship trapped between Scylla and Charybdis, dwelling on my nemeses does not so much as stir the gift. I consult my scrying sphere and obsidian bowls, using everything from wine to milk to drops of my own blood.

But my sight does not budge an inch, sitting tucked and quiet in the very back of my skull like a scorpion concealed beneath a stone.

And so, as I have always done in trying times, I turn to my snakes.

Along with Alecto, Megaera, and Tisiphone, I have acquired so many others that I have not bothered giving them all names. They live along the walls of my banquet hall, kept safely in the series of vivariums I asked Antoine to build for me. I walk among them for a while, trying to match each species with its name.

"King snake, emerald pit viper, coral snake, rosy boa," I whisper to myself, trailing my fingers along the glass. "Regal ringneck, jaguar carpet python, sunbeam, yellow-headed calico."

The hypnotic motion of their bodies, as they weave silkily around one another, captivates my eye. It tickles the gift awake as well, if only just a whit, like a feather run teasingly along its length.

But it is not quite enough to bring forth any real revelations.

"But what if I could see you better?" I muse to myself, pressing my palm against the glass, where a corn snake lifts its little head to flick a searching tongue over the pane. "What if you were free?"

As I envision lifting them from their captivity, letting them slide their way unfettered across the banquet hall parquet, I am rewarded with a brief flash of vision.

My gloved hand tucked into the Sun King's own arm as we meander through the wintry paradise of Versailles.

"Yes," I mutter, lifting one of the vivarium lids as a frenetic excitement pulses to life inside my belly. "Yes, this will be it."

A quarter of an hour later, I stand barefoot amid a shifting sea of snakes.

Most of them are not venomous, as I have no intention of dying in my pursuit of a solution. The ones that are, are also my favorites; specimens I have handled time and again, so often they have become familiar with and fond of the scent of my skin. I let them curl around my ankles and even slither up my calves if they so choose, though most of them are not inclined, content instead to inscribe their winding paths across the floor like runes. I let my eyes go soft and hazy as they seethe around me, a great writhing mass of captivating color.

As if I am some dark pupil, floating in the center of a colossal iris.

When the visions come upon me, they are nothing like what I see for others.

Instead of showing me the future rendered with the hazy texture of a dream, they assail me with a violent mixture of symbolism and sensation. I see blood spiraling through water, a glinting knife raised high above an altar, a brief snatch of Adam's painted devil's face leering against moonlit clouds. There is snow sparkling against a mesh of dark and lacy lashes, a barred door swinging open, a blazing fleur-de-lis tumbling from the sky like a comet run amok.

All of it is shot through with elation and reinforced by a column of cataclysmic fear. And there is a sanctity to it as well, as though I am praying without so much as uttering an imploring word.

Praying to the snakes themselves, and to whatever slit-eyed deity claims them as their own patron.

By the time I lie down among them and let them course coolly over my limbs, I know exactly how I must proceed.

## CHAPTER TWENTY TWO

# The Stratagem and the King

I arrive at Versailles two days later for a private audience with the king.

Despite my posturing for La Reynie, I am stunned that the king would receive me so readily upon my request. As the marquise said, Louis knows me now for Satan's wench. That he would open his doors to me again so willingly is telling.

Though I do not yet know whether it bodes ill or well.

When I arrive, I am escorted at once to the château's famed Galerie des Glaces. The decision to receive me here is revealing, too; this is the château's central and largest gallery, reserved for greeting the brightest of visiting luminaries. With the heavy glass chandeliers still unlit, the gallery glitters with frosty light streaming from the arcaded windows, reflected by the bank of mirrors on the hall's other side. Frescoes of Louis XIV's many triumphs adorn the vaulted ceiling, should a guest be willing to part their eyes from the grandeur of the walls to look up.

The effect is spectacular, as if one stands between the facets of a jewel set into the château's very heart.

As I walk along this corridor of wintry light, I catch glimpses of myself in the partitioned glass of the arched mirrors set between slim marble pilasters. They reflect my curls' foxy sheen, vivid against the pallor of the light; my profile, picked out in sharp silhouette; the swirl of my emerald manteau over the intricate lattice of the parquet. I have taken great care with my appearance, remembering that the king called me a siren of the damned. Today is not a day for drab cloaks nor covered hair.

Today I must present only the very brightest of myself.

At the great hall's end sits the king, in a resplendence of blue silk and cloth-of-gold, ruffles pouring forth like cream from his neck and wrists. His two captains of the guard stand at his shoulders, gimlet-eyed and at the ready.

I dip into a deep curtsy before him, taking care that my face betrays nothing but serenity.

"Sorcière jolie," he says when I rise, his mild tenor surprisingly approachable. Much softer than it was during the ritual. "Welcome back. Has le Diable perhaps sent you to me himself, with some message from the nether realms?"

"No, Your Majesty," I respond. "Nothing so otherworldly as that. I come to warn you of a very earthly plot to end your life."

The captains stir behind him into even greater vigilance, their already stern faces hardening, as though I might be not just a messenger but the threat itself. But the king looks far more curious than afraid, lifting a pensive finger to his cheek.

"Nothing terribly new, I fear—though it has been some time since the last such scheme sprang up." He appraises me, drawing his lower lip through his teeth. "And pray tell, who lurks behind this one?"

"The Marquise de Montespan, I regret to say," I reply. "She fears that you mean to throw her over for the Princesse de Soubise. And she would sooner wish you dead than lost to her."

The king closes his eyes, heaving a long-suffering sigh.

"Pardieu, can the accursed wanton not do without her melodramas for so much as a moment?" he murmurs to himself, pressing his fingertips to his temples, closed lids quivering with strain. "My gorgeous, bedamned Athenais. Ever setting her sights too high, and then overshooting her mark. And I suppose this explains why she has grown so withdrawn and dark."

I hesitate, taken aback by this cavalier reaction, his readiness to believe me without even a desultory doubt. The king seems not only unfazed by my news but oddly unsurprised.

"I would take some air," he says, opening his eyes again. He abruptly seems so weary, for one so gold-touched and young. "I have been cloistered in this gilded cage too long. You will join me on a stroll in the gardens, Madame La Voisin. We have some questions to consider, you and I."

With my gloved hand tucked into his elbow just as I foresaw, I walk with the Sun King alongside the château's frozen canal. Feathery tufts of snow whirl past our faces, as though some celestial bird is shedding its downy coat. The captains of the guard trail us at a healthy distance, far enough behind to be entirely out of earshot.

Part of me is nearly giddy, wonderstruck at being here, strolling with none other than the lord and liege of France. How inconceivably far I have come since my days of toil in the fabrique.

The rest of me is consumed with fear at the audacity of what I attempt.

"So that is it, then, between me and Athenais," he says in a rueful tone, his breath puffing into a cloud before spinning away. "Well past time, but still. I shall miss all that unbridled passion, and her lashing wit. No one else could flay with a backhanded compliment half so well as she."

He speaks with genuine regret, as though his maîtresse is merely leaving his side rather than scheming toward his death.

Perhaps the prospect of being surrounded by murderous intent is truly not so alien to him.

"It must be difficult," I comment. "To know that someone once beloved wishes you so ill."

"Oh, who wishes a king well, save for those who would curry his favor?" he replies with a shrug, ruffling his heavy cape's ermine trim. "And even that is only ever temporary. Each time I elevate someone to a vacant position, I make one ingrate and ten new enemies. It is ever the way of things."

"It sounds rather lonely," I say without thinking, then clap my hand to my mouth at my presumption, horrified. "Forgive me, Sire, I did not mean to imply that your life is . . . inadequate in some way."

"Do not trouble yourself over it," he replies, casting me an amused and slightly wry half smile. "As you are not wrong. My life is well-nigh miraculous—dazzling and delicious in most respects. Having been born to its savor, I would not be content with any other. But there must always be a price. And I pay the tithe by never quite trusting anyone."

I think of what Marie has told me of his ruthless campaigns, his willingness to resort to child espionage. Such brash cruelty is difficult to square with the reality of this refined and sharply self-aware young king.

"Tell me, what is it that she plans?" he inquires, glancing over at me with one eyebrow raised. "Something elaborately vengeful, I'm sure. She would not miss the opportunity to play the role of the scorned woman to the hilt."

I hesitate, knowing that here I must be subtler and more cunning than I have ever been.

"She approached me to craft a deathly spell," I lie, omitting any mention of poison. If La Reynie has not yet identified me as a suspect in the affair, I certainly will not volunteer myself. "A satanic ritual meant to strip you of your vigor and drain you of life over the course of several months. I do not have any such power, of course; I am only a gifted seer, a priestess of the Devil's Mass. But I could see she was in earnest when she asked."

"I see," he says, nodding. "I imagine she must have offered you a goodly sum as well. And yet you walked away from it, and here you are instead. It would seem I am in your debt, madame."

I suppress a relieved sigh, grateful I did not even have to broach the matter of recompense myself.

"Of course you are not, Sire," I say, dipping my head. "You are my king. And as your loyal subject, it was only my duty to warn you."

He waves my humility away with an impatient hand. "That is all very well, but I cannot abide the indignity of an outstanding debt. It is an unseemly position for a king to occupy. Tell me, what would you have of me?"

"I need nothing for myself, truly. But there is a young woman at Vincennes . . ." Again I gloss over the truth, choosing not to mention that Marie is known to me at all, much less a dear friend. "I met her when the lieutenant general requested my help in ascertaining her involvement in some sort of poison affair. She had been badly mistreated at his hands, and yet when I examined her with my sight, I found her innocent. It would please me greatly to know that she was freed, that my scrying was not in vain."

"Easily done," he says with a decisive nod. "You have my word that she will be released. La Reynie has made no headway with her in any case. There is little sense to keeping her jailed when she can shed no useful light on the affair, if one even exists."

"Thank you, Your Highness," I whisper, my knees nearly buckling under the weight of my gratitude. "Truly. I could not be more grateful."

"And now we are left with the outstanding matter of Athenais," he muses, resuming our walk. "Tell me, sorcière jolie, what am I to do with her?"

I frown, wondering why he should bring up the nature of her punishment with me.

"Surely she will be tried for treason?" I say. "To be followed by some form of public execution?"

He shakes his head briskly, pursing his lips.

"Oh, I think not," he says with a sudden icy deliberation that nearly steals my breath. "It would hardly do to have it known that the king is vulnerable to the stratagems of his own maîtresse. What would my enemies think of such a weakness? No, she must be removed much more quietly and swiftly. Her death must appear to have been an unfortunate accident."

He pauses on the path, turning me around until we stand face-to-face. I see a snowflake trembling in the trap of his dark lashes—another fragment lifted from my vision. A runnel of chill trickles down my spine at the cold rage that consumes his face.

Here, then, is Louis XIV as Marie has known him. The one who lays merciless waste to Les Pays Bas, and ruthlessly scourges the cité.

The one who would bring the whole world to its knees.

"And I intend for there to be pain as well," he says softly, barely above a breath. "A sharp punishment for such ultimate treachery. She will be made sorry in her final moments, for having schemed against me while sharing my bed."

"Your Majesty," I force through trembling lips. "Why

do you speak to me of this at all? I fear that knowing such things is not my place."

Slowly, he peels the gloves off both his hands, then gently cups his palms around my face. The warmth of his touch spirals through me, radiating outward like a slug of liquor burning down my throat. I even feel a little dizzy, as if I am truly drunk.

"Do you know, before seeing your Messe, that I despised all things eldritch and arcane?" he says huskily, tilting my face back and forth as if to inspect me. "The last time a comet's passage stirred up the peasantry, I commissioned an astronomer to strip it of its status as some dread portent. Such vulgar beliefs are only fodder for the coarse and narrow-minded, I have always felt. Reason is what must reign supreme."

His dark eyes shift silkily between mine, and he draws the bright ringlets that frame my face through his fingers. My scalp tingles furiously at the touch, as though he is stroking my skin rather than my hair.

He tugs at me like a lodestone, exuding an irresistible compulsion. A magnetic pull unlike anything I have ever felt.

"But you, sorcière jolie," he murmurs, narrowing his eyes. "I believe that you are the exception that proves the rule. Though much of the Messe may have been no more than your compatriot's exceedingly clever illusions, I believe some genuine magic courses through *your* veins."

"Are you . . ." I must stop and clear my throat before I speak again. "Are you saying I might be of some use to you, Your Majesty?"

With a slow finger, he traces a path between my eyes and down my nose, over the crests of my lips and under my chin.

"I am saying that you fascinate me, and that I would know more of you," he murmurs as he slowly closes the distance between our lips. "I am also saying that, from what I have heard from Athenais, your rituals are typically much more savage than the one I witnessed. And that they also rely upon the use of blades."

I think again of my vision, of the raised knife and the droplet of blood corkscrewing through water, the painted devil's visage with its silent, leering laugh.

And as I yield to the king's kiss, I understand what it is he asks of me.

## CHAPTER TWENTY~THREE

# The Plot and the Dream

"So the king wishes you to kill the marquise for him during a Black Mass," Adam says, firelight picking out the luster in his short hair.

We sprawl in front of the fireplace in my study, having reconvened upon my return from Versailles.

"In a way that can be construed as an accident," he continues. "An unfortunate consequence of dancing with the devil."

"Exactly. And he wishes us to invite the foremost peerage, so that her demise becomes something of a public secret. An incident to be swiftly covered up for everyone's benefit." I swallow the salted truffle I am eating, licking the crystals off my fingers. "After all, who would want it to be known that the marquise died at a Devil's Mass, especially one with such an illustrious gathering of guests?"

"Ingenious," Adam breathes. "Who would have thought we had such a devious king?"

"He is . . . remarkable." I struggle to find a better word to capture his mercurial essence, the strange charisma that emanates from him. But I cannot properly describe what I do not even understand. "As though there is more to him than can be seen with the eye alone."

"And you can do what he asks?" Adam inquires more soberly. "I know the marquise is no Claude, certainly far from innocent. But I also know you seem . . . somewhat averse to causing women's deaths."

"It was not so much a request as a command," I reply, though disquiet stirs within me at the question. "And as you say, the marquise is easily as bad as the men whose ends we've hastened. Besides, what choice do I have? I certainly cannot defy the king without risking my head."

"And once she is gone, it sounds as though the king aims to make you his new maîtresse." Adam shakes his head, awed at the prospect of such influence. "Pardieu, this is even better than we planned. Think of what we could accomplish behind the scenes, with you whispering in his royal ear."

"Are you truly not made even a *little* jealous by the prospect of sharing me with him?" I half tease, reaching out to run my fingers through his spiky hair. To my surprise, I find I want him to say yes.

"Jealous?" His brow creases with genuine consternation. "What a notion, Catherine. Why in the world would I be?"

I swallow against the unexpected pain that swells in my throat like a mouthful gone awry. It is not really that

I want him to feel possessive of my affections; in truth, I would not care either if he were to woo someone else, even become another's steadfast lover. The cool respect between us is no closer to the heat of love than it ever was.

But perhaps Marie would have cared, before I ruined everything between us, razed it down to its foundations.

And however she feels about me now that I have at least secured her freedom, I still miss her so terribly.

"Of course you would not," I reply, forcing a smile. "I was only jesting. Now, let us decide how we shall proceed."

As soon as I receive notice that the king has kept his word and Marie has been released, Adam and I set about curating the guest list to our blasphemous festival. We spend the next few weeks meticulously mapping out the marquise's death. I have already secured her participation, having extended her the "honor" of serving as our living altar—a special offering to the devil to secure his blessing of our supposed, secret undertaking, the murder of the king.

As I expected, she had been only too eager to agree.

Rather than a ritual blade gone awry during the Messe, Adam and I settle on the use of a venomous snake instead— a demise even more easily presented as an accident. We also concoct an intoxicant incense, a mixture of belladonna, mugwort, and henbane to confound our audience's senses, render them more credulous. More willing to believe that what befalls the marquise is of the devil's doing. The rest of my time is spent training the chosen serpent—a coral snake so indistinguishable from my own king snakes that the marquise will not be alarmed by its presence—so that it will strike eagerly at the opportune moment.

A week before the Messe, all invitations have been sent and the necessary preparations made. We are ready as we will ever be to execute our plan. Though I am confident in our success, I have been so alive with nerves during our active plotting that I have barely slept for days. But now that there is no more to be done, I retire to sleep early for once, in hopes that I will actually find some rest.

I succumb to sleep as soon as my head touches the pillow and plunge immediately into a dream both vastly terrible and strange.

In it, I look down upon myself as I was at the fabrique—a young starveling with wax burns along her arms, standing in a torn shift against a backdrop of toppled cauldrons and writhing flames. Then the girl that was once me begins to walk, following a twisting path that leads her out of hell. Her road glitters with fragments of green glass, the crushed remnants of the many jars and bottles of ingredients I purchased from the alchemist Blessis. There are coins, too, along the way, warped and half melted, searing hot under her soles.

Though the broken glass and molten metal must torment her, the girl's face remains adamant, betraying not a hint of pain.

I see her continue her journey as the road takes on an incline, beginning to wend around a mountain's sheer face. She climbs and climbs, not sparing a glance for the vertiginous drop, still with that resolute look stamped across her face. By the time she crests the mountain's summit, she has aged fully into a woman, several years older than I am today.

And the king waits for her upon the summit, his glorious hair billowing around him, his hand outstretched.

As soon as she takes it and moves to stand beside him, a black crown materializes upon her head. It wavers like a mirage, as if wrought not of any metal but of a poisonous inky mist, like snake venom turned to breath. Her ragged shift transforms into a grand habit both majestic and macabre, sewn of batwing leather and cobwebs instead of lace. A smile splits her face, wider than wide, a grin so grotesquely broad it contorts her features into something other than human.

Then my perspective shifts—and suddenly it is me gazing outward from the mountaintop, occupying her place. The king's hand burns like an ember in mine, and all of France sprawls out before us: rows upon rows of vineyards with curling vines, swaths of grassy meadow, pools of glimmering lakes. A dark sun blazes above our heads amid a churn of clouds, like an eclipse shedding a noisome light.

And I understand that this no mere dream, but something more. A sleeping visitation of the sight. It tells me that, should I follow through with the deadly Messe, I will become much more than even what the marquise dreamed for herself. Louis will take me as a morganatic wife, a left-handed queen. Wearing his matching crown in all but name.

As triumph grips my heart like some crushing fist, I make the mistake of looking down—to meet the rictus grin of the skull that lies at my feet. Beneath it is another, and another, and another, along with yellowed piles of longer bones clustered haphazardly together.

Because the mountain is made not of stone, but of skeletons. The bodies of my murdered victims, the many dead I climbed over to ensure my own ascension.

And if I pledge myself to Louis XIV, there will only ever be more and more and more.

I rip myself awake with the sound of my own animal howls. My hands twist into my balled-up sheets, and tears sluice hotly down my face.

"Pardieu, what have I become?" I whisper to myself, burying my knuckles into my eyes. Sobs rack through me with a tearing force, fit to split me asunder. Here, then, are all the tears I have not cried since my days at the fabrique, coming upon me all at once. "What bane, what fiend? What bedamned monstrosity?"

And I know at once that I cannot do it. Dieu keep me, but I cannot kill the marquise.

I cannot kill *anyone* again.

Villainous as the marquise doubtless is, I cannot continue to gather power as others' bodies continue to tumble around me; victims fallen to my ambition, innocent and deserving all alike. Though I appease my conscience by styling myself a Fury—for dispensing justice that was never mine to administer at all—in truth, I have killed largely for my own benefit. How many more Claudes must I fell to secure my place beside the king? And when I am finally on that mountaintop, how could I possibly be any better than the marquise?

How would I not be even worse than the dead Prud-homme himself?

I have succumbed to my own hubris like Icarus, flown too close to the king's dread sun. *And all of it, for what?* I ask myself through tears, keening into my pillow. For the false power of being in a powerful man's thrall, when he may discard me whenever he likes?

I do not want to be this person anymore; seizing for myself at any cost, telling myself whatever lies I need to hear. Perhaps I never truly wanted it at all, at least not in the easy and guiltless way that Adam does.

Maybe playacting the part of Satan's priestess in the Messes had some part in this dread transformation, nudged me to stray so far from any path of sanity and reason. Perhaps with all my false prayer and ritual, I truly summoned something infernal and took it into myself.

*Or more likely*, I think bitterly as I unwind myself from the sheets, *this is merely me.* The bitter dregs at my own bottom, all the very worst of myself given its head.

I fling myself from my bed, a pall of dread settling over me as I consider the extent of my predicament. Should the investigation of the poison affair continue, certainly the king will not save me from La Reynie, not once I have incurred his wrath by defying him.

Even if the inquiry does not continue, thinking of the frosty rage in Louis's eyes at the marquise's betrayal convinces me that should I thwart the king's desires, I will not have long to live.

There are no two ways about it.

If I do not kill the marquise, I will likely die myself.

## CHAPTER TWENTY FOUR

# The Predicament and the Plan

I sit on the floor for hours, my back huddled against the bed with my arms around my knees. My mind swooping and darting like a cornered bird at the mercy of a broom.

There must be a way out of this, I exhort myself. There *always* is, even when there seems to be no apparent escape; even walls closing in should not be able to contain a clever enough divineress. Agnesot herself was proof of that. And though I am less inclined than ever to follow in her footsteps by entreating the devil in earnest, for fear of further blackening my already tainted soul, I still have my wits at hand, along with everything I've learned of trickery under Adam's tutelage.

Finally a notion occurs to me, a tiny flame of hope kindling in my chest. It is smaller than a feather, and about as substantial. But it is enough to keep the scourging wind of hopelessness away.

There *is* one thing, after all. One possible way.

Within an hour, I am knocking on the door to Marie's little garret in the cité. As I wait on her doorstep, bouncing on my toes, I am wreathed in fear and uncertainty, unsure that Marie will even let me in.

And why should she, with everything I have cost her, with how little I've given back?

"Catherine?" she exclaims when she finally opens the door, her mouth rounding into an astonished O at the sight of me. "What in damnation are you doing here?"

"I am so sorry to come bursting in on you like this," I say, my chest welling with trepidation, lifting a hand to gnaw nervously on my knuckles. "I know I deserve no succor from you, after all the grievous wrong you've suffered on my account."

"Like the gaol, you mean?" she asks flatly. "I rather suspected you had some hand in my imprisonment. But then the warden informed me that I owed my freedom to you as well . . . so, thank you, I suppose? Truly, the protocol escapes me."

"I would never have let you languish there," I say. "No matter what I had to do. Even so, I do not deserve your help. But I need it, Marie, more desperately than ever. And there is no one else that I would trust, in any case. Not when it comes to my own life."

"Your *life*?" she exclaims, her face darkening. "How in the world has it come to that?"

"I've made mistakes," I say simply, biting my cheek against the tears that spring to my eyes. "Bad ones. The very worst. And now I am afraid it has come time to pay."

She scrutinizes me for a moment longer, her mouth drawn to the side, hands on her hips. Still far too thin, but so beautiful, more beautiful than I even remember. Though I have forfeited any right to her affection, I yearn to close the distance between us, to crush her into an embrace. To press my cheek against hers, bury my face into the achingly familiar scent of her hair.

"Very well, then. I may as well hear you out," she says, stepping to the side and beckoning me in. "I suppose I owe you that much, at least."

As I follow her into the tiny garret, floored with splintered planks and furnished only with a listing table, two stools, and a straw-tick pallet, I find myself desperately wishing I had taken a different path. Rejected the marquise's offer and come to live here with Marie instead, leaving Antoine to fend for himself. I almost even wish Agnesot had never given me the grimoire and instructed me to guard my evil, inspiring me to chase after power at any expense.

How different everything might have been.

Though I cannot pretend that, at bottom, I can truly blame anyone else for this ultimate predicament in which I now find myself. It was my choices that brought me here, one wicked step at a time. And it will have to be my own choices that walk me out of it as well.

"So, what is it that you've done?" Marie asks once she has set a kettle to boil on the cast-iron woodstove and turned to face me with her slim arms crossed over her chest. "Though given what La Reynie accused me of, I suppose I might hazard a guess."

"You will hate me," I whisper, hanging my head. "It is much worse than anything you have ever done. What is it you said once? That your evil was of the smallest sort, the kind just enough to keep you in wine and baguettes? This is not like that, Marie. Nothing like that."

"Why don't you tell me, all the same?" She shrugs, coming to sit across from me. "Clearly you've no other choice, anyway."

So I do, sparing her no ugly detail, laying bare both the flawed and selfish reasoning that has brought me to this juncture, and all the crimes I committed with Adam at my side. I tell her of the false Black Masses and of Prud-homme's death, then of the ones that followed. Even what I was forced to do to Claude, and finally, the king's command that I kill the marquise for him.

"And so you were always right," I breathe once I have finished, afraid to meet the judgment in her eyes. "About me and the grimoire, though it did not imperil my soul itself; I did as much entirely of my own volition. And you were right, too, that such a life would consume me in the end."

It occurs to me that perhaps even Agnesot had some inkling of what end I might come to all those years ago, when she warned me that the freedom I yearned for came at a cost higher than most would choose to pay. Perhaps she should have been more clear as to just what I would be risking; but even if she had been, I doubt I would have chosen differently, forged anything other than my own willing path to here.

Across the table from me, Marie says nothing, turning to stare out her tiny window at the peaked roofs that flock beyond, still glistening with dew under a pewter sky that promises rain. A pigeon wings by her window with a long screech and ruffling of feathers, something painfully melancholic to its shrill cry.

"I see. And what sort of help is it that you would ask of me?" she says in a leaden tone, making no comment on all that I have told her.

I take a deep breath, and then sketch out my plan, detailing her minor but crucial role in it.

"Should it work, I would have to run afterward, of course," I finish. "Paris would never be safe for me again. I would have to reinvent myself elsewhere, disappear from here."

She nods once, teeth worrying at the inside of her lip, then turns back to the window.

"Well, what do you think, now that you have heard it all?" I prompt, my lungs feeling like an overinflated bellows, the taste of metal tanging in my mouth.

"What do I think of what, Catherine?"

"Of the plan. Of me, I suppose. Do you . . . do you hate me, Marie?"

She sighs at that, long and grievous, and when she turns back to face me, her eyes are pools of pain. There is a fatigue to her face, a kind of drawn exhaustion. As if she is beyond weary of contending with my foolishness.

"Of course I do not hate you," she replies with a ghost of a smile. "Perhaps I wish I did; it would certainly be far easier on me. But I don't, because I cannot, Catherine. I know you well enough to understand what it is you thought that you were doing, misguided though it was. And most of all, I cannot hate you because I love you still, foolish and driven and heedless though you have shown yourself to be. I have always loved even the very worst of you."

"You . . . *love* me?" I whisper, my insides swooping with shock, half afraid to draw another breath. "Even now, after everything? Even though I left you?"

"Yes, even now. Such a painful irony, is it not, ma belle? That after all your fear of me, this should be the very freedom you have been questing for all this time," she says ruefully, tilting her head. Her full lips tremble, a wealth of restrained emotion gleaming in her eyes. "That no matter what you do—no matter how far off course you find yourself—you can do anything you wish and still find safe harbor with me in the end."

After my many months of meticulous give-and-take with Adam, I can barely fathom so unconditional a love. Much less that I should somehow be so fortunate as to find myself on its receiving end.

Overcome, but still terribly leery of overstepping, I reach across the table to Marie. When she does not twitch away, I take her hand and gently lift it to rest against my cheek.

"Have I truly not ruined everything with all my foolishness?" I whisper into her palm. "For all that I do not deserve you, you must know that I have loved you always. Loving you . . . it is my first real memory. I know that does not begin to make up for anything. But it is true nonetheless."

"Well, I will not lie and say that we are not badly broken, ma belle," she whispers, tears spilling over her cheeks even as my own drip onto her hand. "But perhaps, with a great deal of luck and time, we might yet be mended. Perhaps even be made whole again."

That is enough, more than enough, for me.

I push back from the table, half stumbling as I reach for her with blind yearning, elation flooding me to the bones when she allows me to wind my arms around her neck. The sweetness of her answering kiss, of the fragrance of her skin and her arms sliding around my waist, is worth all that I have left behind, and much more besides.

Her love is the greatest gift I have ever known, and a freedom freely given.

One that I need not chase down with bloody tooth and claw.

When we pull back from each other, she traces her fingers down my cheek.

"And can you truly give it all up?" she asks, searching my eyes. "I know you have become accustomed to the finery, all the luxurious trappings that come with being the sorceress La Voisin. Will some modest new life with me, in whatever hamlet or backwoods we find ourselves, ever be enough? How can I trust that you will not change your mind? That you will not throw me over for the king himself?"

"So if it should work, what we spoke of . . . would you go, too?" I ask her, nearly trembling with trepidation. "Would you truly come with me?"

"Bien sûr," she says simply, tipping her forehead against mine. "Where else would I wish to be?"

"Then even I can learn from my mistakes, my love," I murmur, drawing her close. "If you can be so generous as to love a murderess, then the least I can do is make myself worthy of your heart."

## CHAPTER TWENTY~FIVE

# The Phial and the Bite

I feel as if I cannot catch my breath the entire week before the final Messe.

Nightmares plague me, of all sinister variations. Sometimes I dream that no matter what I do, the marquise dies in the end; all the dream deaths she suffers are the most awful sort, dreadful combinations of the ones I have inflicted with my poisons. Other times I die in her place, and the last thing I see before I burst awake, my heart pounding like a battering ram, are the clods of soil being tossed into my open grave. Black earth raining onto my cold, dead face.

This is made all the worse by the necessity of keeping Adam in the dark. Fortunately, he is already baffled enough by my abrupt coolness, my utter lack of desire to allow him back into my bed, that personal communication between us has all but petered away. I could not begin to trust him with my plan, not when I know how fervently he wishes all this to pass without a hitch. Our final step to winning the favor of the king.

He would never understand how I could turn my back on all that we have been building and chasing together so assiduously.

And though I like to believe that he cares for me enough to not turn on me, I am well versed in Adam's pragmatic nature, his steadfast devotion to his own interests above all else. No matter that he has guarded my back thus far, I cannot be wholly certain that he would not strive to curry favor by turning me in to the king. I do wish that I could give him a proper goodbye, for all the pleasure and understanding that we have shared between us. But there is no way to do so without arousing his suspicions.

Our partnership will have to end just as it begun, with trickery, deception, and mistrust. We were never meant for more than that, Adam and I.

So I say nothing to him, stewing instead in my own churning mess of fears, while Adam fairly scintillates with nervous energy. He insists on reviewing our steps again and again, though the entire Messe will follow the pattern of every other we have ever held—save for the very end, when I will place the coral snake instead of Alecto on the marquise's chest as part of the sacrament. Once it bites her, Adam and I are both to kick up a dreadful ruckus, blaming the calamity on the marquise having fallen out of the devil's favor. We have used my snakes in ritual many times, and none have ever bitten a participant. So its strike will indeed seem guided by some otherworldly power.

Adam is so singularly focused, so dedicated to the success of our endeavor, that I almost feel badly for him that all will not be going according to our plan.

The night of the Messe, I make my final preparations. I apply my cosmetics with an even more liberal hand than normal; once the time comes, they will disguise the healthy color of my lips and face. Then I tuck the poison I have prepared for myself into the neckline of my corset, nestling the phial that holds my hopes next to my heart.

Only then am I ready to begin the performance of my life.

When Adam and I enter the banquet hall, hand in hand, I am momentarily shocked by how many of the court have come to join our devil's dance. More throng about the hall than we have ever hosted before, in vivacious little knots and clumps, chattering with each other in hushed tones. I see the Vicomte de Couserans, Madame Leferon, and the maréchale all clustered together near the Marquis de Cessac, who stands alone but meets my eyes with a knowing, complicit gaze.

We have invited everyone who has ever attended one of our Messes—the more witnesses to the marquise's demise, the better. After all, if so many peers witness her death at something so forbidden and debased as a Devil's Mass, who would be so bold as to demand an investigation into the affair?

Normally, I suffer from not even a jot of stage fright, but tonight I find myself unnerved by all these nobles' ogling eyes. Their powdered faces glow a dreadful white against the dark swathe of their hoods, beauty patches standing out like pox marks against pale skin, as if they are the restive spirits I feigned for them so many times.

And though this is the same banquet hall I have presided over for so many a Black Mass, the very air in the room seems to have turned ominous and strange, somehow imbued with an unfamiliar horror. The twining vines of the wallpaper seem to surge and coil like unruly snakes, thrown into relief by the lick of candlelight, forming uncanny shapes like leering faces. Once again I am reminded of how often I have entreated darker deities, prayed to demonic powers for their favor in rituals both sincere and feigned. Who is to say that some of them did not hear me and choose to finally attend? Especially tonight, when my very life hangs in the balance as it has never before done?

Why should infernal creatures not teem behind my wallpaper to watch, to see if they may yet sup on my sinner's blood?

What a rich meal my soul would make for them.

I stagger in place a bit, my head rushing with a bout of dizziness, feeling as though I am already halfway to somewhere else; somewhere beyond our mortal plane. Stranded between and betwixt, one foot already planted in hell.

As if he can feel the surging of my unease, Adam squeezes my cold hand, leaning over to brush a kiss across my cheek. I recoil from him a little, barely masking my twitch with a nervous shudder, somehow afraid he will sense my imminent betrayal as if it has a malodorous scent.

"Take heart, my priestess," he whispers into my ear with genuine concern, and for a moment I feel that I will truly miss him. "Tonight will be nearly the same as all the others. And take no heed of their number, when they are as nothing to us. We all but own them already, do we not?"

I swallow hard, but nod, as if I am comforted instead of even more dismayed.

Once we begin, some of my discomfort begins to slip away, soothed by the familiarity of our mock rituals, our wicked kiss before the altar, our well-worn chants. The first departure comes when the marquise goes to serve as the living altar, rather than Camille or me. Adam escorts Athenais to the center and helps her lie upon the table, her golden swoop of hair tumbling to the floor as he sets the chalice upon her chest, the apple on her navel. Then I make my customary rounds about her, tilting a dripping candle over her smooth-skinned form as Adam leads the group in a rousing chant.

She is so beautifully arrayed, so lithe and lovely upon the table, that for a moment I am filled with an incandescent burst of rage. How can the king cast aside something so beautiful simply because it has come to bore him; as if the marquise, capricious and vicious and halfway demented though she is, does not have a feeling heart and soul enrobed by that pristine flesh?

As if she is not a woman but merely one of Antoine's pretty trifles, a *thing* Louis can simply dispense with on a whim, eager for some new amusement with which to divert himself?

It occurs to me that she is doomed no matter what, whether I stay my chosen course or falter enough to carry out the king's original plan.

She will face the king's fury either way, and die all the same.

And though it makes very little sense, for a moment I am desperately sorry to know that Athenais will soon meet her own impending end.

As if she can sense my misgivings, the marquise opens her eyes as I approach her head, my shadow falling across her face. Her eyes glitter against the dark, vivid and unafraid, almost gleeful with malice; as if she can barely wait for the satanic demise this ritual will ostensibly bring down upon Louis's head. Terrible as it is, it centers me a little to be reminded of how lost she is, how utterly depraved.

The marquise is already far beyond redemption, but perhaps I can still save myself.

The remainder of the ritual proceeds precisely as planned. The devil rears in Adam's faux mirror, while Adam's devilmakers fling a diabolic bestiary across the walls, painting them with the monsters I already imagined to be lurking there. All of it perversely calming, remembered steps in a well-practiced dance.

When the chalice makes its way to me for communion, I apply some of Adam's own legerdemain. Slipping loose the dainty phial from between my stays, I bring it to my mouth as I take a sip of wine, tossing its contents back as well. Then I pass the chalice to Adam and drop my hand to my side, letting the empty glass tube slide down the folds of my skirts and to the floor, where I crush it firmly underfoot.

Should some unaccountably upstanding guest think to summon the searcher to establish my cause of death, I do not want the phial found anywhere on my person.

The concoction is bitter as gall, so revolting I struggle to gulp it down. It will slow my heart down to almost nothing and chill my limbs, mimicking the appearance of death—so that when I goad my Tisiphone into inflicting her harmless bite on me, I will appear to perish from the same coral snake venom that Adam and I intended for the marquise.

Once the apple has been shared by all the guests as well, Adam announces that tonight, we seek our master's most profound blessing.

"Just as the serpent twined around Eve," he intones, "so will our priestess's familiar circle our living altar's neck."

This is a ritual we have practiced before, often enough that the more devoted of our guests will recognize it. I even presented it to the marquise as a choice: Did she wish to court the daystar's ultimate favor, by allowing me to place my serpent around her throat? Of course she would never have said no, not when I phrased it in such an insinuating way. And unlike many, the marquise is no shrinking violet. She has never shown any fear of my snakes.

But as I move from the altar toward one of the vivariums, I notice something for which I did not prepare.

The substance is much faster acting than the grimoire led me to expect.

My fingertips are already numb and chilly, my lips tingling as blood rushes away from them. Worse still, my mind begins to cloud and my vision to blur, the flickering candles set all around the room coalescing into a single smeary haze. I should have had at least another five minutes before the concoction did its work; but perhaps I failed to eat enough today. Or I may, by some quirk of the constitution, simply be more susceptible than most to this toxic tisane.

Whatever the case, I can feel that I have much less time than I planned before I fall into my death-mimicking faint. Unfortunate but manageable, I tell myself. I need only dispense with the quick prayer I was meant to lead, gather up Tisiphone, and then goad her into biting me with haste.

But by the time I reach unsteadily for the vivarium's top, I am confronted with a much worse predicament.

Since Adam knows full well that I would never spend an entire ritual with a venomous and unpredictable serpent slung around my neck, I made my substitution by placing Tisiphone in the vivarium where the coral snake normally dwells. Tisiphone is the most mercurial, the least readily handled of my three king snakes; there are certain ways she dislikes to be held. She has even bitten me once or twice when I failed to take her up in a manner she deemed acceptable.

Her bite will do me no harm, of course, but it will leave a convincing mark. Enough to assure Adam and the gathered that I met my death by the coral snake's lethal venom.

But somehow, caught up in sizzling nerves and all my trepidation, I have made a terrible mistake. When I put Tisiphone in the tank earlier this evening, I forgot to remove the coral snake.

I pause in front of the glass for a moment, struggling to gather my rapidly fraying self. The room begins to swim around me, and I have trouble focusing my eyes on the curled snakes below the glass. Were it daytime, this would still cause me no trouble, as I am deeply familiar with my girl's pattern and her shape. And though king snakes and coral snakes are identically colored, there is also a subtle difference to the order of their red, black, and yellow bands.

But the banquet hall is only dimly lit, by firelight and the candle clusters strewn about the room. And with my glazed eyes and wheeling brain, I can barely even make out the snakes' individual hues.

"Red touches yellow, death to a fellow; red touches black, friend of Jack," I mutter under my breath, but it is as if the words have lost their meaning altogether. Their bands blur and waver in the dim light, until I can barely even tell where one color begins or ends. And though the two serpents sit a wary distance from each other, coiled against the vivarium's opposing sides, I simply cannot tell which is venomous and which one my old friend.

I can feel Adam draw near to my elbow, puzzled by my delay. "What are you waiting for, Catherine?" he mutters in my ear, his voice warbling as if it reaches me through water. "Is everything well?"

I swallow hard, because this is my last chance. If I fall now without having feigned my snakebite, Adam is more than clever enough to guess that I took some pernicious substance—which will lead him to wonder about my original intent. Perhaps he will even discern part of my plan, enough at least to know that I did not mean to see our undertaking through.

He will certainly be far too suspicious to make any formal announcement of my passing—much less to allow Marie and Antoine to claim my corpse, once the Black Mass guests have scattered to the winds in their panic—until enough time has elapsed that he is certain of my true death.

Bodies are only given to the undertaker once they have lain for three days in their beloveds' keeping, and I will wake from my deathlike stupor only two days hence.

And if the marquise should leave this Messe unharmed and the king learn that I am still alive, his murderous wrath will fall upon my head.

Only if I can convince them all that I have met my death of snakebite will I be truly safe.

"Of course it is," I whisper back as clearly as I can, though my tongue has grown leaden and my ears shrill with a frightful hornet buzz. The inside of my head lists back and forth like a vessel on high seas. "Quite well."

I reach into the tank, biting on my lip until I taste the rusty tang of blood, my hands drifting toward the snake that *feels* the more familiar. There is something to the shape of her head, and the way that she lies coiled, that makes me think this one is my Tisiphone.

I cannot be certain, but from the way my consciousness already pitches out of my grasp, I know that I've all but run out of time.

I must make my gamble now, or fail to ever win my freedom. Certainly I will not have the chance to become the mistress of my own fate again.

My vision rapidly tunneling, I pick the snake up and coil her around my wrists, letting the bulk of her body dangle in the precise way Tisiphone abhors. The snake objects at once, tensing against my grip. When I only allow more of her to go slack, she hisses furiously, then rears back and sinks her fangs into the tendons of my left wrist.

I had planned to cry out for effect, but I do not have to feign my scream.

The pain is so piercing, so agonizing and vivid, that for a moment it bursts right through the encroaching gloom gathering in my head. It hurts so badly that I wonder if I was indeed mistaken; if what I feel is the fiery venom of the coral snake coursing through my veins.

If my life is truly coming to an end.

"Catherine!" I hear Adam cry out, his voice faint and tinny in my ears. "Mon Dieu, *Catherine!*"

Then the darkness closes ranks inside my head, and my last thought before my body strikes the ground is whether I have finally succeeded in damning myself.

# EPILOGUE

There is darkness all around me. An impenetrable black, clammy with cold, as if I have already been interred. *Am I dead or dreaming?* I wonder dully, my mind plucking at the meaning of the word. And if I am dead, where have I landed?

In le paradis, or l'enfer?

I know which one I believe I deserve, and it makes me terribly afraid.

But then I think I hear the chiming of a beloved and familiar voice, and smell the bright scent of citron and sandalwood. It cannot be hell, then, not if Marie is also here.

I turn toward the sound and risk opening my eyes. The gloom around me is so dense that for a horrible, panicked moment, I fear again that I have perished and found myself trapped in purgatory rather than perdition. But as my surroundings drift slowly into focus, I realize that it is only night; real and very earthly night. And that the squalor around me is a familiar one—the sparse and dusty shambles of Marie's little garret apartment, lit by the few faltering candles she can afford.

I have never felt such joy, nor such heady liberation, to find myself so far away from anything that even remotely smacks of wealth or influence.

Then Marie's face hovers into view above me, warm brown eyes latching onto mine. The relief that overtakes her face would melt even a heart of ice, much less one so battered and tender as mine has become.

"Ma belle," she breathes, leaning down to tip her forehead against mine. "It has been so long since you stirred, nearly four days. I was afraid you might not find your way back to me at all."

I reach up with weak and trembling hands, already pricking fearsomely with pins and needles that have only just begun their torment; the plunge back into life from the chilly depths of a mimicked death is not a pleasant one. I can feel by the feebleness of my muscles, my all-encompassing lassitude, that I have not moved for days and days. As it is, I am only strong enough to briefly cup Marie's cheeks, then slide my arms to wreathe around her neck.

"I would not disappoint you so," I murmur, in a wheezy, creaking voice that truly sounds as though it has ventured beyond the veil before returning. "Never again."

I can see from the fear that still writhes in her eyes that she does not quite believe me. I must have given her a dreadful scare, lying still as cold stone and nearly dead for even longer than expected.

"Swear it, Catherine," she demands, gripping my shoulders and giving me a gentle shake. "Swear you will not be so faithless as to actually die on me."

I eke out a breathy laugh, though even the slow spread of my smile hurts my stiff and chilly cheeks. "I swear it. Not even I would dare be so impudent."

And no matter what lies in store for me, I already know I will never discover any freedom or salvation greater than Marie's answering kiss.

# Acknowledgments

This book was a tough one to write, coinciding as it did with some of the hardest moments I've ever had to live through. I would never have made it without the unstinting help, support, and shoulders to (extensively) cry on, lovingly supplied by my tireless support network. I owe the most heartfelt thanks to:

Everyone at Abrams, especially Anne Heltzel, who was beyond kind and understanding throughout this long and unusually grueling process.

Taylor Haggerty, and the whole Root Lit team of ferocious wonder women. I could never have lived any of this dream without you.

My lovely, lovely friends: you know who you are, and I hope you also know how much I love you.

And always, always my family—especially my husband and my mom, who took care of my newborn baby for many hours while I all but tore at my hair like a Victorian madwoman as I furiously wrapped up edits on this book. And above all, my lionhearted little boy: I promise to teach you everything I know about Assassin's Cabinets in due time.